RYAN RENEWED

NEW YORK RUTHLESS: BOOK 5

SADIE KINCAID

RED HOUSE PRESS LTD

For all the readers who just wanted to read about Jessie and the boys and their happily ever after. This one is for you.

For anyone else, if you're looking for a read that has plot over spice, this may not be the book for you.

All my love, Sadie x

NEW YORK RUTHLESS

Ryan Renewed is book 5 in the New York Ruthless series. It is a dark Mafia, reverse harem romance which deals with adult themes which may be triggering for some, inc but not limited to attempted kidnap, discussion of fertility issues, mention of pregnancy loss, as well as scenes of a violent and graphic sexual nature.

If you haven't read books 1, 2, 3 and 4 in the series yet, you can find them on Amazon

Ryan Rule

Ryan Redemption

Ryan Retribution

Ryan Reign

PROLOGUE

THE RYAN FAMILY GROUP CHAT

Mikey: *Boys, I have an important announcement*
Liam: *What?*
Conor: *We're kind of busy*
Mikey: *Jessie is ovulating*
Shane: *She can't be. It's too early*
Mikey: *She peed on the stick*
Shane: *What the fuck!*
Conor: *But we're all the way downtown. You'd better not be lying Mikey!*
Jessie: *He's not. I peed on the stick*
Mikey: *The stick never lies*
Liam: *Fuck!*
Conor: *Jessie, stay away from him!*
Jessie: *I can't! He's just finished his workout! He looks so good.*
Mikey: *And you know how horny she gets!*
Shane: *We're on our way*
Mikey: *Don't rush though boys*
Shane: *Mikey, keep your hands to yourself until we get back!*
Conor: *Mikey!*
Liam: *Mikey!!*

CHAPTER 1
JESSIE

My skin sizzles with anticipation and excitement as Mikey's arms circle around my waist. His warm breath dusts over my neck, making me shiver. The room is dark and quiet, except for the sound of soft breathing. His strong hands grip my hips tightly and I wonder if he's feeling as nervous as I am.

"You think Shane is going to be really pissed about this?" I whisper as a skitter of fear runs along my spine.

"Probably," he chuckles softly. "But he can never stay mad with you for long, Red. And we'll blame it all on me."

I lace my fingers through his. "No we won't. We're in this together, right?"

"Hmm." He plants a soft kiss on my neck.

"I'm not sure your chosen method of getting him back here was the wisest though."

He laughs and presses his lips against my ear. "There is no quicker way to get Shane back here than the promise of fucking you all night long, Jessie," he whispers, making goosebumps prickle along my forearms.

I'm sure that nobody else in the room heard him, but I blush anyway.

"Stop it!" I breathe as his hand skims my lower abdomen, dangerously close to my pussy. The room is dark, but there are eight other people in it along with us and I'd rather they didn't see, or hear, Mikey sliding his hand into my panties because that is surely where he's headed.

Shane is forty next month. He hates parties. He's refused to even acknowledge the fact that he's approaching his next decade for the past six months. So, as we stand here waiting for him, I'm wondering why Mikey and I decided it would be a good idea to throw him a surprise party to celebrate.

I mean, it started off as a good idea, obviously. We just wanted to do something special for him. For a grumpy asshole, Shane is incredibly selfless when it comes to the people he loves. He works harder than anyone I know. He rarely takes time for himself and he never celebrates his birthdays. But forty is a big deal, right? We couldn't let that pass by unmarked. And this isn't exactly a party. Shane doesn't like enough people to have a party and he certainly doesn't trust enough of them to invite them into our home.

So that is why his aunt, Em, his cousin, Aoife, along with her husband Noel, a couple of his friends from LA along with their wives, and the brothers' longest serving and most trusted employee, Chester, are here tonight to celebrate with him - one month early so that he'll have no idea what to expect when he walks through that door in a few moments' time.

Conor and Liam are in on it too, obviously, and they played along so well with Mikey's ruse to get Shane back here. Not that any of us had much choice since Mikey just put it out there in the group chat without discussing it first. And now I'm wondering if that was the worst decision ever, because not only might Shane be pissed that we've thrown him a surprise gathering for a birthday that he doesn't want to acknowledge, but he'll be expecting a baby-making fuck-fest, which is what he refers to the few days a month when I'm fertile.

But I guess it's too late now.

The sound of the elevator door opening signals they're here and I take a deep breath.

"Jessie!" I hear Shane shout and I pray to God he doesn't say anything inappropriate about me and Mikey fucking.

We really didn't think this through.

Thankfully he doesn't and I expect Conor and Liam have also thought of that and are distracting him while guiding him to the dining room where we're all waiting in the dark.

"Why would they be in here?" I hear him ask as the door opens and the light is switched on.

"Surprise!" we all yell and he stands there, blinking in shock as he scans the room. When his eyes land on mine, he narrows them for a second before he is ushered through the door by Conor and Liam, then he's distracted by everyone rushing forward to greet him and wish him a happy birthday.

I hang back with Mikey, wondering just how pissed he is at us for this. It takes him a few minutes to work his way through the small group because they haven't seen him for a long time and they all want to talk to him. While we're waiting, Liam and Conor make their way over to us.

"What the fuck was that, asshole?" Conor says to Mikey with a shake of his head but a smile on his face.

"You couldn't think of another reason to get us back here?" Liam adds. "He's gonna be so pissed that he's shaking hands and making small talk right now instead of fucking Jessie."

"Liam!" I blush at his words even though I thought exactly the same thing.

"It's true, baby." He flashes his eyebrows at me before he

wraps his arms around my waist and kisses me softly. "He'll blame Mikey though, don't worry," he adds with a laugh.

"You told me he was being kinda slow getting back here, jackass. Everyone was here waiting. What was I supposed to do?" Mikey punches his twin playfully on the shoulder.

"Stop fighting, children," Conor says with a roll of his eyes before he leans in and kisses me softly. "You okay, Angel? You look kinda scared."

"What if he's really mad?" I whisper.

Conor shrugs. "He's always mad about something."

Shane walks up behind him as he's finishing his sentence. "That's because the four of you constantly give me shit to be mad about," he says, but there is no anger in his voice at all and there is a smile on his lips.

Mikey wraps his arms around him. "Happy birthday, old man!"

"You know my birthday is next month, right?" Shane says as he slaps Mikey on the back.

"Yeah, but there's no way we could have pulled this off too close to your birthday. You'd have been too suspicious," Mikey replies.

Shane hugs each of his brothers in turn and they joke good-naturedly. Then he reaches me, his eyes narrowed as he looks at me. "I have a hunch that you were the mastermind behind this, Jessie Ryan!"

I stare at him as wet heat pools in my core. His brothers drift away to speak to the other guests, who are their friends and family too, leaving Shane and me alone.

"So?"

"Yeah," I whisper. "Surprise." I still don't know if he's annoyed with me or not. I mean, he seemed okay with his brothers. "Are you mad?"

"Damn right I am." He nods as he takes a step closer to

me and wraps his arms around my waist. Bending his head low until his mouth is close to my ear, his breath skitters over my skin, making me tremble. "I thought I was coming home to fuck you into tomorrow, sweetheart," he whispers before he presses a soft kiss on my throat that makes my knees buckle.

"But you can do that any time you want," I remind him. "How often do you get to spend time with your closest friends and family all together like this?"

"I've never done anything like this," he says as he glances around the room.

"It will be fun. And I like that we get to see your friends from LA again," I smile. I met them at a wedding earlier this year and got along so well with them all, especially Alana and her adopted daughter, Lucia, who is only eight years younger than her mom and five years younger than me. I couldn't wait for an opportunity to see them again.

That was how this whole thing came about. Alana and I were talking about how it would be great to have another occasion to get together because the boys are so busy with work. Then she talked about how much she missed New York and Shane's upcoming birthday seemed like the perfect excuse.

"Hmm." He pulls me closer to him. "Did you and Alana come up with this? Because Alejandro doesn't do birthday parties either. Well, not unless they involve a bouncy house these days."

"Well, I think his wife is a good influence on him that way too," I purr as I run my hands over the lapels of his suit jacket. "It's good to have fun in between all that working, you know?"

"I have plenty of fun." He grins before he starts to kiss my neck again and warmth spreads through me.

"Not that kind of fun, you deviant," I giggle.

"But that's the best kind of fun, sweetheart."

"Hmm." I wrap my arms around him and he stares into my eyes.

"I hate this kind of thing, Jessie."

"Sorry." I bite on my lip as his eyes burn into mine.

"I'm going to have to punish you for this, you know that, right?" he growls with a mischievous twinkle in his eye.

"I'd expect nothing less," I whisper just before Conor interrupts us.

"Plenty of time for that later," he says with a grin. "You have guests."

"And presents!" I squeal, remembering that he has a pile of gifts to open, including the beautiful watch that I bought him.

Shane takes a deep breath and turns to face the room, keeping his hand on the small of my back as he does.

"Let's do this," he says with a flash of his eyebrows.

CHAPTER 2

SHANE

The moon is full as I sit on the roof terrace looking at the view and enjoying the quiet. I left the party about ten minutes ago because I needed some fresh air and some peace. I don't celebrate birthdays. They only remind me that I'm getting older and closer to death, while I still have so much to do with my life. They make me reflective in a way that I don't like.

I could have strangled my brothers earlier. What the fuck they were thinking agreeing to throw me a surprise party I'll never know. But then I saw her face and I knew she was behind it, and how the fuck do I stay mad at her, or any of them, when I know that they did this out of love for me? I'm not sure I'm worthy of the kind of devotion that I have from Jessie when I've done nothing to deserve it.

I spin around when I hear footsteps behind me and see Alejandro Montoya walking toward me, holding the bottle of whiskey he bought me in his hand. He and I have been buddies for a long time, and back when we were both single, along with his best buddy, Jackson Decker, we had plenty of nights out where we got drunk and picked up hot women. Understandably, none of us have any desire to do that any longer given we're all happily married.

"I thought you might want to crack this open?" He holds out the bottle of Midleton Chapter One.

"Is that why you bought me a forty thousand dollar bottle of whiskey for my birthday, so you could drink it yourself?" I grin at him.

"Maybe," he replies with a shrug and a smile before he takes a seat beside me and hands me the bottle. "Now crack it open."

I break the seal and he holds out his empty glass. I pour each of us a generous measure before placing the open bottle on the table and leaning back in my chair. I take a sip and the rich liquid burns my throat.

"So, forty, huh?" Alejandro says with a chuckle.

"Not yet, buddy," I remind him and he laughs harder.

He arches an eyebrow at me. "I never figured you for the birthday party kind of guy."

"That's because I'm not."

"Ah, *Jessie*," he says.

"Yup." I take another sip of my whiskey. "I never figured you for this kind of guy either."

"I'm not."

"Alana?"

"Yup."

"What are we letting these women do to us, buddy?"

"Make us better men," he says with certainty and I realize he's right. Everything about my life is better with Jessie in it. Everything about me is better.

"Where are the boys?" I ask him. He and Alana have three year old twin boys. They would usually stay with Lucia and Jackson when Alejandro and Alana are out of town, but they're both here too.

"They're with my mama and papa. We're flying back first

thing tomorrow before they give their grandparents a heart attack."

I laugh out loud at that. I remember how challenging Mikey and Liam were at that age. I practically raised my twin brothers and I still haven't recovered from the ordeal.

"I miss them too much to stay away," he says as he takes a sip of his whiskey. "Dario is so like his mom, but Tomás is just like me when I was a kid. He's going to make me gray before I'm forty."

"You're forty next year!"

"I know!"

"You ever miss your life before you had them?"

"Not for one fucking second." He turns to me and winks. "You worried you might?"

"I don't know," I say with a sigh.

"How are things going?" he asks. Jessie told Alana that we were trying for a baby when she met her back in LA.

"Not great," I admit. "I mean I love the baby-making part..." I take another sip of my drink.

"Well, yeah," Alejandro nods his agreement.

"But I hate the effect it has on her. Every month..." I shake my head.

He knows. Alana had trouble conceiving and they had their twins through fertility treatment. Jessie was convinced she'd fall pregnant as soon as we started trying. But then her period arrived that first month and she was devastated. I suppose we were all a little disappointed. But, we kept on trying, and we try hard. Now every month when her period arrives, she's heartbroken all over again and I feel powerless to help her.

"It's hard, amigo. I remember how upset Alana used to get. How helpless I felt not being able to fix it for her. She put so much pressure on herself."

"Jessie does the same. It feels like our lives have become about getting pregnant. And don't get me wrong, I love trying to get her pregnant. I want a kid with her. But it's starting to affect everything else. How do you stop it creeping into every aspect of your life? It's like we're just repeating the same cycle over and over again."

"That's because you literally are," he says with a tilt of his head.

"Yeah."

"I don't know, Shane. It's hard when that's what she wants. I remember how fucking heartbroken Alana used to get. How sometimes it made sex feel like something we had to do and it kinda took the edge off at times, you know? I mean fucking my wife is my favorite thing to do in the whole world, but I don't miss the pressure."

"Hmm."

"You need to find a way to take the pressure off. I mean Jessie is only twenty-seven, right?"

"Yeah."

"So there's no rush?"

"I know that, but she keeps thinking there's something wrong with her."

"There's no easy answer, amigo. I wish there was."

More footsteps behind us make us turn as his wife, Alana makes her way toward us.

"Hey, princess," Alejandro says as he wraps his arm around her waist.

"Hey," she stifles a yawn. "Your aunt is looking for you, Shane."

I down my drink and place the glass on the table before checking my watch. It's after two.

"We should probably get going if you want to get any sleep before our flight," she says to her husband.

He stands up and smacks her on the ass, making her giggle.

"A hotel suite to ourselves? We won't be sleeping, princess." He smiles at her and her cheeks flush pink.

"Thank you for an epic evening, amigo," he says, holding his arms wide, and I stand too so he can hug me.

"Thank you for coming, buddy, I really appreciate it."

"Any time," he replies.

When he lets me go, I hug Alana too.

"You and Jessie and the boys will have to come visit us again soon," she says. "Jessie told me you have a club near us now. We should go?"

"No!" Alejandro barks as he pulls her to him and wraps his arms around her. "Not a chance, princess."

I laugh out loud because he sounds like Conor. We own a string of exclusive, private members' clubs – or 'sex clubs' as they are more commonly known – across the US and Europe, including one in New York and one in LA. Conor refuses to let us take Jessie to one either.

"We'll see," she flashes her eyebrows at him and I know that he'll give into her eventually because the look in his eyes when he's staring at her is all too familiar to me. It is the look of a man who would do anything to make her happy.

I SEE the last of our guests out and walk into the den to see Liam and Mikey asleep at either end of the sofa. There is an empty bottle of tequila on the floor, which explains their comatose state. Jessie and Conor are cleaning up.

"There you are," Jessie says, blowing a strand of hair from her face. "Did you say goodbye to everyone? Em, Aoife, and Noel are flying back tomorrow, but they said they'll stop by for some breakfast first."

"I did. I just spoke with them." I walk toward her. "And now I want to go to bed."

"I just need to finish here." She smiles at me as I pull her into my arms.

"We'll do it tomorrow," I insist as my hands drop to her ass and I squeeze.

She flutters her eyelashes at me. "It won't take long."

"I'll take care of it. You two head to bed," Conor says and I wink at him in appreciation. He's such a good brother.

"Are you sure?" Jessie says but I hoist her over my shoulder and she squeals with laughter.

I slap her ass and walk out of the room, heading straight to her bedroom because it's closer than mine. "He just said he'd take care of it."

Once we get inside, I throw her down on the bed and start to pull off my clothes.

She looks up at me, her blue eyes shining as she arches an eyebrow at me. "I thought you were tired?"

"I never said I was tired. I said I wanted to go to bed. I've been desperate to fuck you since I got home eight hours ago. Now take off your clothes and spread those legs wide so I can see my beautiful pussy."

"You're so bossy," she pouts but she sits up and pulls her dress off over her head before taking off her bra and panties. Then she lies back and looks up at me while I finish undressing.

"Spread them, sweetheart," I remind her.

Her cheeks flush pink as she does as I ask.

"You're soaking already, Jessie," I say as I crawl onto the bed.

"I know," she breathes.

I pepper soft kisses on her ankle, working my way over her calves, her knees and her thighs, edging closer to where I want to feel her the most. I can smell how wet she is and it's making my cock weep for her.

"Did you like your birthday gift?" she purrs.

"I haven't tasted it yet," I chuckle.

"I mean your watch."

I stop what I'm doing and crawl up the bed to her. I'm wearing the watch now. It's a Breitling. It's fucking beautiful, but I love it because she chose it for me, and because she had it inscribed. "Yes, I do. Thank you." I settle between her thighs and kiss her softly. "It's perfect."

"I'm so glad you liked it," she breathes. "The inscription..."

"I know what it means," I whisper.

"Your Aunt Em helped me get the Gaelic right. Or Gaelige, that's it, right?"

"Yes."

"I mean it."

"I know." I kiss her softly. "I think we're a part of the same star too."

"You do?" She smiles at me.

"Hmm." I start to trail kisses over her neck, down to her breasts and she moans softly as I suck a pebbled nipple into my mouth. "Now how about we become part of the same body instead?"

"That doesn't make sense," she laughs softly.

"It will when I'm inside you," I murmur against her skin as I move lower, closer to where I was a few moments ago when she interrupted me. She whimpers as I edge closer, pressing soft kisses over her mound as I push her legs wider apart. "Damn! You smell so fucking good, Jessie," I say before I swirl my tongue over her sensitive clit and she bucks her hips against me.

"Shane!" she moans and my cock throbs. That is the sweetest fucking sound in this world. I want to take my time eating her because she tastes so fucking good, but I can hardly wait to get inside her. My cock is aching for her pussy. I slide two fingers into her wet heat and the groan rumbles through her entire body as she rocks her hips against me.

"You feel so good," she whimpers.

"You taste so fucking good," I mumble as I lap up her sweet juices. I suck and lick and finger-fuck her hard until she comes all over my hand and my mouth, her cum soaking me.

When her legs stop trembling, I slide my fingers out and suck them clean. My balls draw up into my stomach as her sweet, salty arousal coats my tongue.

"Shane," she purrs as she reaches for me and curls her fingers in my hair.

"You need more, sweetheart?" I look up at her beautiful face, her cheeks flushed pink and her bright blue eyes dark with desire.

"I want all of you."

"Hmm." I wipe my mouth and crawl up to her, resting on my forearms as I edge the tip of my cock into her dripping cunt. "More?"

"More," she groans as she wraps her legs around my waist and her arms around my neck, pulling me closer and deeper until I sink all the way into her smooth wet heat.

Fuck me, she feels too damn good. I can never get enough of her.

She gasps as I rock my hips and reach that spot deep inside her. Her walls pulse around me, milking my cock with her hungry little squeezes. I press my lips over hers, sliding my tongue into her mouth and letting her taste herself on me. Her soft moans ripple through my body, making me even more desperate for her. Waves of hot pleasure roll through my chest and core as I sink deeper into her with each thrust. I'm torn between my need to nail her into the mattress and wanting to draw this out for as long as possible.

I have never been so close to another person as I am to her. Our bodies couldn't be any more a part of each other's than they are right now. She is the ray of light in the dark world we live in and I would rather die than live without her.

"What are you thinking about?" she breathes as she runs her fingers through my hair and I realize I'm staring into her eyes.

"How much I love you."

She blinks away a tear and then gives me one of her incredible smiles. "How much do you love me?"

"You know already," I growl as I drive harder and she shudders in my arms.

"I love you too," she whispers.

"I know," I mumble as I bury my face against her neck. It took me a long time to let her inside the walls I spent a lifetime building.

It took me an even longer time to trust her again after she left us, but I feel her love for me in every single thing she does and says.

"Shane!" she whimpers as she clings to me while I keep fucking her slowly, drawing out the pleasure for both of us for as long as I can.

CHAPTER 3
JESSIE

My heart is fluttering like a bird trapped in a cage as I ride the waves of my last orgasm. Shane kisses my neck softly as he fucks me through it. I love this side of him. Sex with us is rarely slow and soft like this, but tonight it is exactly what I need from him.

"You're so needy tonight, sweetheart," he whispers. "Your pussy is milking my cock." He rolls his hips and hits the sweet spot inside me, making me whimper his name. "Lucky for you I'm still nowhere near done."

"Hmm," I purr as my senses start returning and I wrap my arms around his neck. "Whiskey always makes you frisky." I giggle at my own poetic genius.

"You make me fucking frisky," he growls.

Neither of us notice Conor walking into the room until he's standing beside the bed taking off his clothes.

Shane rolls his eyes and looks at his brother. "What are you doing in here?"

"Getting naked so I can fuck my wife," Conor says with a grin and I giggle. I think I drank way too much tequila with the twins. I'm such a lightweight when it comes to alcohol.

"Well, I'm kinda busy with her right now."

"So?" Conor replies with a shrug as he lies on the bed beside us.

"It's my fucking birthday."

"No it's not. As you told us at least a dozen times tonight, your birthday isn't for another month," Conor replies and Shane shakes his head in exasperation.

"He does have a point," I whisper making Shane turn his attention back to me.

He narrows his eyes at me. "Don't be taking his side."

"I would never take sides." I bite on my lip and stifle a giggle, wondering if he's going to allow Conor to join us.

"Then stop talking," he growls as he starts to fuck me again.

Conor lies back on the bed with his arms behind his head. "I can wait."

I have to clamp a hand over my mouth to stop myself from laughing.

"For fuck's sake," Shane groans, feigning his exasperation but he has a wicked glint in his eye that tells me he is more than happy for his brother to join us. He grabs me by the hips and rolls us onto our sides, hooking my thigh over his so that we don't lose contact.

He brushes my hair back from my face and smiles at me before he looks over my shoulder at his brother who has already rolled onto his side behind me. "It's my fucking party though, so this pussy is all mine." He winks before he seals his lips over mine and begins to fuck me so deliciously slowly and deep that my core turns to molten lava.

"So unfair," Conor chuckles.

Shane wrenches his lips from mine, leaving me gasping for him. "Although, as it's my birthday..." He looks at Conor over my shoulder with pure devilment in his eyes. "You know, I've been wanting to try that thing the twins did in Ireland?"

"No," Conor says.

"What? Right now?" I ask as my stomach flutters with excitement.

"Come on, Con. I'm only gonna be forty once? If Jessie is up for it?" Shane looks at me, his eyes dark with longing and how the hell am I supposed to refuse him?

"It *is* his birthday," I whisper as I turn my head to Conor.

"I know I'm pretty buzzed off that fancy whiskey, but..." Conor shakes his head.

"What?" Shane frowns.

"Our cocks will be touching." He shudders, making me giggle.

"Your cock will also be squeezed into Jessie's pussy tighter than it's ever been before and is ever going to be again. Besides, no one will ever know. It will stay between the three of us."

Conor's hand slides over my hips and ass and he groans. "I must be drunk because I can't believe I'm agreeing to this."

I take a deep breath, my walls squeezing around Shane and making him groan as both excitement and nerves ripple through my body.

"You ready for this, sweetheart?" Shane growls.

"Yes." I swallow hard and Shane wraps his arms around me and rolls onto his back.

Conor pushes himself up and crawls behind me while Shane keeps me pressed close to his chest. His cock twitches inside me, filling me completely and I wonder how Conor is going to squeeze inside me too. My body trembles in anticipation, laced with just the tiniest bit of fear.

"We've got you," Shane says softly as he brushes my hair from my face. "If it doesn't work, we'll stop."

"I know," I breathe.

Conor leans over me, peppering my back and shoulders

with soft kisses. "I won't hurt you, Angel, but you tell me to stop if it gets too much and I will. Okay?"

"Okay." I nod, my cheek brushing the hot skin of Shane's chest.

"She wet enough for this, bro?" Conor asks his brother and heat flushes across my cheeks.

"I've had her in this bed for half an hour. I'm offended you'd even ask," Shane chuckles.

"Hmm," Conor mumbles as his fingers skim over the edge of my entrance which is currently being stretched wide by his older brother. "How the fuck am I gonna fit in here with you though?" he asks as he edges the tip of his finger inside me.

"Holy fuck!" I hiss as he pushes in further, twisting his finger against Shane's cock and stretching me wide.

"You okay?" Shane whispers as he brushes my hair my face.

"Uh-huh," I pant as my heart races and excitement skitters through my body. When Conor adds a second finger the only noise I can make is a guttural moan as the pain and pleasure burns through me. My walls squeeze around them both as I release a rush of wet heat.

"Fuck, she likes that," Shane hisses.

"Do you, Angel?" Conor groans as he works his fingers slowly in and out of me. "You think you're ready for my cock now, too?"

"Yes," I pant. "Please?"

Shane's fingers dig into my hips as he holds himself still. "I can't wait to fuck you with him," he grunts in my ear.

I suck in a deep breath because I'm so turned on right now I feel like I'm about to spontaneously combust. I never imagined the two of them would ever do this, but maybe it's the whiskey, or the fact that Shane is almost forty – or a combination of the two. Whatever it is, I am *so* here for it.

Conor pulls his fingers out of my pussy and I groan in both frustration and relief. He holds onto my hip with one hand as he guides his cock inside me with the other.

"Oh. My. God!" I grind out the words as he pushes inside me, stretching me wider than I had ever imagined possible.

"God can't save you now, sweetheart," Shane chuckles.

"You need me to stop?" Conor pants as he stops moving.

"No," I shake my head. "Please don't."

"Good, 'cause this is so fucking hot," he growls as he pushes in a little deeper, his breathing hard and fast.

"How you doing back there?" Shane groans as he remains still, his cock throbbing inside me.

"There's no way I'm getting all the way in, bro," Conor replies. "I'm halfway and I think this is my limit."

"It is." I nod my agreement as tears prick at my eyes and my pussy throbs around them. "For the love of God can you both fuck me?"

"My pleasure," Shane growls as he rocks his hips upward and the pressure of having Conor's cock inside me as well means that Shane's is directly pressed against my G-spot. My entire body trembles and I whimper shamelessly.

"That's my girl," Shane soothes in my ear and my eyes roll back in my head. I'm not sure how much I can take of this before I pass out or explode in one huge, life-altering orgasm.

"You feel so good, Jessie," Conor hisses as he holds onto both my hips now and gently slides his cock halfway in and out of me. "You're squeezing me so tight."

I don't even recognize the sound that comes out of my mouth when my orgasm bursts out of me like a river breaking its banks. I soak the three of us and through the sound of the blood rushing in my ears, I vaguely hear Shane and Conor groaning their appreciation and calling me a good girl.

I lie on Shane's chest, completely boneless and in an

orgasm-induced haze as the two of them go on fucking me together. Shane comes first and when he's done, he pulls out of me, wrapping his arms tightly around me and pressing soft kisses on my forehead as Conor takes the opportunity to push deep inside me, causing me to moan softly into Shane's chest.

"Fuck me, Angel, I would spend my entire life buried in this pussy if I could," he groans as his own orgasm hits.

He grinds his release out into me and when he's done, he lies over me, resting his weight on his forearms as he rests his lips against my ear.

"That was fucking amazing," he whispers.

"I know," I breathe.

"Hot as fuck," Shane agrees.

"I... can't..." I mumble as my eyelids flutter closed.

"We're gonna have to stop fucking our girl into a coma, Shane," Conor chuckles and I smile.

"What? No. She looks so fucking sweet when she falls asleep like this."

"Hmm," Conor mumbles and then the two of them go on talking but I don't hear what they say, just the comforting murmur of their voices as I drift off to sleep.

WHEN I WAKE in the dark a few hours later, I am sandwiched between Shane and Conor who lie on either side of me. We've all moved to the other side of the bed where it's dry and I'm wearing a soft t-shirt that smells like Shane's cologne. They must have cleaned me up a little and slipped this on me while I was passed out in a tequila and orgasm-induced daze.

I listen to the sound of their soft breathing and smile. I take Shane's hand and pull his arm around me as I snuggle against Conor's chest and close my eyes.

This is perfect.

My life is perfect.
Well, almost.

CHAPTER 4
JESSIE

I groan as my eyes blink open and my head throbs with a dull ache. I'm lying on Conor's hard body and he wraps an arm around me.

"You okay, Angel?" he murmurs.

"No. I've got my very own private marching band in my head right now," I groan.

"I told you to lay off that tequila," he says with a soft chuckle.

I blink and look around the room. "Where's Shane?"

"He got up about a half hour ago to make a start on breakfast."

I push myself up and look into his eyes. "Don't either of you ever get a hangover?" I whisper as I press my palm against my forehead.

He shakes his head. "Nope."

"Urgh. Now I know why I hardly ever drink."

Conor tucks my hair behind my ear and narrows his eyes at me. "You didn't seem that drunk?"

"Well, no. I wasn't. But Liam and Mikey... Tequila..." I groan loudly. "I only had a couple of shots."

Conor laughs softly. "Let's go get you some coffee and some toast and you'll feel better."

"Hmm," I manage a smile. "Did we do anything while I was wasted?" I press my lips together to stop myself from laughing when I see the look on his face.

He frowns at me. "What? You don't remember?"

"Remember what?" I giggle and it makes my head throb again.

"Jessie!"

"Of course I do. I'm just playing."

"*Thank fuck,*" he breathes.

"It was amazing by the way." I smile at him and my cheeks suddenly burn with heat at the memory of both him and Shane taking me together.

"It sure was, Angel," he says with a soft groan as though he's remembering too.

"We can do it again sometime, right?" I whisper because he said it could only be a one-time thing.

"Yeah we can do it again for my birthday." He winks at me before rolling out of bed.

THE BROTHERS' Aunt Em, cousin Aoife and her husband, Noel arrived shortly after Conor and I got out of bed. I woke the twins too, who were passed out on Liam's bed still wearing their clothes from the night before. A pint of water along with a cup of coffee and a slice of toast eased my hangover but I'm not sure theirs will be as easy to shift.

Now, we're all sitting at the kitchen table eating pastries and toast and jelly and talking about how much fun we had at Shane's surprise party last night.

Mikey almost snorts coffee out of his nose when we remind

him that he fell on his ass after he challenged Lucia Montoya to a dance-off and decided to try a Magic Mike style dance to *Pony* using one of the kitchen chairs.

"You made us all call you Magic Mikey," I giggle.

"I forgot about that too," Liam says as he holds onto his sides.

"You're lucky you landed on your ass, Magic Mikey," Shane tells him with a grin. "You almost face-planted the tiles."

He rubs a hand over his jaw. "And it would have been a damn shame to damage this handsome face."

"It sure would," I agree.

"We should have more parties," Mikey says with a huge smile on his face.

"Well, as long as they're not for me," Shane replies as he takes a sip of his coffee.

"Aw, you loved it." I ruffle his hair and he smiles.

"Did you have any idea at all they were planning this?" Aoife asks him.

"No," Shane says with a shake of his head. "The four of them didn't give anything away. These two played their parts like Broadway actors when they were trying to get me back here." He nods toward Conor and Liam, and I close my eyes as I remember the reason Mikey used to get him back to the apartment.

"I obviously missed my calling," Liam says as he take a bite of a pastry.

"Hmm. Assholes," Shane says with a grin.

"What time does your flight leave?" I ask Em.

"Just after one," she replies as she glances at her watch.

"That is some plane you guys have got yourselves," Noel says with a low whistle.

"It's a beauty," Mikey replies with a smile. "And it comes in handy when you want to fly your family across the world for a surprise party."

"I really appreciate you all coming all this way for this," Shane says.

"We wouldn't have missed it," Em replies, smiling as she places her hand over Shane's.

"Besides, it's good to have two nights away from the tiny..." Noel starts to say but Aoife glares at him. "Our darling son," he quickly corrects himself.

"Good save," Conor whispers as he pats Noel on the back.

"I mean. I love him with every ounce of my heart and soul, but that kid has a pair of lungs on him that would put a world class soprano to shame." Noel chuckles and even Aoife smiles at that.

"Is Archie with your parents, Noel?" I ask.

"Yeah. They love having him."

"I can't wait to see him," Aoife says with a soft sigh.

"Yeah. Me too," Noel agrees.

Talking about baby Archie changes the mood in the room and I feel a sense of sadness and disappointment washing over me. Liam is sitting beside me and he reaches beneath the table and gives my thigh a reassuring squeeze.

"Do you think you'll be coming back to Ireland any time soon?" Aoife asks, unaware of the undercurrent of tension between her cousins and me that has started to ripple through the atmosphere.

"No plans to," Shane replies with a shake of his head.

"Oh no. Really?" Aoife asks.

"Aoife," Em says with a warning look.

"I know. It's just that Patrick is dead now..." she says quietly and it's as though even the mention of his name brings his ghost into the room with us.

The brothers all stiffen. Conor clears his throat. Noel shakes his head softly and Em shoots me an apologetic look.

"Ireland is beautiful," I say with a smile. "I loved it there, but now we have the jet, I'd love to visit the rest of the world. We went to the Caribbean for our honeymoon. Have you been there? The sea is the most incredible shade of blue." I sigh. "Like something from a movie."

"No. I'd love to though," Aoife replies and I can tell she is thankful for the change of subject.

"We had an amazing time, didn't we?" I say.

"That was a fucking incredible vacation," Conor says and his brothers agree and suddenly the mood is a little lighter again. I mean how could it not be? We spent two weeks on a luxury yacht doing nothing but lying in the sun, eating incredible food and having super-hot sex.

"Jessie wore nothing but a string bikini for two weeks," Mikey says with a wistful sigh.

"Mikey!" I admonish him as everyone else around the table laughs.

"What, Red?" He winks at me. "Anyway, speaking of vacations, that reminds me..." He looks at Liam who leans forward in his chair.

"Oh, yeah," Liam replies with a grin. "We have a proposal."

"This sounds fucking dangerous already," Conor says with a groan.

"Did you come up with this proposal last night while you were juiced on tequila?" Shane asks.

"Yeah, but it's still perfectly valid," Mikey replies.

"Yeah," Liam agrees.

"So put us out of our misery," Conor says.

"We want a Jessie-cation," Mikey proudly announces.

"A what now?" Shane asks with a frown as everyone else around the table looks at them in confusion.

Liam grins at his oldest brother. "Conor got the road trip from Arizona. You got your time alone in Ireland. Me and Mikey should get a trip with Jessie too."

"A Jessie-cation!" Mikey declares and I can't help but laugh.

"No way," Shane says with a shake of his head.

"Shane!" the twins shout in unison.

"I think this is our cue to leave." Em laughs softly and she stands. "Thank you so much for arranging all of this. It's been wonderful to see you all."

Shane gets up and walks around the table to give his aunt a hug.

"This discussion isn't over," Mikey says as everyone starts to say their goodbyes.

WHEN EM, Aoife and Noel have left, we head back to the kitchen to start clearing up.

"We were serious about some time alone with Jessie," Mikey says as he loads the dishwasher.

"A Jessie-cation?" I arch an eyebrow at him and he smiles at me.

"We've never had that and you both have," Liam reminds his older brothers.

"They have a point, bro," Conor says with a sigh.

"But..." Shane starts to say but then he looks at me. "What do you think?"

"It sounds good to me," I admit. I mean I get a vacation and some time alone with the twins. What's not to like?

"How many days?" Shane snaps as he stuffs his hands into his pockets.

"Well, you both had four and there's two of us, so eight?" Mikey suggests.

"Fuck, no!" Conor snaps and I giggle.

"One!" Shane offers.

"Um. No," Liam replies.

"How long then?" Mikey asks, his face serious now.

"Two?" Shane suggests.

"Fuck that, Shane. Be serious," Mikey replies.

"Three?" Conor suggests.

"Four and it's a deal," Liam adds.

I jump up onto the kitchen counter and watch the four of them negotiating over me like I'm a car or something. I should probably hate it, but I don't.

Shane narrows his eyes at them. "Where are you taking her, first?"

"The lake house," Liam replies.

Shane visibly relaxes when it's clear we won't be traveling far. "Can we visit?" he asks with a grin.

"No!" Liam and Mikey reply.

"Do we have to agree to this, Con?" Shane groans.

"Kinda," Conor says with a shrug.

"And it's all fine by me by the way," I pipe up. "In case any of you were wondering."

Mikey grins at me and walks over to me, wrapping his arms around my waist and pulling me to him until he's standing between my thighs. "Jessie Ryan, would you please come to the lake house with me and Liam for four whole nights so we can worship and adore you all to ourselves?"

"Yes," I whisper as even the thought makes warmth spread through my core.

"When is this Jessie-cation taking place?" Conor asks.

"End of the month?" Liam suggests.

I see Conor and Shane working the dates in their heads. That will be a few weeks after ovulation time.

"Fine," Shane eventually agrees.

"Yes!" Mikey punches the air. "This is going to be fucking *epic!*"

Liam laughs softly while Shane and Conor roll their eyes.

"I can't wait," I whisper.

"Me neither, Red," Mikey growls before he seals his lips over mine.

CHAPTER 5

MIKEY

J essie squeals as I pick her up and toss her over my shoulder while Liam grabs our bag from the car. The lake house is our second home so we didn't bring much, besides if I have my way we won't be needing a lot in the way of clothes. Four whole days with Jessie to ourselves. I can't fucking wait.

I put her on her feet as soon as we're inside the house and she rewards me with a soft, deep kiss.

"I am so fucking excited for our Jessie-cation," I tell her.

"Me too," she breathes, her eyes dark with heat.

I swallow hard. *Fuck*! I'm not even going to make it through the next ten minutes without fucking her. I don't know if any of us are going to be able to walk out of here when this week is through.

Liam walks in behind us and drops the bag onto the floor. He sees Jessie in my arms and the look on her face and he whistles softly. "Are we even bothering to unpack yet, baby?" he asks with a soft chuckle.

"No." She shakes her head.

"Where do you want us to fuck you first, Red?" I growl as my cock starts to harden.

"Right here is fine," she purrs.

"Right here, huh?" Liam asks as he steps behind her.

"Yeah," she moans softly as my twin pulls her hair to the side and starts to pepper soft kisses over her neck.

"Let's get you naked," I whisper as I reach for the edge of her sundress. She raises her arms in compliance and I pull it off over her head until she's standing in her white cotton bra and panties.

"Fuck, Jessie. Where did you get these?" Liam growls as he tugs on the waistband.

"From the store. Why?" she whispers.

"Because they look so fucking sexy on you," he groans as he fists his hand inside them and I chuckle. He and I are so fucking different. The tiniest scrap of black lace does it for me, but my twin has a raging boner for her comfy cotton pants.

"I think we're gonna have to leave them on while we fuck you," he says and I grin at him over her shoulder.

"Liam," she gasps, spreading her legs wider as she rolls her hips against me and I assume he's got a finger or two inside her.

I slide my hand down her body and into her panties until I reach her clit and rub softly. She wraps her arms around me and buries her face into my neck, whimpering as our hands work together to bring her to the edge.

"Oh, God!" she hisses as we press her between us.

"You close, baby?" Liam murmurs in her ear.

I slide a finger inside her to join my twin's and her legs tremble as her walls squeeze around us, pulling us deeper. "Oh, there it is," I chuckle as her body shudders and bucks and she moans a combination of both of our names as she comes hard for us.

When she's ridden the final waves of her orgasm we pull

our hands from her panties and I pick her up, wrapping her legs around my waist and carry her through to our bedroom with Liam close behind.

I throw her down onto the bed as Liam is already pulling off his clothes. I quickly follow him but he's done before me and he crawls onto the bed beside her. He takes off her bra and gives each nipple a brief suck before he rolls onto his back.

"I want you to suck my cock while you're being fucked in those panties," he growls.

"You love these panties, huh?" she giggles as she rolls on top of him and starts to trail soft kisses over his chest. I climb on the bed behind her, slapping her juicy ass before I bend my head and take a huge bite of it that makes her squeal.

Liam's hands fist in her hair, guiding her to where he wants her as she swirls her tongue over his skin.

"Fuck, baby, get that pretty little mouth on my cock," he hisses while I grab onto her hips to hold her steady for me, pulling her into the perfect position so I can rail her while she sucks him.

I leave her panties on for him, fisting the soft material in my hand and pulling it to the side so it stretches taut over her perfect ass and reveals the most beautiful pussy I have ever seen in my life. It glistens with her cum and as she sucks Liam's cock into her mouth, I dip my head to have a quick taste of her. Running my tongue over her hot entrance, she groans loudly around him.

Fuck! She tastes so sweet, I could eat her all day, but right now my cock is weeping to be inside her hot, tight cunt.

I grab her hips again and line up at her entrance. Then with a roll of my hips, I drive all the way inside her, pushing her further onto my twin's cock and making them both groan loudly at the same time.

Her pussy squeezes me like a vise as I drive into her, using the panties as leverage to go deeper and harder. I could live ten lifetimes and never get enough of this woman. As my balls draw into my stomach I think about all the times I've blown my load in her and how one day I'm going to put my baby in her too.

"Fuck, Jessie. You suck cock so good," Liam pants. Sweat glistens on his torso and his abs tighten as he's reaching his release. I've been fucking women with my twin for as long as we were old enough to fuck and I know when he's on the edge.

I drive into her harder and she sucks his cock deeper until he roars her name while I keep on fucking her through his climax. When she finally comes up for air, she wipes her mouth and purrs like a fucking kitten.

"You want to give me a hand?" I wink at him and he grins back at me.

"Come here," he says, pulling her to lie on his chest as I push her down. He pulls her legs either side of his hips so she is stretched open for me. Then he slides his hand between their bodies and rubs her clit while I pound her pussy, the wet sucking sounds loud enough to be heard over our heavy breathing and moans.

"You hear how wet our girl gets for us?" Liam asks and I growl my agreement as my balls draw up into my stomach and warmth spreads through my core. I circle my hips, hitting that spot deep inside that makes her whimper because I need to make her come before I do.

"Oh! Mikey," she breathes as her pussy squeezes me tighter. She buries her face into Liam's neck as her orgasm ripples through her body and her hungry little squeezes grow more insistent until I can't hold off a second longer and I fill her with my cum.

I lie on top of her when I've emptied every last drop into her.

"This vacation is going to be so much fun," she giggles.

"You better believe it, Red," I sigh as I rest my face against her back, holding my weight on my forearms so I don't crush her against Liam.

"Love you two," she says softly.

"We love you too, baby," Liam says as he tucks her hair behind her ears.

"Hmm," I mumble my agreement before I roll onto my side, pulling her with me so she's lying on her side between the two of us. We each wrap an arm around her waist and I look at her beautiful face and feel more at peace than I ever have in my entire life.

CHAPTER 6
LIAM

I walk into the master bedroom to find Jessie but I can't see her. It's our second night at the lake house and it has been without a doubt two of the best days of my entire life. I love sharing her with my brothers, but I also love getting her to myself for a while too. Both Mikey and I have managed some time alone with her and I know he loves it just as much as I do.

The light from the bathroom is on and the door is half-open so I walk inside. She's putting a box of tampons back on the shelf but she must hear me coming in because she turns and looks at me. When she does, my heart breaks for her. Tears are running down her face and she wipes them away with her hand.

I cross the room in two strides and wrap my arms around her, picking her up so she can wrap her legs around me too.

"I'm sorry, baby," I whisper in her ear.

She sobs into my neck as she clings to me. This has happened every month for the last seven months and I swear each time she gets even more heartbroken than the last and it kills me to see her so upset. I walk back into the bedroom as

Mikey walks in. He looks at us both, his eyes wide as he wonders why our wife is sobbing in my arms.

"She got her period," I whisper as I carry her to the bed.

"Fuck, I'm sorry, Red," Mikey says as he walks to us, hugging her from behind until she is the Jessie-meat in a Ryan-brother sandwich.

"I'm fine," she sniffs but her hot tears keep falling onto my neck.

I flash my eyebrows at Mikey and he nods his understanding. We need to take care of our girl. Shane and Conor will want to know but they'll only worry about her if I call them now.

Mikey presses a soft kiss on the back of her neck. "You got cramps too, Red?"

"Yeah," she whispers.

He rubs her back. "I'll go make you some of Conor and Shane's stinky stuff."

"Thanks, Mikey," she mumbles.

With a final kiss on the top of her head, he walks out of the room to go make her one of our older brother's famous healing poultices. They stink, but they are great for muscle pain. They are also the best thing for period cramps according to Jessie – well aside from orgasms, but she's clearly not in the mood for any of them right now. Not that she ever is on her first day. The cramps are worse in the first twenty-four hours; it's the second day when she gets hornier than a teenage boy at the beach.

I crawl onto the bed and lie down, pulling her on top of me. She's stopped crying and she just lies there on me while I rub my hands over her back.

"It will be okay, baby," I whisper, brushing her hair from her cheeks where it's gotten stuck to them with her tears.

"What if it's not, Liam?" she whispers.

I cup her chin, tilting her face so I can look into her beautiful blue eyes. "What do you mean?"

"What if I can't give you all a baby?"

I frown at her. "But you will. You know what the doc said. It could take up to a year or more."

"But what if there's something wrong with me?" Her voice sounds so small and quiet. Seeing my feisty, stubborn wife this broken is too fucking hard to deal with. "There is nothing wrong with you, Jessie. And we don't care about a baby as long as we have you."

"You're just saying that to make me feel better," she sniffs.

"I'm not."

"But I thought you all wanted a baby?"

"We want you, Jessie. A happy you. We should never have started with those stupid ovulation tests."

She blinks at me and I wince. I shouldn't have said that aloud, but it's true. I've been thinking for a couple of months that there's too much pressure attached to this whole baby-making thing, for Jessie at least. Not that fucking her senseless for three days a month isn't fun, but we do that pretty much every day regardless.

"Mikey!" Jessie groans softly and my eyes snap open. She's lying on her side in between the two of us, facing me with her back pressed up against him. But why is she moaning his fucking name in my ear? She never gets us mixed up.

It's hot and we don't have any covers over us. Glancing down, I see my twin's hand in her panties and everything becomes clear.

"You pair of fucking deviants," I chuckle.

"She's got cramps, haven't you, baby?" Mikey whispers.

"Uh-huh," she groans as she bites down on her lip.

I turn onto my side and keep watching them, his hand

fisting in her panties as he rubs her clit. She drapes her leg over mine and grinds herself onto me.

"Are you close, baby?" I ask as I brush her hair back from her face.

"Yes," she moans as she looks up at me through her long, dark lashes.

I lean forward and kiss her, sliding my tongue inside her as she wraps an arm around my neck and pulls me closer until I feel Mikey's hand working her now as it's wedged between us. Her body tenses as her orgasm draws closer and she sucks me deeper into her mouth, clawing at my neck as my brother tips her over the edge. I swallow her whimpers and moans as he keeps on rubbing her clit until she melts into us both. She pulls back, gulping in air.

"You're so fucking horny, Red," Mikey chuckles.

"Me?" She giggles. "You're the one who woke me up with your hand in my panties."

"Because you were grinding that fine ass of yours on my cock," he protests. "You knew exactly what you were doing, Red."

"Hmm, maybe," she purrs and my cock throbs at the sound.

"How are your cramps?"

"A little better," she breathes.

"You need some more help?" I arch an eyebrow at her and she nods.

I suck my two fingers, coating them with spit before I slide my hand between us, beneath the waistband of her underwear and to her hot pussy until I find her clit. I apply gentle pressure and she gasps as I keep circling the swollen bud of flesh with my fingers. I'm as hard as iron and I am fucking desperate to pull that tampon out of her and fuck her, but I know she'll be too sore for that right now. She reaches into my shorts and squeezes my dick, making me suck in a breath.

I look at my twin over her shoulder and he knows exactly what I'm thinking. He takes hold of her wrist and pulls her hand away, lacing his fingers through hers.

"Just relax and let us take care of you, Red," he growls in her ear.

"Hmm," I murmur as I trail soft kisses over her jaw as Mikey does the same to her neck. "This can just be about you. Okay?"

"Okay." She smiles and her eyelids flicker as I bring her close to the edge again. She is so fucking selfless when it comes to us and I love being able to take care of her. I kiss her again as I rub my fingers over her swollen clit, circling the delicate bundle of nerves as I tongue-fuck her mouth. Her nipples are hard against my chest as she presses herself against me. Her skin is hot and damp as she lies sandwiched between me and my twin. Mikey pulls her hips back slightly, to allow my hand more room, and no doubt so he can grind his cock on her beautiful ass while he sucks on her neck.

"Fuck, Liam!" she moans into my mouth, grinding herself onto my hand as her orgasm hits. She shudders, bucking against me and whimpering as I keep on working my fingers until every last tremor has ebbed away.

I break our kiss and pull back so I can get a good look at her. Her eyes dark and her cheeks flushed pink. "God, you are so fucking beautiful, baby."

Her blush deepens and she smiles at me. "So are you," she whispers.

"You feel better now, Red?" Mikey asks.

"Yes," she breathes as she stretches her body. "Thank you, both."

I cup her chin in my hand, rubbing the pad of my thumb over her cheek. "You sure?" I ask her and she blinks at me. We both know I'm not just talking about the cramps.

"Yeah," she says with a soft sigh. "There's always next month, right?"

"We've got all the time in the world," I say with a wink and she presses her head against my chest until I'm looking into the concerned face of my twin.

He shakes his head softly. Our girl is heartbroken and I wish I could fix it for her.

CHAPTER 7
JESSIE

I stand in the shower with the hot water running over my body. I've had a lovely day with the twins. Mikey made us pancakes for breakfast and then we watched movies all morning on the huge screen in our cinema room. After lunch, we went for a swim in the lake that ended in the three of us fooling around on the deck when we got out.

My cramps have all but gone. I'm in our beautiful lake house with two of my favorite people in the whole world, who have done nothing but take care of me since yesterday evening when my period arrived. So, why do I still feel like this? I can't even describe what it is. An emptiness maybe? Disappointment tinged with failure. What if there's something wrong with me? What if I can't give my incredible husbands the one thing they want?

I close my eyes and let the water wash over my face. I don't hear the sound of the bathroom door opening. The first thing I hear is his voice and it sends shivers along my spine.

"Hey, Angel," he says as his hands slide over my hips until they're resting on my stomach.

"Conor?" I wipe the water from my eyes and turn in his arms. "What are you doing here?"

He brushes a strand of wet hair back from my face. "The boys told us." He looks down at the shower floor and there is a faint trickle of blood pooling at my feet. "They said you were upset."

"Us?" I look behind him to see Shane pulling off his pants and boxers. The rest of his and Conor's clothes are strewn across the bathroom. A ball of emotion swells in my chest and I swallow it down before I start to cry.

Periods always make me so damn emotional. This was supposed to be the twins' chance to spend some time alone with me – our Jessie-cation – but they are so sweet and selfless that they called their brothers because I've been so upset. And now I feel guilty that I've spoiled our alone time.

"Move over," Shane says with a grin as he steps into the shower too.

"You didn't think we could stay away after Liam told us how upset you were last night?" Conor says as he turns me until he's standing under the water and Shane can press his body against my back.

"I'm okay," I lie and Conor narrows his eyes at me.

Shane pulls my long hair to the side and presses his lips against my ear. "It's natural to be disappointed, sweetheart," he breathes.

"Are you guys disappointed?" I look up into Conor's dark brown eyes.

"Only because you are, Angel," he replies.

Meanwhile, Shane traces the shell of my ear with his lips. "But don't for one second think that any of us are disappointed in you, Jessie. You are the only thing that matters. You got that?" he growls before he starts to pepper soft kisses down the side of my neck.

"Okay," I whimper as Shane's hand slides over my stomach, reaching between my thighs.

"Besides, we weren't sure the twins could handle you alone on your period," Conor says with a grin.

"Why not?" I blink at him as he runs a hand through his wet hair. God, he looks so freaking delicious it makes my ovaries ache in an altogether different way.

"Because you get so fucking horny, that you're even more insatiable than usual," Shane answers, murmuring against my skin as he continues nibbling my neck.

As if to prove his point he slides a finger through my folds and pushes inside me, making me moan softly.

Conor chuckles before bending his head low and sealing his lips over mine. He kisses me softly, his lips gently opening mine to allow his tongue inside. I curl my arms around his neck and lean into him while Shane gently thrusts his finger in and out of my pussy. I spread my thighs wider apart and Shane growls his appreciation in my ear as he adds a second finger. "So fucking needy, sweetheart."

I push my ass back against him, feeling his hard cock pressing into me and suddenly I'm desperate for both of them. I pull Conor closer until I'm sandwiched between the two of them so tightly I can barely breathe. But this is what I want. What I need.

"Our girl wants fucking, Con," Shane groans as my walls squeeze around him.

"Then let's oblige," Conor growls as he puts his hands on my waist. He and Shane have done this so many times, they're as in tune as the twins are when it comes to fucking me together. Shane slides his fingers out of me and Conor lifts me, wrapping my legs around his waist before he reaches back and shuts off the water.

Then he starts walking out of the shower and my eyes

widen in horror. "Where are you going? We need to stay in here," I gasp.

"Nah," Conor shakes his head. "We want to fuck you in bed."

"Yup," Shane agrees as he opens the door to the master bedroom.

"You can't," I look between them both.

"Why not?" Shane arches an eyebrow at me.

"You know why!" I hiss. "We'll need new sheets. Maybe even a new bed."

"Then we'll get some," Conor says with a shrug.

"But there will be..." I don't finish the sentence but I don't have to.

"You think a little blood is gonna bother us?" Conor winks at me before he throws me onto the bed and I bounce into the middle.

I look up at the two of them. Their hard, muscular bodies glistening with water and their huge cocks standing to attention. I have no idea what I did to deserve their devotion. They and their brothers make me feel like the luckiest girl in the world.

"It will be more than a little," I breathe as I brush my wet hair back from my face.

"Who gives a fuck?" Shane growls as he advances toward me first, grabbing hold of my ankles and pulling me to the edge of the bed before he drops to his knees. "Even two days without this pussy was too much," he says before he bends his head and swirls his tongue over my clit.

"Shane!" I blush as he pushes my legs wider apart and buries his head between my thighs.

"You taste so fucking good, Hacker," he groans as he licks and sucks my delicate flesh so good that I no longer care about the fact I'm on my period. He obviously doesn't.

I press my head back against the soft duvet as the waves of pleasure roll through me. When Conor crawls onto the bed beside me and sucks one of my hard nipples into his mouth, I groan as I experience a rush of wet heat.

"Fuck," Shane hisses as Conor's hand slides down my body and he starts to circle my clit.

"Just one before we fuck her?" Conor says with a grin.

I bite on my lip. I love it when they talk about me like I'm not here.

"Uh-huh," Shane mumbles against me as they work together with Conor sucking on my nipples and rubbing my clit as Shane licks and sucks around his brother's fingers. I whimper with need as they bring me close to the edge before easing me back down again.

"Please!" I cry out as I chase the orgasm they are deliberately withholding.

"You think she's had enough teasing, bro?" Conor asks with a chuckle.

I look down and all I can see between my thighs is the top of Shane's face and head. His eyes are closed but he opens them and winks at me as he pushes a finger deep inside me. I cry out as my climax washes over my body in a huge, rolling wave.

"Good girl," Conor mumbles as he trails hot kisses up to my throat and I think they're both going to kill me with hot sex and praise. Shane lets go of my ankles and plants them on the bed, so my legs are still wide open in front of his face and I can still only see from his eyes up. Then he takes a dark towel from the floor and wipes his face and that's when I realize they are so prepared for this. I glance to the side and realize the bed sheets have been changed too. We usually have white ones in here, but these are dark navy blue. There are more towels on the nightstand and a huge jug of water. When did they even have time to do this? I was only in the shower for maybe five minutes before they joined me. The twins helped! God, they are so fucking incredible.

"You want her ass or her pussy?" Shane asks Conor as he pushes himself up into a standing position.

"Pussy. Always," Conor winks at me and heat floods my body.

Shane looks down at me as I lie trembling, both from the incredible orgasm they just gave me and the anticipation of what's to come.

He flashes his eyebrows at me. "Your ass is mine then, Jessie."

I gasp out loud as I suck in a deep breath. God this is going to get so messy.

Shane sits on the bed beside me, narrowing his eyes as they search my face. "If you've still got cramps, sweetheart, we don't have to do anything you don't want to."

"No, I want to. It's just..."

Conor chuckles softly as he runs his fingertip over my cheek. "We'll jump in the tub straight after. Okay?"

"Okay," I whisper.

Shane frowns at me. "We always fuck when you're on your period. Why is this any different?"

"Because we usually do it in the shower, or the tub, or the lake." I arch an eyebrow at him. "Or there's only one of you and I wear a tampon until, you know... We've never done this before," I whisper.

"Hmm, well you get a period every four or five weeks and they last for three to four days, so it was only a matter of time, right?" Shane says with a wink. "It'll be fine."

"Hmm," Conor agrees as he lies down on the bed. "Come here." He holds out a hand and I take it, allowing him to pull me up until I can straddle him. He grabs my hips in his powerful hands. "How wet are you?" He licks his lips as he looks down at my pussy.

"Soaking," I whisper.

"I bet you are, my horny little angel. Slide onto my cock so I can feel you," he growls.

I shift my hips, taking hold of his shaft with one hand so I can lower myself onto it. I glide on easily, taking him all the way to the hilt until he's touching that sweet spot inside me. There is a delicious ache in my cervix that throbs when he thrusts his hips and goes that little bit deeper.

"Fuck, Jessie!" he hisses as he keeps a grip of my hips, holding me in place while he drives upward, probing deep inside and causing another rush of searing wet heat.

"Jesus, Conor," I whimper shamelessly as I grind down on him as much as I can.

"You love my cock, don't you, Angel," he groans.

"Yes. I love the way you fuck me." I moan loudly as the plea-sure vibrates through my body, causing the throbbing deep inside me to intensify. I need some release and I need it now. I close my eyes, only vaguely aware of Shane crawling onto the bed behind us. But when he grabs my waist, his hands directly above Conor's, shivers of pleasure skitter along my spine. His breath is on my ear, hot on my cool damp skin. "Lean forward, sweetheart so I can get inside you too."

I nod and bend forward until I'm lying on Conor, my chest flush against his and my head tucked into his neck as he stills his movements to allow his brother to ease inside me. He edges the tip in first, sticky and wet with lube, and I moan softly.

"More," I urge and he presses deeper. I will never get used to the feeling of being stuffed full of their huge cocks. It is exquisite – ecstasy bordering on the brink of pain.

"More?" he growls. He wouldn't usually be so gentle with me but I love that he is when I need it.

"Uh-huh," is all I can manage as my brain stops being able to function.

Shane takes his cue to push deep inside me and I moan into Conor's neck. Shane leans over me, until I'm sandwiched between him and his brother. "You ready, Con?" he hisses as he stays still, his cock throbbing in my ass.

Oh dear God!

"Yup." Conor grinds out the word, the effort of not moving making his heart beat fast against my cheek.

Then they start to fuck me. It's slow and gentle but raw and primal at the same time. They hold back as much as they can at first, one moving in while the other slides out until my walls are squeezing and pulsing around them both. They start moving faster, going harder and deeper as I teeter on the edge of oblivion.

"We gonna make you squirt, Angel?" Conor whispers in my ear as he brushes my hair back from my face.

"Yeah," I groan because I can feel it building. The intensity is mind blowing. Stars flicker behind my eyelids as every nerve ending in my body aches and throbs for the delicious release that constantly remains just a breath away. I'm so close for so long that I feel like I might pass out.

"You take us both so well," Shane growls in my ear. "Such a good fucking girl the way you let us fill you with our cocks."

Holy fuck! I'm going to pass out.

When Shane burrows his hand between us and rubs my clit, my orgasm detonates through my body like my veins are filled with black powder and he just lit the fuse.

I can't even speak any words, I just moan loudly as the rush of my climax bursts out of me, soaking the three of us.

"Good girl," Shane whispers in my ear as I pant for breath, completely spent and boneless, and in an orgasm-induced stupor.

I lie between them with a huge smile on my face as they grind out their own releases, stoking the embers of my climax with every thrust and sending soft fizzes of pleasure skittering through me.

When they're both done, they pull out of me slowly. Everything is wet and sticky, but I don't care. I lie on Conor's chest as Shane pushes himself up and climbs off the bed. I'd be happy not to move for the rest of my life.

My eyelids flutter closed.

"I think we fucked our girl into a coma," Shane laughs and Conor's responding chuckle rumbles through his chest and makes me purr like a contented cat.

"TIME FOR SLEEPING LATER, Angel. We need to get cleaned up," Conor whispers as he cups my chin in his hand and tilts my head so I can look into his eyes. "Shane has run the bath."

I blink at him. "Already?"

"You fell asleep," he says with a smile.

"Oh. I guess you really did fuck me into a coma." I smile back at him.

"Hmm. Gonna fuck you into another one later."

Then he sits up in bed and takes me with him. Standing up, he carries us to the bathroom. Shane is already in the tub waiting for us as Conor walks up the two steps, and gently places me inside before he climbs in himself. I didn't look down at either of us while he did, but the water around us turns a deep pink color. I'm sure my cheeks flush the same shade as I bite on my lip and Shane chuckles as he pulls me to sit beside him.

"You're so fucking cute when you pretend to be all sweet and innocent, Jessie."

"I'm not pretending. I *am* sweet and innocent," I protest making him and Conor laugh out loud.

I glare at both of them in feigned indignation, suddenly feeling much more awake.

"Well, you're definitely sweet," Conor says with a wink.

"Definitely not innocent," Shane adds.

I tilt my head to one side and bite on my lip as I look between them both. "Hmm. I suppose I'll take that."

Shane pulls me onto his lap and wraps his arms around me. "You'll take whatever we give you, won't you, sweetheart?" he growls.

"Yeah," I giggle.

"Good girl."

CHAPTER 8
MIKEY

I hear laughter coming from the bathroom and Liam and I walk inside and it makes me smile to hear her giggling. It was the right decision to call Shane and Conor here, even if it did put a huge dent in our Jessie-cation.

Liam and I start pulling off our clothes as soon as we get into the room. We had this tub specially built when the house was constructed. It's deep with a bench seat around the edge like a jacuzzi, and it's big enough that it fits all five of us easily. Despite that, I'd prefer only three of us to be in it for the next hour.

"You two are on dinner duty seeing as you gatecrashed our vacation," I say as I step into the hot, bubbly water.

"We didn't gatecrash. We were invited," Shane replies with a flash of his eyebrows.

"Whatever. You still gotta make dinner." I slide into the water next to Jessie and pull her to sit on my lap.

"Fair enough," Conor replies as he stands and starts to climb out of the tub. "Come on," he says to Shane and our oldest brother rolls his eyes but he stands too, giving Jessie a soft kiss on the cheek before he climbs out of the tub.

"You guys want anything in particular?" Conor asks as he grabs a towel and wraps it around himself.

"Hot dogs and nachos," Jessie squeals as she wraps her arms around my neck and smiles.

"Jessie Ryan," Conor leans down and kisses her forehead. "You have the culinary tastes of a fifteen-year-old boy."

"But we're on vacation," she purrs.

"Toss a salad too," I say with a shrug. "Then we've got all the food groups covered."

She smiles at me and my cock twitches. It's already semi hard from her naked ass on my lap but now I want her. I want my cock inside a part of her body. Like *now.*

I ignore my brothers and keep my eyes fixed on Jessie. Her eyes darken as she looks back at me while Liam slides into the tub beside us.

"We got anything for dessert?" Conor asks.

"Get the fuck out, Con," I growl and both he and Shane laugh as they leave the room, leaving Liam and me alone with our girl.

"I want my cock inside you now, Red," I groan as I rub my hands over her hips.

"Me too," Liam kneels on the floor of the tub in front of us, his eyes as dark as my own and the need for her written all over his face.

I know she'll just have been fucked by Conor and Shane together and she's always a little more tender around this time of the month, so I lift her off my lap and push myself out of the tub until I'm sitting on the edge.

I look down at my cock and she does too, licking her lips as she does. It stands thick and proud, desperate to feel her. She leans forward, starting at my balls she trails her soft, wet tongue the length of my shaft and I shudder. Then she swirls her tongue over the tip and I fist my hands in her hair as she sucks me into her silky smooth mouth, making a groan rumble through my chest.

She looks up at me, her blue eyes dark with lust as she sucks my cock.

"Take it all, Red," I growl.

While she's sucking me off with all the skill of a highly trained call girl, Liam edges up behind her, positioning himself so that he can fuck her pussy while I fuck her mouth. The moment Liam slides inside her, she groans around me, the sound muffled by my cock in her throat.

"Fuck, baby. You sure love sucking Mikey's cock because your pussy is fucking soaking here," Liam says.

She mumbles her agreement but then she goes on sucking and licking me as Liam fucks her and it doesn't take long for my balls to draw up into my stomach as I blow my load against the back of her throat.

I hold her head still as I pump out the last of my release into her mouth and she drinks it greedily, sucking every drop from me until I slide out of her. She looks up at me, her eyelids flickering and my cum dribbling from her lips, and I have never seen her look more beautiful. I wipe her chin with the pad of my thumb.

"Where the hell did you learn to suck cock so good, Red?" I arch an eyebrow at her. "You make me blow my load quicker than a horny teenager."

She smiles at me. "You guys give me plenty of practice."

"Damn right," Liam groans as he kisses her neck.

I slide back into the tub and look at Liam over her shoulder and he stops fucking her long enough so I can lift her onto my lap. "Come here, Red," I growl as I pull her to straddle me again so I can suck the sweet soft skin of her neck as my twin rails her.

"Oh fuck, you two..." she groans as he brings her to the edge.

"You love being fucked like this?" Liam asks her.

"Uh-huh."

I slide my hand down between her thighs and rub her clit until she whimpers with need.

"Your pussy is so fucking hot, Jessie," Liam growls in her ear. "I can't get deep enough inside you."

"I want you deeper," she moans softly as her eyelids flutter.

"Fuck!" Liam hisses as he drives harder and I increase the pressure on her clit before I seal my lips over hers and claim her mouth. Swirling my tongue against hers I can still taste myself on her.

Every time he thrusts inside her, he presses her against me, her hard nipples grazing my chest until she's pressed so tightly between the two of us that I feel every tremor ripple through her body as she comes for us. I swallow her soft whimpers as her orgasm ebbs away and when she's finally stopped trembling I let her up for air, pushing her damp hair back from her face.

"You're so fucking hot, Red," I hiss as I stare at her. My cock is twitching again already. I want her so fucking much. No amount of time with her is ever enough. In less than a minute, my cock is going to be as hard as iron again. How easy it would be to slide into her pussy and fuck her again. And how her eyes would darken if I did, because she is just as fucking insatiable as I am. But we need food and she needs a break.

"You're pretty hot yourself," she whispers and then she snakes one arm behind her, wrapping it around Liam's neck and pulling him to her so she give him a quick kiss on the lips. "I love you both so freaking much."

"Love you too, baby," Liam whispers.

"Thank you for inviting Shane and Conor here. I'm sorry if I spoiled our break by getting all crazy and emotional."

"Hey!" Liam snaps before he grazes his teeth over her shoulder blade in warning.

"You didn't get crazy, Red," I cup her face in my hands. "And you have every right to be upset."

"And you didn't spoil our Jessie-cation," Liam adds.

"Nope," I shake my head in agreement. "And now we have an excuse to have another one."

She giggles and the sound vibrates through my bones. Damn, I would fucking die for this girl.

"Shall we go see if Conor and Shane have managed to rustle up something vaguely edible for dinner?" I suggest.

"Hmm," she purrs softly as she leans forward and rests her head against my chest.

"You tired?" Liam asks as he rubs her back.

"Not tired exactly," she murmurs.

"Fucked?" I offer with a flash of my eyebrows.

She laughs again. "Exactly."

"Let's get out of here before Mikey fucks you again then." Liam laughs too and he goes to stand but she reaches for his arm and pulls him back to her until she's sandwiched between us again.

"I don't know what I'd do without you boys," she whispers.

"You'll never have to know, baby," Liam says as he presses a soft kiss between her shoulder blades and she purrs contentedly.

"Yeah. Stuck with us for life, Red."

"I'd better be," she says with a smile.

CHAPTER 9
JESSIE

I lean back in my chair and rub my hands over my stomach. "I'm so full," I groan loudly.

"You've barely eaten," Conor says as he looks down at the half-eaten hot dog and the small pile of nachos I've left. I've eaten plenty, but I usually have a huge appetite.

"I have," I protest. "And now I'm full."

"Well, we can't have this good food go to waste," Mikey says as he reaches over the table and takes my plate.

"You don't want dessert then?" Conor asks.

I look at the fudge cake in the center of the table and lick my lips. "I'm sure I could squeeze in a little slice shortly."

"Hmm. Thought you might," he says with a wink.

Shane is sitting beside me and he drapes an arm around my shoulder. "Are you feeling okay now, sweetheart?"

"Yeah. I'll be fine. Thank you all for looking after me."

"That's kind of our job, Angel," Conor says softly.

I smile at him. Right now I do feel fine, if slightly too full. I'm still disappointed but I count myself lucky that I have these four incredible men to share that with and to remind me that our life is about so much more than baby-making. And my period isn't kicking my ass too much either. It's definitely lighter than usual and apart from some initial cramps in the night, I haven't had any further.

"We were talking earlier when you were drying your hair," Shane says and my stomach drops. Serves me right for feeling too happy and smug.

"What about?" I whisper.

"We think we should stop with the ovulation testing."

"What?" I blink at him. "Why? Don't you all want a baby now?" My lip trembles as I speak and I curse myself for being so damn emotional.

"Yes, we still want a baby," Shane replies and his brothers voice their agreement.

"We just don't want you driving yourself crazy every month," Conor says as he reaches across and takes my hand.

"I'm not..." I say as a tear rolls down my face and I swat it away. What the hell is wrong with me?

"We all love the baby-making part, Red," Mikey adds.

"Yeah," Liam agrees as he takes my free hand in his. "But we don't want you to feel so much pressure, baby. It'll happen when it happens."

"But w-what about... W-we won't know when the time is right..." I stammer.

"Like you said yourself when we started this, there isn't a day goes by without you being fucked by at least one of us. We're not going to miss the window," Shane assures me.

"I know you said this is for me," I sniff, "so why does it feel like a punishment?"

"Jessie," Conor says with a sigh as both he and Liam squeeze my hands tighter.

"It's not a punishment at all," Shane replies. "But we all think it's for the best."

I pull my hands from Conor and Liam's. "So it's decided then?"

"No, Red. It's up to you," Mikey replies but I see the looks that his brothers shoot him. It is decided, whether I like it or not.

"But none of you want to keep doing it?" I swallow as emotion balls in my throat.

"Jessie," Shane cups my chin in his hand and turns my head so I can face him. "We don't want you to keep on doing those tests every day and putting so much pressure on yourself to get pregnant, but we do want to keep trying for a baby. We all still want this with you, but just with a little less pressure. Tell me you understand that," he frowns.

"I understand," I whisper and the room is full of silent tension, because this hurts me and I can't explain why.

"Cake?" Mikey offers in a desperate attempt to lighten the mood.

I force a smile. "Sure."

CHAPTER 10
SHANE

We've been back from the lake house for two days and Jessie has stopped with the ovulation testing. I know that she wanted to continue, but I hope in time she sees that it's the best for all of us if we take our feet off the gas a little. It's not like we fuck her much less when she's not ovulating anyway.

I look up from my computer screen to see her walking into my office and closing the door.

"Something wrong?" I look behind her at the door. She rarely closes it, no matter what we're doing.

"I wanted to talk to you about something," she says, biting her lip as she takes a seat opposite me. It's not the sexy lip biting she does, either, but the one when she's feeling anxious about something. It makes the hairs on the back of my neck stand on end. An anxious Jessie is never a good thing.

I close my laptop and rest my hands on top of it as I look at her, trying to read her mind so I can be prepared for whatever bombshell she's about to drop, because she looks to be in that kind of mood. She stares back at me, her bright blue eyes fixed on mine as I give her my full, undivided attention.

"What is it?" I ask.

She sucks in a deep breath before she speaks, another sign that she is nervous. "I've been thinking about the baby thing."

I try to keep my face neutral as I groan inwardly. I'd been wondering when she'd bring this up and I suppose two days of her not doing that was more than I'd hoped for. Every month when her period arrives I watch her get upset and disappointed, but each month her disappointment grows deeper, and because I know her so well, I see the feelings of guilt creeping in too. Not that she has anything at all to feel guilty about, but there's no telling her that.

I lean forward slightly. "What about it?"

"About why it hasn't happened yet," she whispers.

"Because it takes time," I remind her.

"I know that, but..." she swallows hard as though the words are lodged in her throat.

"But what, sweetheart?"

"I know it can take time for like normal couples..." Her voice trails off.

I keep staring at her because I don't know where she's going with this bit.

"But there are four of you. I ovulate every month. I'm always full of..." Her cheeks flush bright pink and I can't help but smile at how she blushes so easily around me and my brothers, like she isn't as much of a horny deviant as we are.

"Cum?" I offer.

"Yes," she whispers. "So why hasn't it happened yet?"

"You were on birth control for years. Doesn't that shit take time to leave your system?" I ask with a shrug.

"It's been seven months, Shane."

I stare at her. Do I tell her Mikey's theory, or will that only make her more upset?

Since we decided to try for a baby, my younger brother has

researched baby-making with a fervor that would put a Harvard student to shame. Jessie's periods aren't entirely regular and can come anywhere between four and five weeks. They're pretty heavy too and she gets bad cramps that incapacitate her for at least a day a month until they ease off. On our second month of trying, her period arrived after five weeks and one day. Her bleeding was even heavier than usual and the worst of her cramps lasted a full two days.

She put it down to the birth control hormones coming out of her system, but Mikey has a theory that she may have been pregnant and it was so early that we didn't notice that she lost it. It's just a theory. We will never know if it was true, but apparently it's much more common than people realize. But as Jessie is already upset enough, I don't land that one on her today.

"We spoke to Lisa about this," I remind her. Lisa is our personal physician. She removed Jessie's implant and then talked us all through what to expect. Not getting pregnant immediately was a part of it. "She said it could be up to a year before we conceive. I know it's upsetting, sweetheart, but it will happen when the time is right."

She leans forward in her seat as her eyes search my face. "But that's just it, Shane. What if it doesn't?" she asks quietly and the anguish on her face almost breaks my heart.

What the fuck do I say to that? "Then we'll deal with it," I offer.

"But wouldn't it be better to deal with it now?"

I rub a hand over my jaw and sigh. "What are you talking about, Jessie?"

"There are tests—"

"No," I interrupt her before she can finish the sentence.

"Not for you guys, for me," she says with a frown as though I've mistaken her meaning.

"I know what you mean, Jessie, and the answer is still no."

"But..." She stares at me, her mouth opening and closing like a fish in a bowl.

"You are twenty-seven years old. We've only been trying for seven months."

"But if there's something wrong?"

"Why are you so convinced there's something wrong with you?" I frown at her. I fucking hate seeing her driving herself crazy like this. I knew this baby-making would bite us in the ass. We shouldn't have started those damn ovulation tests.

"Because it can't be all of you, can it?"

"It's probably not you either, Jessie. Why is it such a big deal that you're not knocked up already?" I snap and regret my tone.

"Because it just is, Shane! Are you sorry you even agreed to try now?" she snarls, her eyes narrowed and her fists clenched at her sides.

"I'm going to pretend you didn't just say that," I snarl back.

"Then I'm getting the tests done."

"The fuck you are!" I shout, louder than I had intended to and she blinks at me in shock. I don't know why this pushes my buttons so damn much, but the fact she immediately jumps to the conclusion that something is wrong with her makes me pissed.

She pushes herself up from her chair. "You're an asshole!" she snaps as she heads for the door.

"Is that the only comeback you ever have for me?" I challenge her. I'm irrationally pissed now and that was probably uncalled for, but I don't care.

She spins on her heel until she's facing me again and flips me the bird. "Fuck you!" she snaps before she storms out of my office leaving me staring after her wondering how the hell we just got into an epic argument again.

CHAPTER 11
JESSIE

I blink away the tears as I march down the hallway to my bedroom. I don't know why I'm such an emotional wreck lately, but Shane is a complete jerk. I don't know what I was thinking going to him to talk about this. I mean, I get that he's an asshole a lot of the time, but he's also logical and rational too, so why the hell did he get pissed as hell about the fact that I want to have a few blood tests to rule out any physical reasons why I'm not pregnant yet?

I wipe the tears from my cheeks and sniff loudly. None of the other boys are home. Not that I think they'd be any more sympathetic to my cause. They just don't get the pressure I feel under every month when my period arrives. It makes me feel like a failure, even though my rational brain knows that's not true. The value of a woman, and a person, is so much more than their ability to procreate, so why the hell is it bothering me so much? Why is it consuming me?

Even as I ask myself the questions, I know the reason why. It's because I'm scared they'll change their minds. They're all excited by the thought of it right now, but I see their faces every month when I get so upset – it takes a toll on them too.

What if they decide they're happier as we are?

What if Shane decides that he was right not to want a child for all those years after all? Because that is my biggest fear, that I will have my perfect family ripped away from me again. Right now it is only a promise of a home full of children, and promises can be broken, right?

WALKING out of the bathroom after my shower, I see Mikey lying on my bed. He gives me a huge grin as I walk into the room, his eyes roaming over my body which is covered only by a small towel because all of the huge bath towels seem to have disappeared from my bathroom. I have an idea the hot, mischievous devil smiling at me had something to do with that.

"Hey, Red."

"Hey." I smile back at him as I approach the bed but then I see there is a mini dress and some black lace underwear laid out on it and I frown. "What's this? Are we going out?"

"You're going out," he says with a deep sigh. "But not with me. I was asked to get these ready for you." He fingers the lace of the panties and as he does, I see they're crotchless and my pussy floods with warm heat.

"But I'm under strict instructions not to even touch you," he adds with a roll of his eyes.

"What?" I flash my eyebrows at him as I sit beside him on the bed. "Since when do you guys obey rules like that?"

He runs a fingertip down my cheek, following my jawline and throat until it reaches the edge of my flimsy towel. Goosebumps prickle over my skin.

"Well, ordinarily, you know I wouldn't." He winks at me. "But Shane is currently in one of his *don't even look at me funny* moods."

"So he thinks I'm going out with him?" I roll my eyes. "He

hasn't even asked me. What if I'd rather stay here with you?" I move quickly, straddling him as he lies on the bed.

He rests his hands on my hips and shakes his head. "No way, Red. You're not getting me into a heap of trouble. You know the rules. You two have had a fight so you need to work it out. Don't be using me as a distraction." I close my eyes and Mikey sits up and wraps his arms around me. "Even if it would be the best distraction ever," he whispers in my ear. "Because I wish it was me you were wearing those panties for tonight, Jessie."

I open my eyes and look at him.

"But you know that you and him need to work this out."

"Did he tell you what we argued about?" I ask quietly.

"No."

"Aren't you curious?"

Instead of replying, he seals his lips over mine and kisses me, softly at first until I start to grind my hips against his hardening cock. A growl rumbles through his chest and he slides his tongue into my mouth as I rake my nails down his muscular back. Warmth pools in my core as he kisses me, rolling my hips over his cock until I'm moaning into his mouth. I shift my hips, trying to gain some friction on my pulsing clit, but he holds me still. When he pulls back from me, I'm left panting for breath and wanting more.

"I need to stop because I want to fuck you so bad," he breathes.

"You didn't answer my question," I remind him.

"What you two fight about is between you and him, Red. Right now, you should get ready because Shane wants you to meet him in the basement in a half hour."

I swallow hard. Part of me wants to tell Shane to go to hell. He doesn't get to act like an asshole and then start ordering me around like I'm his obedient servant. But the other part of me knows that this is his attempt at making things right. Besides, for the most part I enjoy him being a bossy alpha-hole.

"Fine," I say with a sigh as I climb off Mikey. "Hadn't you better leave then?"

Mikey laughs loudly. "No way. Just because I'm not supposed to touch you, doesn't mean I can't watch you getting dressed, Red. And if you could just wander around here in only your panties for the next half hour, that would be fucking perfect." He winks at me again and I clamp my lips together to stop myself from smiling.

"You're a deviant, Mikey Ryan." I shake my head.

"Only for you, Red."

A LITTLE OVER a half hour later I walk into the basement. There is no sign of Shane, but there is a sleek black limousine with its engine running near the elevator and a driver standing beside it. He opens the door as I approach and I peer inside to see Shane sitting on the back seat. He's dressed in a suit and a white dress shirt, open at the collar so that the tattoo of my name on the base of his throat can be seen. I'm still so mad at him, but that doesn't stop my pussy throbbing in anticipation at the sight of him.

I climb inside and sit on the opposite end of the seat so I'm as far away from him as I can reasonably be. I've got to make him work a little, right?

"Jessie!" he says, his tone full of frustration.

"Shane!" I snap back.

"Come here," he sighs as the car starts to move.

I remain in my seat so he moves along the bench instead and I suppress a smile. It may seem like a small victory, but making Shane Ryan bend is a huge feat and we both know it. He sits beside me, his thigh pressed against mine and the heat from his body, coupled with the thick tension in the confines of the car, makes goosebumps prickle along my forearms.

"Where are we going?" I ask, trying to keep my tone sharp, but he rests his hand on my thigh and it sends a jolt of electricity straight to my pussy.

"To dinner."

"At a restaurant?"

"Yes." He frowns at me.

"Oh?" I breathe. I can't help feeling a wave of disappointment. When he chose the crotchless panties, I thought I might be getting to visit The Peacock Club. The brothers own a string of exclusive, private members' sex clubs. I've been there before, but only during the day for a meeting. I've never been there in the evening yet, although I'm desperate to.

"You were expecting somewhere else?"

"Maybe," I whisper.

He laughs softly. "If I take you to a sex club wearing crotchless panties, Conor would come in and drag you out of there."

I turn to him and smile. That is so true. The reason we haven't been there yet is because Conor is so resistant to the idea. I'm sure he thinks it's some kind of free-for-all, when in fact it's probably safer than their regular club. Anything might go in a sex club, but as a rule it's a very safe and respectful place. Everything is consensual, unlike in some clubs when a girl can find herself getting groped just trying to get across the dance floor.

"We'll go there soon. Promise." He winks at me and I have to turn away from him because I want him so freaking bad. I swear he and his brothers have turned me into the horniest woman alive. Making out with Mikey earlier has left me needy and on edge and I know that Shane could resolve the issue in a matter of minutes, but until he apologizes to me I'm going to continue to be petty and resist him.

"You still pissed at me, sweetheart?" he asks in that tone that makes me hot and needy.

"Yes," I snap as I stare out of the window.

"I'm not apologizing, Jessie."

That certainly gets my attention and I turn back to him.

"Really?"

"What exactly do you expect me to be sorry for?" He arches an eyebrow at me.

"For being an asshole!"

"According to you, I'm always an asshole," he says with a shrug.

"Well, yeah. But you were extra asshole-y today."

He shakes his head in frustration.

"If you're not apologizing then what's all this for?" I narrow my eyes as I glare at him.

He reaches over and grabs me by the hips, pulling me until I'm straddling him. I gasp because I wasn't expecting that, but I make no effort to wriggle from his grip. We both know where this is heading and I'm powerless to stop it now. Being alone with him only ever leads to one thing.

"This is because I know you're upset. I know that you're pissed at me even though you know I'm right..."

I open my mouth to tell him that he's not right but he palms the back of my head and brings my mouth crashing down onto his, kissing me so hard I almost lose my breath. I waited a long time for one of Shane Ryan's kisses and they were worth every second. They are possessive and all-consuming.

Despite my anger at him, my body melts into his until I'm sagging against his chest and practically whimpering into his mouth. The feminist in me shouts at me to stop being so weak, but she's shouted down by the horny demon that the Ryan brothers have let loose.

He wraps his free arm around my waist, pressing me tighter

to him until I feel his hard cock pressing against my pussy. I wrench my mouth away from his, gasping for breath as pleasure rockets around my body and wet heat slicks between my thighs.

"I hate when you're pissed at me," he says as he brushes my hair back from my face. "Let me make it better."

"Shane," I breathe. "You can't just fuck me and pretend that today didn't happen. You completely dismissed my feelings."

He narrows his incredible green eyes at me. "That wasn't my intention," he finally says. "So if I did that, then I'm sorry."

I blink at him. An apology from Shane Ryan is a rare thing.

"And also I have no intention of fucking you before dinner." He grins at me.

"You're an asshole," I whisper.

"So you keep telling me," he says before he starts to trail soft kisses over my throat and I groan softly. "You're so needy tonight though, sweetheart. I can tell by the way you're grinding yourself on my cock. What did Mikey do to you?" he growls as one hand slides between my thighs and he dips a finger into my pussy.

"Nothing," I hiss.

"But you're fucking soaking. He must have done something."

"He kissed me. That's all," I whimper as I bear down, trying to get more of him inside me, but he pulls back so he can continue taunting me.

"That must have been some kiss." He withdraws his finger and runs it through my slick folds instead.

"It's these damn panties," I groan. "You know they make me horny."

"Hmm." He chuckles. Whenever he takes me out on a date he makes me wear crotchless panties and then he spends the rest of the night teasing me until I'm a trembling, dripping mess. "Well, I did just offer to make things better but you called me an asshole." He dips the tip of his finger inside me again and wet heat floods my pussy.

"Shane?" I plead.

"I'm going to enjoy teasing you all night," he whispers. "By the time I get you back in this car after dinner, you will be begging me to let you ride my cock."

I stare at him, chewing on my bottom lip. It used to be that I thought he had all the power in our relationship, but that has shifted significantly in the time we've been together. He's no longer just the grumpy alpha-hole who constantly pushes me, he's my husband, one of my best friends and he makes me believe I am his equal in every way.

Despite our argument earlier, I know that we will work out a solution eventually.

"I'm pretty sure you'll be doing some begging of your own," I purr.

He smiles at me. "Damn straight." He kisses me softly before he pulls back again. "You want me to make you come first though, sweetheart?"

Is this a trick question?

"Yes, please," I purr as I grind my hips against him.

"Good girl," he whispers as he drives two fingers deep inside me and that coupled with his words makes wet heat slick his fingers. "You like that, huh?"

"Shane!" I groan loudly, wrapping my hands around his neck and grinding shamelessly on him as he finger-fucks me in the back of the car.

"You hear how wet you are for me?" he growls. "How the fuck am I going to get through dinner without fucking you?"

"Then don't," I gasp. "Fuck me now!"

"I can't, Jessie. I want to eat this pussy on our way home later, and I much prefer it when it's only your cum I'm tasting."

"Then pull out," I offer as he rubs his thumb against my clit and stars begin to flicker behind my eyelids.

He laughs softly. "You know I can't do that. Besides where else would I come? I don't want to spoil your beautiful dress."

"I don't care," I gasp as I ride his fingers, chasing the orgasm that I know he's deliberately withholding now.

"You would when we got to the restaurant, Jessie. Trust me," he chuckles as he pulls me closer to him, stilling my hips so he can push deeper inside me and press that sweet spot that makes my entire body tremble.

"Shane!" I shout as my climax washes over me in delicious rolling waves.

"That's my girl," he chuckles in between peppering my neck with soft bites and kisses.

CHAPTER 12
JESSIE

The car rolls to a stop and I peer out the window and smile. This is the little Italian restaurant in Brooklyn where we came for pizza the night the boys proposed to me. Back in Ireland, Shane made me an offer that his brothers still don't know about and they never will. He suggested that I could marry Conor and have a regular life with a husband and babies, and he and the twins would step back if that was what I truly wanted.

It was the day of their father's funeral when I finally gave him my answer – and that was that I wouldn't marry one of them unless I could marry all of them. I have never been able to choose between the four of them and I never want to. I was happy to go on with the four of them as we were, because marrying four people is still illegal in the state of New York. However, I underestimated my husbands. I mean the Ryan brothers don't operate within the limits of the law for anything else, why would they care about doing that when it came to marriage?

So one night shortly after we came home from Ireland, they brought me here. The place was lit entirely by candlelight and it was empty except for us and halfway through our meal, the four of them dropped to their knees and proposed to me. I have never said yes to a question more quickly in my life.

The place isn't closed to the public tonight though, and there are diners sitting outside in the warm evening sunshine.

"You're really bringing the big guns tonight?" I arch an eyebrow at him.

He leans forward, his lips dusting over my ear. "You've seen nothing yet," he growls and my stomach flutters with excitement.

I'm about to ask what else he has planned when the car door is opened by our driver.

Shane climbs out first and holds out his hand to me. "You ready Mrs. Ryan?" he winks at me as I reach for him and my heart swells in my chest. I will never get tired of being called that.

"Sure am," I grin as I step out of the car, pulling the hem of my short dress down once I'm outside on the street.

Shane slides an arm around my waist and we walk into the restaurant, where the owner, Tony, greets us enthusiastically and seats us in our usual booth near the back. He leaves us with our menus and then walks away with a huge smile on his face. He's practically squirming with delight and I frown as I watch him walk to the kitchen. Tony knows us and he's always smiley and happy to see us, like with all of his customers, but he is downright giddy this evening.

"Did he seem like super-buzzed to you?" I ask Shane as I turn back to him.

He is looking at his menu. "Hmm. Didn't notice," he mumbles without making eye contact.

"What are you up to, Shane Ryan?"

He looks up from his menu and I arch an eyebrow at him.

He doesn't answer, instead he looks behind me. I turn in my

seat and almost fall off it as I see who's walking toward us. No wonder Tony was practically squeaking with excitement.

"Is that Carl Paxton?" I whisper as I stare at the silver haired guy in a chef's uniform making his way to our table.

"Maybe," Shane replies.

"Oh. My. *God*! How did you swing this, Shane?" I gasp as I keep my eyes trained on Carl. He's one of the most famous chefs in the entire world. He's been on a tour of South Asia recently for his hugely popular cooking show and he only got back to the States yesterday. I know this because I stalk him on Instagram. I spend hours salivating over the images of his dishes, because he's not just a famous chef, he is world renowned for his desserts. This man can do things with butter and sugar that should be considered illegal. Mikey and I have tried to recreate some of them with varying levels of success.

Tony hovers nervously behind him as Carl finally reaches our table. Some of the other diners also notice him and they swivel their heads and their chairs so they can stare at him too. As well as being known for his incredible culinary skills, he can also be seen cooking shirtless with his toned, tattooed torso on full display to the delight of his millions of followers – both male and female.

Gasps and whispers rumble through the small restaurant as the superstar walks through it with a towel casually slung over his shoulder.

When he finally reaches us, he smiles widely, showing a set of perfect white teeth. Then he holds out his hand to me.

"You must be Jessie?" he says with a wink.

I take his outstretched hand but I don't speak. I stare at him open-mouthed and he laughs softly.

"And Mr. Ryan?" his eyes drift to Shane and I remember that my super-possessive and jealous husband is sitting opposite me. "Thank you for inviting me."

"Well, my wife loves your show," he replies and I glance at him, looking for any signs that he is annoyed with me for fangirling over a sexy chef, but his face is unreadable right now.

"You do?" Carl looks back to me.

"Yes. I watch it every week. Me and my husband make your banana waffles all the time."

Carl glances back to Shane again. "Have you tried my passionfruit crepes yet?" he asks us both, understandably thinking that he is the husband I'm referring to and not one of my other three. Neither Shane nor I correct him.

"Not yet, we're working our way through your *Naughty but Nice* book first," I babble. "We want to make sure we try every one so we don't miss anything."

"Wow! Now there's a blast from the past." He laughs again. "I almost forgot about that book."

I stare up at him, aware that I have a huge goofy smile on my face but I don't care. Since he got mega-famous, some of his dishes and his cookbooks got a little too pretentious and fancy for my tastes. I much prefer his earlier stuff that was the kind of food most ordinary people could attempt to make. Now you need three dozen exotic ingredients to make one of his recipes. I have no doubt that they would taste just as amazing though.

"I love your old stuff," I blurt out. "I used to watch your *Cooking with Carl* show all the time."

He rubs a hand over his jaw as he stares at me, his brown eyes twinkling as he narrows them. "That was at least ten years ago. You really are a fan."

"Yep. You're like my hero," I say and immediately regret those words. I didn't mean like in any other way than making delicious desserts. *Fuck!*

He nods his head and puts a hand over his heart. "I'm honored."

By now, some of the other diners have edged closer to our

table, cell phones in hand, as they stand and wait for a chance to grab a selfie. He notices them and then rolls his eyes.

"Duty calls. I'll just deal with this and then I'll be back to discuss your options," he says with a wink before he turns his megawatt smile back on and spins around to face his adoring crowd.

I turn back to Shane, wincing as I wonder how pissed he's going to be.

He is staring at me but his face is still unreadable. "What the fuck?" he growls.

"I'm sorry. But he's like..."

"Your hero?" He arches an eyebrow at me.

I close my eyes and suck on my lip. God, I really said that. I'm such an idiot.

"I only meant as like a dessert-hero," I whisper.

"A dessert-hero?" he rests his chin on his hand as he continues to stare at me. "My mistake. I didn't realize there was such a thing."

I bite back a laugh. "You know how much I love dessert," I whisper.

"Hmm. And I know why you used to love that show," he says and I realize he's not mad at all. When I was sixteen, I was kidnapped and held hostage by an assassin named the Wolf. I used to watch Carl's show on morning cable TV because it was one of the few channels we had. I would pretend he was cooking just for me and answer his questions as though he was actually in the room. Back then he was warm and friendly – at least on TV. Now he sometimes comes across as an arrogant asshole, but he's still a great chef.

"I didn't mean to babble like a teenage girl," I say as a blush creeps over my skin. "I promise I wasn't flirting."

"I know that, sweetheart," he growls as he leans closer, placing his huge hand over mine. "Because if I thought you were, I would have bent you over this table, taken off my belt and your panties and spanked your ass right in front of him."

"Shane!" I hiss even as wet heat pools in my center.

"Then I'd make you come on my fingers while he watched so that when you moan my name, he would know exactly who you belong to."

I suck in a breath as heat creeps over my chest. "You're a devil."

He laughs softly. "You're wet thinking about it though, aren't you?"

"Yes," I admit.

"But *he* was flirting with *you*," he goes on.

"He wasn't," I shake my head. "He's got like an army of adoring female fans."

"Like you?" he frowns at me.

"I adore his cooking ability. Nothing more. You know that."

We're interrupted by Tony bringing a bottle of red wine to our table before he takes our order. I order a small fillet steak and asparagus so I can save plenty of room for whatever delights Carl is going to prepare, while Shane orders a T-bone with all the fixings.

When Tony has left, I look at Shane. "Thank you so much for this, Shane."

"You're welcome."

"How did you even pull it off?"

"His agent owes me a favor," he replies with a shrug.

"That must be some favor."

"Hmm." He takes a sip of his wine.

"Oh, God. You didn't threaten to kill him or something, did you?"

"Jessie!" He frowns at me and I giggle.

"Sorry. I'm just messing with you."

"You know I adore you, right?"

"Yes," I breathe.

He leans closer, standing slightly until his lips brush my ear. "But make no mistake, if you flutter your eyelashes at Carl Paxton again when he smiles at you, I *will* spank your ass in the middle of this restaurant and then I will break every bone in his hands."

I look at him and swallow as he sits down. He's being completely serious now and it's still as hot as hell. Not the breaking Carl's hands part, obviously. I would die if he did that because of me.

"I'll be good. Promise," I whisper.

He nods as Carl makes his way back to our table. He stands beside us and claps his hands together. "So, I thought the zucchini and chocolate mousse with the cherry foam? What do you think?"

I swallow and look between him and Shane. I don't want to offend him, but the sound of cherry foam makes me feel a little nauseous. I mean I just don't get the point of foam on a plate. It's like air. And zucchini is a freaking vegetable. It does not belong in a dessert. "Actually, I would prefer your churros with the peanut butter and chocolate dipping sauces," I say.

He stares at me and for a second I wonder if I've deeply offended him, but fancy desserts really aren't my thing.

He narrows his eyes at me. "You know, I don't even remember the last time I made them."

"The zucchini thing is fine if that's all you have prepared," I say quickly.

"No. Churros are good. I'll make churros. And for you, Mr. Ryan?"

Shane shakes his head. "Nothing for me. I'll try some of Jessie's."

"Then I'll make extra," he says. "I'll leave you both to enjoy your wine."

As soon as Carl has left the table, I give Shane my full attention. "You know I adore you, right?"

He narrows his eyes at me. "Yes."

"But you take one bite of my dessert and I will stab you with my fork." I grin at him and he chuckles softly.

"In that case, I'm going to have to tell Mikey that you got all swoony over some asshole chef and told him he was your dessert-hero."

I open my mouth in feigned indignation. "You wouldn't."

"Try me, sweetheart."

CHAPTER 13
SHANE

Jessie could hardly finish her dessert so I helped her and even I have to admit Carl Paxton can cook. It still doesn't excuse him being an arrogant asshole and smiling at her the way he did. I should have punched his teeth down his throat, but I know that she has no interest in him, and she would have been pissed at me if I had. So, I let it go because I'm secure enough to know that she is devoted to me and my brothers.

I shake my head at the thought, because I can hardly believe it myself. Even six months ago I would have responded completely differently. Jessie Ryan has changed me in ways I would never have imagined.

"That was incredible, Shane," she says with a soft sigh as she rests her head on my shoulder as we walk to the car.

"I'm glad you had fun."

"I love you," she purrs.

"I know," I say, giving her shoulder a squeeze.

"You know most people's response to that would be *I love you too?*"

"Hmm, but I'm not most people," I remind her.

"You're certainly not."

Our driver opens the door as we reach the limo and she climbs inside first. Her dress rides up to almost the bottom of her ass cheeks and I bite my lip because I have been desperate to fuck her for hours now. I thought about taking her into the restrooms, but the place got super-busy once word got out that Carl Paxton was the dessert chef for the evening. His agent agreed he could spend an hour there and to his credit he made dessert for all of the other diners too, so maybe he's not as big an asshole as I give him credit for.

She sits on the long bench seat near to the window and I sit on the opposite end.

"Come here!" I order as soon as the door closes behind us.

She bites on her lip as her cheeks flush pink. It amazes me that she can look so sweet and innocent when she is behaving like a brat. She's my brat though and I fucking adore her.

"Now, Jessie!"

She does as she's told, edging closer until I can reach her. I grab her hips and pull her to straddle me, wrapping my arms tightly around her waist so I can hold her in place. Her dress rides up to the very top of her thighs and I can smell her wet pussy. It's driving me fucking crazy.

"I love you too," I whisper.

"I know," she says with a grin.

I dust my knuckles over the soft skin of her cheeks. After everything we've been through, sometimes I can hardly believe that she's mine.

"You remember the very first time I fucked you?"

"Of course I do," she breathes. "We were sitting in your office, just like this."

"I have never been so desperate to get inside someone as I was that day with you," I say, brushing a strand of hair from her face.

"You hid it well," she giggles. "I thought you hated me."

"I sure fucking tried to," I admit, but she doesn't seem bothered by the comment. She knows better than anyone how hard it was for me to let her in.

"I guess I'm just too damn lovable," she says with a flash of her eyebrows. "You might even say I'm irresistible."

"You *are* irresistible," I growl as I start to peel off her dress. "And I want you naked right now."

She lifts her arms in compliance so that I can pull the dress off over her head. I run my hands over the soft skin of her back and unclip her bra before pulling that off too and letting her gorgeous tits spring free.

I suck one of her hard nipples into my mouth, making her groan and grind herself on my cock.

"You said we'd be just one night, do you remember?" she breathes as I move to her other nipple. I bite her gently and she purrs like a kitten.

I do remember and at the time I even convinced myself that it was true. "Yes," I growl.

"See how that worked out for you," she giggles and I bite deeper but that only makes her grind harder against me. My girl loves a little pain to go with her pleasure, and I love to give it to her.

"And then you said you were only interested in my pussy," she teases me.

"Right now, I *am* only interested in your pussy." I wink at her.

"Liar," she breathes as she presses her tits against me.

My hands coast down her back until I grab her ass and squeeze hard. "You're right. I want this too."

"You do?" she purrs.

"Yeah." I slide my hand between her thighs and drag a

finger through her dripping folds. "When we get home I'm going to spank it and then fuck it."

Her eyelids flicker and she clings to my neck. "Why not here?" she whimpers.

"I don't want to do that in the back of a limo." Those things are too intimate to do to her when my driver might hear. I slide two fingers into her cunt and she clenches around me. "Not enough room to swing my belt."

"Shane," she whimpers.

"I love how much you love my belt, Jessie." I start to unbuckle it.

"I thought you weren't..." she whimpers as I keep finger-fucking her with my free hand.

"I'm still going to fuck you, sweetheart," I growl, then I pull my fingers out of her, causing a rush of her cum to dribble out. I pick her up and lie her down on the seat. "After I eat my dessert."

Pressing my hands flat on the inside of her thighs, I push them down against the seat, spreading her wide open for me. I swear she has the juiciest, pinkest pussy I have ever seen. I kneel on the floor, leaning closer to her as I listen to her heavy breathing while she waits for what she wants from me.

I press my nose against her folds, running it up from her hole to her clit and breathing in the scent of her. I close my eyes and savor it before I eat. Carl Paxton might be some fucking dessert magician, but nothing in the world could top this. She is the sweetest thing I have ever tasted in my life. I could feast on her pussy every day and I'd still never get my fill. My cock is busting to get inside her but I need this first.

"Shane," she whimpers as her fingers curl in my hair. "Please?"

"You're so fucking wet," I murmur against her skin, my lips dusting over her folds. "Why are you soaking already?"

"Because you made me wear these panties..." She gasps as I start to swirl the tip of my tongue over her clit. "You've just had your fingers in me," she groans loudly as I slide two back inside her. "And now you're about to eat my pussy too."

"Hmm," I mumble as I suck and lick, savoring every drop of her sweet cum. "It better all be for me, sweetheart."

"It is!" she gasps. "You know it is."

"Good girl," I growl before I suck her clit into my mouth. Her hips roll as she rides my face. When I graze the sensitive bud with my teeth she comes hard for me, bucking and shaking as I press my fingers deeper inside and the rush of her slick heat coats them.

"Oh, fuck! Shane," she pants for breath, her hands in my hair as the last of her climax rolls through her body. I sit back on my knees and pull my fingers out of her before sucking them clean.

She pushes herself up onto her elbows and blows a strand of hair from her face as she stares at me. Her eyes are dark. Her cheeks flushed pink. "Did you enjoy your dessert?" she giggles softly.

"Hmm. Your dipping sauce is way better than Carl Paxton's." I wipe my mouth as I grin at her.

"Shane!" She flushes a deeper shade of pink.

"It's true," I reach for her hips. "Now come here." I pull her onto the floor of the limo, turning her around until she's facing the seat so I can bend her over it. I look down at her. Her crotchless panties stretched taut over her perfect peach of an ass so that her pussy and backside are on full display. I think about how that asshole chef smiled at her. How the anger burns in my veins when I think of her with any man other than my brothers. I can keep it in check these days but I still feel it. I swallow hard as one word keeps on repeating over and over in my head.

Mine!

She has done nothing wrong, but I'm going to fuck her like she did anyway. I drive my cock into her silky wet heat and she groans loudly as she's pressed against the seat.

"Jesus, Shane!" she hisses as her walls tighten around me.

I lean over her, my lips dusting over her ear. "This pussy is mine, Jessie," I growl. "Don't ever forget it."

"How could I? You're such a possessive asshole." She grinds out the words as I nail her to the seat.

"You. Love. It." I drive into her with each word.

"Fuck, yes," she moans as I wrap my hands around her waist, gripping her tightly as I fuck her hard and deep.

CHAPTER 14
JESSIE

I have no idea what caused the sudden change in Shane, but he went from being kind of sweet and funny to fucking me like he was pissed as hell. Not that I'm complaining. I mean, angry sex with him is super-hot, but I'd kind of like to know what I've done – if indeed I have done anything.

As soon as we got home, he carried me to my bedroom and practically tore off my clothes while barely speaking a word. Now I'm cuffed to the headboard, lying face down on the bed with my ass in the air waiting for whatever the hell he has planned. I'm pretty sure it involves his belt because I heard him taking it off about five seconds ago and it sent shivers along my spine.

The bed dips behind me and his warm, rough hand rubs over the skin of my back. I arch it in pleasure, pressing into his touch. I turn my head to see him and he's kneeling on the bed behind me, in just his suit pants, staring at my ass.

I swallow hard. "Shane?" I whisper.

He seems to snap out of his trance. "Yeah?"

"Are you mad at me?"

89

Sometimes he spanks me like he's mad even though he's not, and it is hot. Sometimes he spanks me because he is mad at me, and that's hot too. And often I don't care if he's pissed at me or not, because the outcome is always the same and neither of us remember what we were even mad about. But sometimes, like tonight, I feel a need to know one way or another. Maybe because we fought earlier today and because the whole baby issue makes me feel so raw and vulnerable.

He frowns at me as he lies beside me until his face is close to mine. "No," he whispers.

"Good."

He narrows his eyes at me. "You want me to untie you?"

"Nope." I grin at him.

"You know you're everything to me, right?"

"Uh-huh. Written in the stars."

"We sure are, sweetheart," he says before he gives me a quick kiss on the lips. "But now I'm about to spank that beautiful ass like you're the biggest brat I've ever met."

Wet heat floods my core. "I *am* the biggest brat you've ever met, aren't I?" I purr.

"Hmm." He rubs a hand over his jaw. "You did flip me the bird this afternoon. And remind me what you said as you were leaving?"

My cheeks flush pink.

"Do you remember?" His hand glides down my back and skims over my ass.

"Fuck you?" I whisper.

"Fuck me?" He flashes his eyebrows at me. "Yes, that was it."

I roll my lips together to stop myself from giggling but he sees me.

"You think that's funny?" he growls, but there is a wicked

glint in his eye that makes my thighs tremble with anticipation and excitement.

"No, Sir," I purr.

"Fuck! You know I love it when you call me Sir," he groans and then he springs up from the bed.

The jangling of his buckle as he picks up his belt makes wet heat flood between my thighs and I brace myself for the first strike. He smacks me with his hand first, right on the fleshy part of my ass and I groan loudly. This is going to be all about pleasure.

"You want to be punished like a brat?" he growls as he spanks me again.

"Yes," I whimper as he goes on, warming up my skin in preparation for the soft leather. Heat sears between my thighs as I push my ass higher, wanting more from him.

"You want my belt now, sweetheart?" he growls.

"Please?"

The sound of the door opening makes both of us look up to see Mikey sauntering into the room.

"Wow, Red, what did you do?" he asks with a laugh.

"Nothing," I groan as I wait for the first crack of the leather. When it lands on my skin a few seconds later I cry out.

"Did she flirt with Carl Paxton?" Mikey opens his mouth, feigning his horror.

"No." Shane grinds out the word as he spanks me again.

Mikey lies on the bed beside me, his face just inches from mine and a mischievous look on his face.

"You knew about that?" I ask.

"Of course."

I wince as Shane spanks me again and my juices run from my pussy.

"If you haven't been naughty, then why are you getting a

spanking?" Mikey asks with a flash of his eyebrows before he pushes himself up and stands beside his oldest brother.

"She didn't flirt," Shane says as he brings the belt down again. "But she did say he was her hero."

My cheeks flush with embarrassment. "Shane!" I protest.

"Oh sorry. Her dessert-hero," Shane adds.

"Oh, Red," Mikey says with a devious chuckle. "I thought I was your favorite dessert chef? All those hours I spend in the kitchen making you banana waffles and fudge cake and you called another man your dessert-hero."

"I didn't mean—" I gasp but Shane spanks me harder and I lose my ability to speak.

"Fucking brutal, right?" Shane says.

"I've never felt so hurt in my life," Mikey replies.

"You want to take out your pain on her ass?" Shane asks.

"Hmm. I can think of better things to do with Jessie's ass than spank it, bro," Mikey replies.

"Such as?"

"Eating it. Fucking it."

"Well you get to do both of those after you've spanked her if you do it right."

"What if I hurt her?" Mikey whispers.

"You won't."

"I might, bro. I mean she's so small compared to us. Do you just like really hold back or something?"

Shane laughs out loud and I can't help but giggle.

"I can guarantee, no matter how hard you hit her with that belt, she can take it." He rubs a hand over my ass and a shiver skitters up my spine.

"Thank you," I whisper.

"That doesn't mean you try and hurt her," Shane warns as he hands his younger brother the belt. "But you want to make it hurt."

"Fuck, Shane! How do I make it hurt but not hurt her?"

"Just spank her with the belt, Mikey," Shane says, frustration creeping into his voice. "Because you're kind of killing our mood here."

"Yeah," I agree.

"I'm sorry, Red," he says before he brings the belt cracking down over my ass cheeks, but he gets the angle slightly off and it stings like a bitch.

"Jesus!" I hiss.

"Fuck! I hurt her," Mikey mumbles.

"I'm fine," I breathe.

"You just aimed too high is all. She can take way more than that. But you want to aim for here, see?" Shane traces his finger across my ass. "Where the lines already are."

"Okay."

"Try again and don't apologize to her before you do it. You wouldn't be doing it if she didn't want you to."

"Sor..." Mikey starts to say but then he clears his throat and I smile.

Mikey spanks me again and he hits exactly the right spot with the right amount of pressure and I groan loudly and wet heat rushes between my thighs.

"Fuck!" Mikey groans.

"That's the kind of response you're aiming for," Shane chuckles.

"Have you ever made her come from a spanking?" Mikey asks.

"Yup," Shane replies and I close my eyes as I recall the times he's done that.

"Damn!" Mikey hisses.

"You have to spank her pussy for that though," Shane chuckles.

"Her pussy?"

"Don't worry. You're not ready for that yet."

"No," Mikey agrees as he hands the belt back to Shane.

"So, are you joining us here, or are you just at a loose end?"

"Do we get to eat and fuck her after?"

"Of course we fucking do," Shane growls and I chuckle.

"Then I'm in."

I LIE on Mikey's hard chest and smile. My ass is stinging. My pussy is throbbing and I am completely wrung out with orgasms.

"This ass is so fucking beautiful," Shane growls as he crawls onto the bed beside us and rubs his hand over my flaming skin. Then he presses a soft kiss there before he begins to rub arnica gel on the parts of me he's marked with his belt.

"I kinda get the whole belt-spanking thing now," Mikey chuckles.

"Told you," Shane replies.

"Still prefer just to eat and fuck you though, Red," he whispers in my ear.

"Hmm," I mumble as I concentrate on Shane's firm hands rubbing my ass and Mikey's huge biceps wrapped around me.

"I hope you're comfortable, kid, because she'll be asleep in about thirty seconds," Shane laughs softly.

"Are you kidding? I could stay here forever," Mikey replies.

"Yeah, well I want her back as soon as I'm done here."

"Take your time then," Mikey replies as he holds me tighter and my eyelids flutter closed. "But I'm staying in here with you both."

"Fair enough," Shane agrees. "But she sleeps between us."

I giggle softly. I love them so much.

"Hey, you didn't kill our favorite chef, did you, Shane?" Mikey whispers as though I won't be able to hear him.

"No," Shane replies. "He was flirting with her though. Asshole."

"So why is he still breathing?" Mikey asks.

Shane stops rubbing my ass. "Look at her, Mikey," he says with a sigh. "If I killed every guy who smiled at her or wanted to fuck her, we'd have to buy a cemetery to hide all the bodies."

"Hmm," Mikey chuckles. "But she's always been this hot, so what else has changed?"

I smile against Mikey's chest. I mean, of course I know they think I'm hot, but it never gets old to hear them say it.

"I just get it," he finally replies.

"Get what, bro?"

"How much she loves me. That prick was flirting with her and I know how much she admires him, but she didn't look at him the way she looks at me. At us."

"Nope. She's something, right?" Mikey says as he kisses the top of my head.

"She sure is," Shane replies as he goes back to rubbing arnica on my ass and I drift off to sleep.

CHAPTER 15

CONOR

I frown at the screen in front of me as the numbers start to merge into each other before my eyes. I've always done the books for our businesses. We have an accountant too, but I like to look over everything myself to make sure everything is in order. I know Shane is grateful for me having oversight too, because that suspicious fucker trusts other people to do a job even less than I do.

There have been some anomalies in our accounts recently. Payments not adding up to what they used to and a deposit going missing. It's nothing too major and with an operation as big as ours, we have to allow some room for human error, but it still bugs me. And there is always the possibility that it's part of something bigger.

I run my hands through my hair and lean back in my chair. I've been at this for three hours and my eyes need a break. Right on cue the door to my office opens and the best break in the goddamn world walks straight through it holding a plate of food in one hand and a bottle of water in the other.

"Hey, big guy," she says with a huge smile on her face as she kicks the door closed behind her and walks toward my desk.

Fuck, she's like a sexy little bundle of sunshine. Shane took her out on a date last night and I missed her.

"Hey, Angel." I hold out my hand to her and she sets the water and food on my desk before she laces her fingers through mine. I glance at the plate and my stomach growls. It's one of Mikey's famous Philly cheesesteak sandwiches.

"You've been holed up in here for hours and I thought you might be hungry?" She arches one eyebrow at me and I pull her onto my lap, lifting her so she is straddling me.

Running my nose along the column of her throat, I inhale her sweet, intoxicating scent. "I am hungry," I growl and she giggles.

"I mean for food, Conor," she says as she places her hands on the back of my neck.

I grab hold of her hips, pulling her closer to me until I can rub my cock against her pussy and it starts to harden instantly.

"You come in here wearing this tiny little summer dress and think that I don't know what you're really after?" I wink at her and her cheeks turn pink.

"It's over eighty degrees outside. That's why I'm wearing a summer dress. You need to eat."

I grin at her as I slide my hand up her back until I can palm the back of her head and push her face close to mine. "Oh, I'm going to eat, Jessie. You can fucking count on it."

"A man cannot survive on pussy alone," she breathes.

"Your pussy is all the sustenance I need," I chuckle and she rolls her hips over me as her breath catches in her throat.

"Conor!" She feigns her protest even as she's grinding herself against me.

I slide my hand beneath her dress, feeling the supple smoothness of her skin as my hand runs up her thigh until I reach the edge of her panties. Sliding my hand beneath them, I cup her ass cheek and squeeze. "Tell me this is what you really came here for, Jessie," I growl as I trail my lips over her neck. "Because I know if I put my fingers in you right now, you'd be dripping wet for me wouldn't you?"

"Actually, I've got lots of work to do today," she purrs. "I don't have time to fool around with you."

So she wants to play? "Is that so, Angel," I hiss as I stand, pushing my laptop and the plate of food out of the way before lifting her onto the desk until I'm standing between her thighs. I reach for my belt and unbuckle it as she sits there chewing on her lip.

"You're just going straight for it, big guy?" She looks down at my hands working fast to open my zipper next.

I narrow my eyes at her. She's looking for an ass spanking and I might just give it to her. "You just said you don't have time to fool around, but make no mistake you won't be leaving this office until I've fucked you, so we might as well get on with it, right?"

She tilts her head to one side. "I suppose."

"Just a quick fuck until I fill you with my cum and then you can go back to work," I growl as I pull my cock out of my boxers with one hand as I tug her panties to the side with the other.

Then I wrap an arm around her waist as I pull her closer to me and drive deep inside her.

"Conor!" she hisses as she wraps her arms around my neck.

"Fucking soaking," I groan as her walls squeeze around me.

"You planning on coming in me before you eat me then?" she breathes as she rakes her nails down my back.

"Are you looking for a spanking, Jessie?" I groan.

"From you? Always," she whispers in my ear.

"Tell me why you came down here?" I growl as I pull my head back and glare at her.

She flutters her eyelashes at me. "To bring you your lunch."

"My lunch?"

"Hmm. But it is two courses," she giggles.

I glance at the sandwich. "Two?"

"Hmm." She leans forward and traces her lips along the skin of my neck. "Your first course is my pussy, obviously."

"Obviously." I smile at her.

"And I already finished my work for the day so I'm all yours," she purrs.

"Already?" I frown at her. She was looking into the financials of an old rival of ours. I wanted to rule out their involvement in any of our recent business anomalies. I forget sometimes how incredible this woman is at her job.

"Yup."

"So, why did you tell me you were too busy?" I growl. I tilt my head back as her soft tongue dances over my skin, making my cock twitch in her pussy.

"Because I wanted to make you mad at me so you'd bend me over this desk and spank me."

"Fuck, Jessie!" My balls draw up into my stomach and I pull out of her before I blow my load.

I pull her off the desk and spin her around until she's facing it. Her breathing comes harder and faster as she realizes I'm about to give her exactly what she wants.

Placing my hand between her shoulder blades, I push her down until her face is pressed against the desk. Her legs tremble as I pull her dress up over her hips and run my hands over her ass. "This ass is so fucking beautiful, Jessie. I don't know whether to worship it or eat it."

"Conor!" she pants as I reach the waistband of her panties and start to tug them off over her legs. I don't have any more time for her teasing. I'm too damn hungry.

I slide off my belt, palming the buckle and wrapping half of the leather around my fist before I rub a hand over the soft skin of her ass.

She whimpers at my touch and it makes me smile as I draw my hand back before I bring the soft leather down over the plump flesh of her cheeks, making her groan in pleasure. I'm gentle the first few times as I build up to the level that we both thrive on, but nevertheless each strike with my belt leaves a satisfying pink stripe on her perfect ass.

"You look so good bent over my desk waiting for me to fuck you," I growl as I land the next blow, harder this time.

"Please, Conor," she begs me and she knows how much I love to hear her pleading for me. This woman makes me harder than titanium.

"You think you deserve to be fucked? Coming in her interrupting me while I'm working? Trying to make me mad enough to spank you?"

"Yes!" she gasps as I strike her again.

"Why do you love my belt so much, Angel?"

"Because you fuck me so good when you use it?" she groans and she's right. Something about doing this to her makes me fuck her harder and for longer.

It took me a long time to let this side of myself loose with her, but now that I have, I live for the days when she's like this. Begging me for a little hurt to go along with her pleasure. I still love to fuck her soft and slow too and she is the only woman to ever get that side of me, but this right here is so fucking hot. I swear I could come just watching her ass turn red and listening to her desperate whimpers for more.

When her ass is striped like a candy cane and she has taken enough, I drop to my knees, ready to worship at the altar of her dripping pussy and her perfect peach.

"Conor, please," she moans as I push her thighs wider apart and spread her pussy lips with my thumbs to see her cum dripping from her. The smell of her sweet juices makes my cock throb painfully but I need to taste before I can fuck her.

I plant my hands on the back of her thighs and drag my tongue the length of her, from her clit to her delicious ass and she shudders, her thighs trembling in my hands.

"This is the best thing I've ever fucking tasted," I growl as I go back for more, sucking and licking her, lapping at her cream as it dribbles from her opening.

"Conor!" she squeals as I push my thumb into her ass and start to fuck her slowly with it. A few seconds later, my girl is grinding on my face and coming all over my tongue and I lap her up like she's my last meal.

While the tremors of her climax are still rippling through her body, I stand and grab hold of my cock, rock hard and weeping to be inside her. Grabbing her hips with my free hand, I drive into her wet heat and she moans loudly as she squeezes me. I lean over her, wrapping her hair around my fist and pulling her head back until my lips are dusting over the shell of her ear. "My belt makes your pussy taste so fucking sweet, Jessie," I growl as I nail her to my desk, fucking her so hard that the bottle of water topples over and rolls onto the floor.

"Oh, fuck! Conor!" she hisses as she squeezes me tighter, pulling me deeper even as I can't get any further inside.

"You gonna come on my cock now too?" I hiss.

"Uh-huh," she breathes.

"That's my good girl," I hiss as her juices coat me and her walls milk my cock as I pull another orgasm from her. The sound of her moaning my name tips me over the edge and I drive into her one last time as I find my own release.

"Conor!" she groans as I pull out of her and our cum drips down her thighs.

"You're so fucking hot, Angel!" I growl as I pull her up and spin her around to face me. Her cheeks are pink and her eyes glazed as she smiles at me.

"You're pretty hot yourself, big guy," she pants as she wraps her arms around my neck again and places a soft kiss on my throat. "Now where are my panties?"

"You're not getting them back," I chuckle.

"You're getting to be worse than Mikey for stealing my panties."

"I didn't steal them. They were willingly given," I remind her.

"Hmm," she purrs, fluttering her eyelashes at me. "If you give them back to me, I'll help you go over the accounts."

"But you're going to do that anyway, and it will be much more fun having you working in here with me if you're not wearing any panties."

"You're a deviant," she says with a wicked grin.

"Because you got me pussy-drunk." I squeeze her ass and she squeals.

As she opens her mouth to give me a snappy comeback, we're interrupted by a knock at the door. I straighten her dress but I keep my arms around her waist as she turns to face the door.

"Come in," I bark, annoyed at being disturbed when I'm alone with her.

A second later, our head of security for the club, Chester, pops his head into the room. "Sorry, Boss," he says with a wince as he realizes he's interrupted us. "But someone is here to see you."

"Tell them to make an appointment with my secretary," I snap and she shivers in my arms. Chester shakes his head in frustration. I don't have a secretary.

"Actually, it's not you he's here to see," Chester goes on. "I was talking to Jessie."

My arms tighten instinctively around her. She rarely has visitors and the few she's had in the past have always led to trouble.

"Who the fuck is it?" I snarl before Jessie has a chance to speak.

"I don't know, but he asked for Jessica Ivanov," Chester replies and my blood freezes in my veins. Nothing good has ever come from hearing that name. We buried Jessica Ivanov and her entire legacy over twelve months ago. Nobody has called her by that name since.

"Fuck!" I hiss, anger rumbling through my chest as I pull her closer.

"What does he look like?" she asks.

"Just a kid. Maybe twenty-one. Looks young enough to be carded if he tried to get in here while the place was open for business."

"Is he Russian?" I ask.

"Sounded American to me."

"What the fuck did you say when he asked for Jessica?" I snap, barely able to contain my anger.

"I brought him into the club and left him at the door with two of our bouncers. I figured you'd want to at least speak to the guy?" Chester replies.

"Hmm." I run a hand over my jaw. "Sit him at the bar and I'll deal with him shortly."

"Sure, boss," Chester says with a nod and then he walks out of the room leaving us alone again.

"Conor, who the hell could this be?" She blinks at me, searching my face for answers as she places her hands on my chest.

I brush her hair back from her beautiful face. "No idea, Angel, but if he is any threat to you, he won't be breathing when he leaves this club, I promise you."

I lean over and switch on the security monitor, then we both watch as Chester escorts our intruder to the bar and leaves him sitting on a stool.

"You recognize him at all?" I ask.

She peers closely at the screen. "Nope."

He looks young. Maybe fresh out of college. He has dirty blonde hair and he wears glasses. He doesn't look like much of a threat but I know that looks can be deceiving and if he's looking for Jessica Ivanov then he obviously has some dangerous connections.

I take my cell from the table. "I'm gonna get Shane and the boys down here too. You want to speak to him, Jessie, or you want us to deal with him?"

"No, I want to hear what he has to say, but I'm happy for you to do the talking," she replies and I feel a wave of relief. We need to know who this guy is and why he's asking for a woman who is supposed to be dead. Because this woman here in my arms is Jessie Ryan. Jessica Ivanov is the true heir to the Russian Bratva empire, and she hasn't been her for a very long time.

CHAPTER 16
JESSIE

Conor returned my panties as soon as Chester left the room. Now, I sit between him and Shane as the twins escort our visitor into the office and close the door behind them. His face is pale and his eyes dart around the room, like a frightened rabbit trapped in the lair of a wolf. I suppose that Liam and Mikey are a pretty intimidating pair. I watched on the security camera as the twins placed their hands on his shoulders and the poor guy looked like he was about to pass out. And now he is confined in a tiny room with all four terrifying Ryan brothers – no wonder he's as white as a ghost.

His eyes land on me and I offer him a faint smile and regret it immediately because we have no idea who this guy is, but something about him looking so terrified endears him to me. I have been where he is many times myself.

Mikey pushes him roughly onto a chair and all five of us stare at him while he keeps scanning our faces, blinking rapidly as a bead of sweat runs down his brow.

"Who are you?" Conor barks.

"H-Hayden Chambers," he stammers.

"So, Hayden Chambers." Conor clasps his hands together,

placing them on the desk in front of him as he leans forward. "What the fuck are you doing in our club asking about a dead woman?"

Hayden blinks and shakes his head. "She's dead?" he whispers.

"Why are you asking about her?" Conor snarls again.

Hayden's Adam's apple bobs in his throat as he swallows. "I think she might be my sister," he says, the crack in his voice apparent.

My heart starts to hammer in my chest and I gasp quietly. Shane places a hand on my thigh and squeezes gently, distracting me enough to allow me to regain my composure. Ordinarily I have a great poker face but that was the last thing I expected to hear today.

"Jessica's brothers are dead," Shane says calmly.

Hayden nods. "I heard that. I suppose I'd be her half-brother really. I believe Alexei Ivanov was my father, too."

"You looking for a slice of his empire, kid, then you're looking in the wrong place," Conor snarls.

"It's nothing like that," he stammers. "I was just looking for my sister. Since my mom died last year, there's just me and I just wondered if I had some other family out there, is all."

"You said you believe he's your father, but you don't know for sure?" I ask him and he turns to face me, giving me his full attention and offering me a chance to study his features. He has dark eyes like Alexei, but then plenty of people do. I see a resemblance when I look closely, but perhaps I am seeing one because I'm looking for one.

"My mom left Russia with me when I was a baby. I don't believe he even knew I existed, but she told me he was my father before she died. I could hardly believe it when I discovered who he really was. I suppose that was why she never wanted me to know him, but she gave me dates and told me where they met and it all seems to add up. I don't see why she would lie to me then after keeping it a secret for all those years."

"Why did you come here looking for her?" Conor asks, his knuckles white as he clenches his fists on the desk.

"Because this is where the trail ended," he says. "This was the last place she was known to be."

"And who told you that little snippet of information?" Shane growls.

"Some Russian guy I met at a bar. He didn't give me his name."

"What bar?" Conor snarls.

"The Black Bear."

"Never heard of it," Shane says.

"It's in Newark. It got closed by the cops last week."

"Convenient," Liam snorts.

"It's true," Hayden adds.

"So you never asked this guy's name?" Shane asks.

"No. He didn't seem like the type of guy who appreciated me asking questions about who he was. I was happy not to know."

"And you think we do look like the kind of guys who appreciate complete strangers turning up at our place of business and asking questions about dead Russians?" Conor barks and Hayden jumps in his chair.

"No." He shakes his head. "I'm sorry. I didn't know. Is she really dead?" he whispers.

"She no longer exists," Shane answers, "so it seems you've had a wasted journey."

Hayden swallows hard and I'm sure I see tears in his eyes. "I understand. I'm sorry I took up your time." He pushes himself up from his chair.

Mikey places a large hand on his shoulder and pushes him

straight back down. "Nobody said you could leave, fuck-face," he snarls.

Hayden visibly trembles as he looks between Shane, Conor and me.

"If we let you leave here," Shane says, his fiery green eyes narrowed and fixed on Hayden, "we expect you never to come around here asking questions again. You got that?"

Hayden nods furiously. "Yes, Sir."

"Let him up," Shane inclines his head to Mikey who takes his hand from Hayden's shoulder before escorting Hayden from the room.

As soon as Mikey is back inside and he closes the door I let out a long, deep breath that I feel like I've been holding in for the past five minutes.

"You okay, sweetheart?" Shane asks as he takes my hand and squeezes it in his.

"Yeah," I breathe. "You think he was for real?"

"No," Liam replies and his brothers turn and glare at him but he shrugs. "Just some loser looking for some easy money."

"Maybe he was telling the truth though?" I suggest. "It's perfectly plausible that Alexei had another child he didn't know about."

"You're saying you believe that guy, Red?" Mikey asks.

"I'm saying it wouldn't hurt to look into him a little more and see what his story is – whether he's genuine or not."

"I agree. Then we can find out who the asshole was who gave him your former name too. Because I'm going to cut out his fucking tongue," Shane snarls.

"Now that I can get behind," Mikey agrees.

"Hmm. Now if only we knew a super-hacker who could get her hands on that kind of information," Shane chuckles before he stands and plants a soft kiss on my forehead.

"I'll make a start as soon as I've helped Conor with the

books." I smile up at him and he winks at me before bending his head until his lips are grazing my ear. "Don't be too long, I miss you working in my office with me."

"I won't."

"We should all get back to work," he adds as he looks at his younger brothers.

Mikey nods his agreement and stands too but Liam remains in his seat and stares at me. "You weren't actually taken in by any of his bullshit, were you, Jessie?" he asks with a frown.

I frown back at him. It's not like Liam to be the unreasonable one amongst his brothers. "All I'm saying is there's a possibility he's telling the truth."

"And what if he is?" he snaps.

I blink in confusion. Why does it seem like he's so pissed at me?

"I don't know what happens then," I tell him honestly.

He opens his mouth to speak but Shane puts a hand on his shoulder. "Enough. There's no point arguing about it until we have more information. Let Jessie do her thing and then we can decide what to do next. All of us." He turns to me as he says that last part and I know it's mostly for my benefit, because in the past I have been known to be a little impulsive and make reckless decisions. But that was the old me. I'm much more considered now – at least most of the time anyway.

"Of course," I agree.

CHAPTER 17
JESSIE

I've spent the entire afternoon looking into Hayden and he's a pretty quick study. I didn't get a chance to look into him yesterday after he dropped his bombshell and it was probably a good thing because I was so rattled by his revelation I'm not sure I'd have been at my most clearheaded.

I turn the computer off, pick up my notebook and head to the den to meet the guys. We have a group date night once a week, but every four weeks, we stay in the apartment and have a movie or game night – all five of us, with no work and no interruptions. Cell phones are switched off. Laptops, tablets and computers are left untouched and we pretend like there is nobody else in the world but the five of us. It used to almost kill Shane because he's such a workaholic but I think he looks forward to them more than any of us now.

I walk into the den and drop my notebook onto the coffee table.

"Where have you been, Red?" Mikey says as he reaches out and pulls me onto his lap as he sits on the sofa. "We're waiting to start the movie."

"Sorry. I was just finishing up," I whisper.

We're all distracted by Liam and Conor as they walk into the room carrying bowls of fresh popcorn. Placing them on the table next to my notebook before they sit on the sofa with Mikey and me. I stretch my legs out over Conor's lap and he lifts my foot to his lips and presses a soft kiss on my ankle.

Shane sits on his usual spot in the armchair. He holds the TV remote in his hand. "And are you finished?" he asks me.

I roll my lips together. I was hoping he'd ask me that. I know we're not supposed to talk work tonight, but this isn't exactly work, is it? "Yes."

"Finished what?" Conor asks before he tosses some popcorn into his mouth.

"Looking into Hayden," I reply and I see Liam's shoulders stiffen.

"And?" Shane asks.

"No work. It's movie night," Mikey protests.

Conor frowns at him. "This isn't work."

"No. It's not," Shane agrees. "We can wait a few minutes to start the movie."

Mikey groans and rolls his eyes. "Fine. Make it quick, Red," he says with a wink as his arms tighten around me.

"There wasn't a lot to find. His story checks out though. His mom moved to the US from Russia when he was three months old. She married some guy from New Jersey called Jon Chambers and he raised Hayden as his own until he died nine years ago of lung cancer. Hayden is smart. He got a scholarship to UCLA, but he dropped out in his second year when his mom got really sick. She died of lung cancer last year too. Just like he said. He lives alone in a tiny apartment in New Jersey. He makes fifteen bucks an hour waiting tables at a bar in Queens. Has a couple of friends from his job. Stays at a girl named Heather's place in Queens a couple of nights a week, but checking their social media they're not in a serious relationship. I mean I got plenty of other stuff. I know his favorite food and how often he visits the laundromat too, but I'm pretty sure the movie would be more entertaining than that."

Shane narrows his eyes at me. "Any red flags at all?"

I suck in a breath. "One," I admit.

"And that is?"

"He owes over a hundred thousand dollars in unpaid medical bills from when his mom was sick."

"So he's after money," Liam says with a scowl.

"Maybe?" I shrug.

"Maybe? Of course he is, Jessie. He finds himself in massive debt and all of a sudden he finds his rich long-lost sister?" Liam snaps.

"I'm not rich," I remind him, earning me a scowl from the rest of his brothers too. "And you know, so what if that was his motive for finding me? There are far worse reasons he could be looking for help. If he even is looking for any. It's not like he's in debt because he partied his inheritance away or owes money to some nasty people. He couldn't pay his dying mom's medical bills. I mean it's freaking awful that people even have to pay to die," I shout, fidgeting on Mikey's lap in frustration, but he keeps his arms firmly wrapped around me.

"I don't trust him," Liam adds, his arms folded across his chest like a moody teenager.

"Well, I want to speak to him. If he is my half-brother then I want to know."

"Why?" Liam snaps. "Why do you need a half-brother?"

I shake my head in annoyance. "I don't need one, Liam, but I might have one and that means something. How can you not see that?"

"Red..." Mikey starts to say but Liam interrupts him.

"And what if he is your brother, what then? You expect us to let a complete stranger into our home? Have him over for dinner once a week? Sleepovers?"

"Yes!" I reply.

"Don't be ridiculous, bro," Mikey says at the same time.

I turn to him and frown. "Why is that ridiculous?"

"What?" He blinks at me. I know he was probably only trying to help me out, but why is the prospect of my family being here so unthinkable?

I untangle myself from his arms and stand up. "So, I'm supposed to call this place home but it's not really my home is it?" I shout as the four Ryan brothers stare at me. "There would be no question of your family coming for dinner or sleepovers, but when it's mine then it's ridiculous?"

My hands are balled into fists at my sides as I wait for them to tell me that I'm wrong.

"That's not what he meant, Angel. Calm down, and—" Conor says.

"Don't tell me to calm down," I interrupt him. I mean in the history of the world, has actually saying that to someone ever had the desired effect?

Conor frowns at me. "We have no idea who this guy is yet and you're getting pissed about something that might never be an issue."

"And that's the problem. This will never be an issue for any of you because this is your home and if you invited somebody here nobody would give a shiny rat's ass. But I have to ask permission like a child? Like I'm just renting a room here with you guys until..." I swallow because I've gone too far and I don't even know how to finish that sentence.

"Jessie Ryan!" Shane snarls in that quiet, animalistic growl he has that makes the hairs on the back of my neck stand on end. "Sit your ass back down."

I swallow hard, not daring to turn and look at him. Instead I look at the three faces of his brothers who stare at me, willing me to do as I'm told before their oldest brother's temper explodes and ruins movie night for good.

"Now!" Shane barks.

Mikey holds out his arms and I sit back on his lap.

"Look at me," Shane commands and I turn my head and stare into his fiery green eyes.

"Until he proves otherwise, Hayden will not be trusted by any of us. Not in our homes. Not with you. Not with anything."

I open my mouth to reply but he shoots me a warning glare that makes me close it again. "But this *is* your home. In case you haven't noticed, we rarely have any visitors here. We do not like strangers here."

"I know," I whisper.

"But," he licks his lips and glares at his brothers and me, "if Hayden is your half-brother, and if he proves himself trustworthy, of course he can come here whenever you want him to."

"And how would he prove himself?" I ask.

"Only with time, sweetheart," he says softly. "Until then, you're just going to have to run his coming here by us."

"Okay," I nod.

"We all okay now?" Mikey asks with a half-hearted laugh, trying to lighten the mood.

"Yeah," I say as I lean against his chest.

"I'm sorry if I made you feel like this wasn't your home, baby," Liam reaches over Conor and squeezes my hand. "It's only home now because you're here."

"I'm sorry too," I whisper.

"Great. Now can we please put this fucking movie on? I've been waiting to watch it all week," Mikey asks.

"It better not be a pile of shit like the last one you picked," Shane replies as he presses play on the remote.

"Yeah, sorry about that one," Mikey chuckles. "This one will be better. Promise."

The opening credits come on and we all settle back to watch the movie. Liam holds onto one of my feet, rubbing the pad of his thumb over my toes and sending tiny waves of pleasure rippling through my calves and up my thighs. I love to have my feet massaged. Conor holds onto my hand, his fingers laced through mine while I lean against Mikey's hard chest. I look over at Shane and he's watching us instead of the movie. He winks at me and I smile back as warmth floods my core. This is exactly where I belong. My name might not be on the deeds of this property, but this is my home in every way that matters.

CHAPTER 18
JESSIE

Mikey and Liam wake me as they climb out of bed. It's their turn to make breakfast this morning. "You need any help?" I ask as I blink in the dark room.

"No, they don't," Shane growls as he wraps one of his huge biceps around me. "You're staying here."

"Okay," I whisper as I stretch my legs. My body aches from last night's exertions. Movie and date nights always end the same way – with the five of us in bed together – and I love it.

Conor rolls into Liam's vacated spot and snuggles up behind me. "Morning, Angel," he whispers before he kisses my shoulder blade softly.

"Morning, big guy," I whisper.

"How's that ass?" Shane chuckles as he rubs a hand over it.

"Fine," I purr as the memory of Shane spanking me last night makes wet heat pool between my thighs. "It was a pretty tame spanking by your usual standards."

"Hmm." He rubs his jaw over my neck and his stubble tickles my skin. "It wasn't supposed to be a punishment, that's why."

"I know," I whisper.

"But if I ever hear you saying that this place isn't your home again, sweetheart..." he growls, not needing to finish his sentence because the threat is implicit.

"I know." I swallow as he trails soft kisses over my throat.

"Actually, I've been thinking about that," Conor says and Shane looks up at him.

I turn to lie on my back so I can look at the two of them.

"What about it?" Shane asks.

"Well, if Jessie was legally married to one of us, then she would be legally entitled to a claim on our assets," Conor says.

"I can't just be married to one of you though," I whisper.

"It would only be for legal purposes," Shane assures me.

I shake my head. "I don't care about that stuff though."

"If anything happened to us..." Conor says but I glare at him.

"Nothing is ever going to happen to any of you. I am not marrying one of you because I am married to all of you. You all agreed that the piece of paper didn't matter."

Shane sighs softly but Conor starts to chuckle. "I knew she wouldn't go for it, bro. So I have another idea too."

"We just get her name put on all the paperwork? The houses? The bank accounts? The businesses?" Shane arches an eyebrow at his brother.

"Yup." Conor nods his agreement.

"What? That's like way too much. No. I don't need that," I insist. "I don't want your money."

"Jessie," Shane says as he brushes my hair from my face. "Some day very soon you're going to be the mother of our children as well as our wife. We are all in this until the end. There is no getting rid of any of us, so we're doing this. Okay?"

I stare at them. It's true that I don't want their money, but if we have children, I do want their futures to be secure. "As long as Mikey and Liam agree, but just the apartment. Or one of the clubs? Not everything."

"What do you give us?" Conor asks as he pins one hand to the side of my head while Shane does the same to the other. Then they both start to trail their hot delicious mouths over my skin, leaving trails of fire in their wake.

"I don't know," I mumble as I squirm beneath their ticklish kisses.

"You do," Shane murmurs against my skin. "What do you give us, Jessie?"

I close my eyes. I really don't know the answer.

"U-um..." I stammer as they move lower and now their free hands are running over my abdomen and down between my thighs. I part them in anticipation and they both smile against my skin.

"Still waiting on that answer, Angel," Conor says as his fingers skim my pussy. "Tell us and we'll take care of you."

"I don't know what you want me to say," I mumble as they start to drive me crazy with their delicious teasing.

"Answer the question," Shane says as his lips move lower to join Conor's fingers. "You're gonna have to give her a clue because I need to taste this pussy, Con."

Conor chuckles in response and then he lifts his head to look at me. "Think about what you have to give and then tell me what you give us," he arches an eyebrow at me.

Fuck! This is a riddle. I have nothing really. No assets. I mean I can get my hands on money if I need it. But I give them my time. My love. My... Damn. I got it.

"Everything?" I offer as Conor's hand slides between my thighs.

Shane looks up at Conor. "Our girl got it," he grins at him.

"She's as smart as a whip," Conor chuckles.

"That was the answer?" I pant as my body sizzles with hit sweet, anticipation.

"Yep. Everything. So let us do the same for you, Angel," Conor whispers as he sinks one finger deep into my pussy while Shane's tongue dances over my skin until he reaches my clit.

"You already do," I pant but the two of them are too focused on what they're doing to me to hear, bringing me to the edge of orgasm as they work my body perfectly together.

An hour later, we're sitting in the kitchen eating breakfast when I decide to raise the issue of Hayden again. Everyone is full of Mikey's delicious pancakes and have smiles on their faces, so I figure now is the best time to do it.

"So, are you all okay if I reach out to Hayden and see what his angle is?" I ask as I take a sip of my coffee.

"Of course," Shane answers before any of his brothers can object and I feel like kissing him. "But you do nothing without running it by us first and you do not meet him alone under any circumstances. Deal?"

"Deal," I agree.

"I'm free today if you want to stake him out?" Mikey offers with a flash of his eyebrows.

"I can take a few hours off too," Conor adds.

"If these two don't put him off then he probably is your half-brother," Shane says with a chuckle.

"Oi," Mikey gives him a gentle nudge. "We'll be on our best behavior, won't we, Con?"

"Yup," Conor nods his agreement.

"You both promise?" I wrap my hands around my coffee mug and stare at them.

"It could be worse, Liam could be going with you," Mikey replies and Conor and Shane start to laugh.

"Why is that so fucking funny?" Liam snaps.

"Because you have got your panties in a real bunch about this guy, bro," Mikey chuckles.

"Fuck you all," Liam says with a sigh and slight shake of his head.

I walk around the table to him and sit on his lap and he reluctantly wraps his arms around me as I take his face in my hands. "I love that you have my back, but I got this. I promise."

He stares at me with his huge brown eyes before he nods softly. "I know, baby. I just want you to be safe."

"I will be," I say before I seal my lips over his and kiss him softly. He fists his hands in my hair as he deepens our kiss and I open my mouth, allowing him to slide his tongue inside.

"Not at the breakfast table," Conor groans.

"You were happy to eat her on it the other morning," Shane reminds him.

"That was different. That was me," Conor chuckles and I'm vaguely aware of the three of them clearing the table and moving to the other side of the kitchen leaving Liam and me alone.

I pull back from our kiss and look at him as he pulls me closer to his chest. "I promise I won't do anything reckless," I whisper. I mean with my track record, I get that he is anxious about Hayden.

"Okay," he smiles at me. "I promise to try and not lose my shit every time his name is mentioned."

"Okay," I giggle. "I love you, you know that right?" I ask, because out all of his brothers he is the one who doubts his own worth, and sometimes I wonder if that makes him question how much I love him. When we found out that his and Mikey's biological father was the man who slaughtered my family before kidnapping me and making my life hell for two years, he struggled so much with accepting that I could see him the same way I always have.

"Yeah. I love you too, baby."

"I know."

CHAPTER 19
CONOR

Mikey and I sit in the front of the SUV while Jessie fidgets nervously in the back. We're parked outside Hayden's apartment in New Jersey. We know he's in there because my super-smart and incredibly hot wife is tracking his phone.

"He should be getting ready to leave for his afternoon run by now," she says, her brow furrowed in annoyance.

Mikey arches an amused eyebrow at me and I suppress a smile. I have to admit when this guy showed up at our club looking for her, I was less than impressed. In fact, I was ready to slit his throat for even daring to mention her previous name. And if I'm completely honest, I've been hoping this kid isn't her half-brother, but my reasons are entirely selfish, because I don't want to share her affections with anyone other than my own brothers. Seeing her now though, jittery with nerves and excitement, I'm starting to bend a little. I mean she has nobody except us, and while I want to believe that she doesn't need anyone else, I see how much having a sibling would mean to her.

"You want us to just go in there and get him, Red?" Mikey asks.

"No, you can't do that to the poor guy. He might have a heart attack or something," she says with a shake of her head and I laugh. I'm not sure it's going to be that much less terrifying when Mikey and I drag him into our car.

I turn to Mikey to suggest maybe we try and not make the kid shit his pants but Jessie shouts down my ear, "Here he is."

I turn in my seat to her pointing out the window at the door to the run-down apartment building. Sure enough, Hayden is walking out of there dressed in shorts, t-shirt and a baseball cap. He grabs hold of his ankle, stretching his hamstring as he prepares for his run.

"Showtime, big guy," Mikey says with a grin before he jumps out of the car. I follow him and we approach Hayden from either side in case he decides to use those running shoes he has on.

The kid looks between us both. Fear etched all over his face. Fuck! I think he actually will shit his pants if we go with our original plan of just bundling him in the car.

"Hey." I hold my hands up. I'm not used to this diplomacy shit, but then I've never had a wife who I live and die for before either, so I suppose I'm becoming a new man. "We don't want to hurt you, kid. We just have someone who wants to speak to you is all."

He bounces on the balls of his feet as though he's getting ready to run. Jessie is under strict instructions to stay in the car and not even show her face in case this is some kind of trap and anyone is watching. I know she must be itching to roll that goddamn window down and talk to him.

"You're getting in that car one way or another, kid," Mikey says. "So why not just walk in like a man before my brother and I make you cry in front of your whole neighborhood?"

Hayden's Adam's apple bobs as he swallows.

"Get in the fucking car, kid," I snarl and he nods before he takes a few tentative steps toward it. When I open the door, Jessie's smiling face is right there and it seems to ease his nerves a little. I mean how could it not? She's like a ball of fucking sunshine.

"Hi Hayden. Get in," she says and he climbs into the car as she scoots back along the seat. I close the door behind him before Mikey and I climb in.

"I'm sorry we had to surprise you like that," Jessie says as he sits in the back seat staring at her, still unsure what the hell we want with him.

He doesn't speak so she goes on talking. "I'm Jessie. And these are my husbands, Conor and Mikey. Well, two of them anyway, but you met the other two in the club a few days ago."

"You have four husbands?" he asks. "Is that like even legal?"

Mikey turns in his seat while I keep my eyes on the road. "We don't really care much for the law," he says with a smile but there is an edge to his voice. Hayden must pick up on it too because he says no more on the matter. I mean, I can't blame the kid for asking. Having four husbands isn't exactly the norm.

"I know it's kind of unusual but it works for us," Jessie says.

"Sure does, Angel," I agree with her, looking in the rearview mirror and giving her a cheeky wink that makes her cheeks flush pink.

CHAPTER 20
JESSIE

"Jessie?" Hayden says, clearing his throat. "Are you Jessica?"

"I knew her. A long time ago."

He frowns at me and I'm not sure he understands. I mean, he's a smart kid from what I found about him, but I suppose book-smart and regular-smart aren't always entirely compatible.

"You can relax, Hayden. I just want to talk to you," I say with a reassuring smile.

"Okay," he eventually replies and settles back against the seat. "What was she like?"

"Do you know anything at all about her?"

"Only that her family were murdered when she was young and then she went missing after."

"But you thought she was still alive? Why is that?"

He clears his throat. "Well, she was never found, so I thought maybe she had survived, but it wasn't until I started looking for my father that I found out she had."

Conor fidgets in the front seat as he drives, his knuckles turning white on the steering wheel and the tension in the car suddenly grows thicker.

"Who told you that?"

"Like I said the other day, some guy in a bar."

"A guy in a bar?" I arch an eyebrow at him but I keep my voice calm and steady, trying to put him at ease and to prevent either Mikey or Conor reaching back and throttling the truth from him. "I'm going to need a little more than that from you."

His Adam's apple bobs as he swallows. "I don't have any more. I was asking around about Alexei and, well," he pulls at the collar of his t-shirt, "as you can imagine people weren't too happy about me doing that. I was about to get thrown out when this huge guy came over to me and stopped them. I thought he was going to fucking kill me. Then he told me that Alexei was dead but that his daughter was still alive. He said her name was Jessica and I'd find her at Emerald Shamrock. When I found out it was a nightclub, I thought maybe she worked there. That's all I know."

"What was the name of the bar?" Conor barks.

"The Black Bear. Like I said," he says.

I stare at him. A bead of sweat runs down his brow and he wipes it away.

"What did the guy look like?" I ask.

"Terrifying," he replies with a shudder. "Huge. Greasy. He had really dark hair and it was slicked back with like oil or something. He had a beard. I honestly don't remember that much. He told me to get out and I did. I swear, I was just happy not to have been shot at. This," he looks around the car and then his voice drops to a whisper, "is not my world."

I lean back against my seat and stare at him. I can't get a good read on him and that worries me.

"You want to come for dinner?" I ask.

His eyes widen and he looks between me and my two bodyguards.

"They'll behave. I promise." I wink at him.

"Are you...?" he asks again.

"Look, kid, she told you Jessica Ivanov was dead," Mikey barks.

I put my hand on Mikey's shoulder. "It's okay. I got this."

Hayden stares at me, his face pale and his eyes wide with terror. This really isn't his world. That much I believe. "I'm Jessie Ryan," I tell him. "Jessica Ivanov is dead. She died along with her parents and her brothers and we won't speak of her again, okay?"

"Okay," he says but he blinks in confusion.

"But that doesn't mean you don't have a half-sister."

Hayden keeps blinking at me.

"He's not getting this, Jessie," Conor snaps.

"He is," I say with a reassuring smile. "It's just taking a while, right?"

Hayden swallows. "Right."

"You want to come for dinner at our place then?" I ask again.

"Yeah," he says with a nod of his head.

"Good," I smile at him and I squeeze Mikey's shoulder. "Mikey here is a great cook."

"I make a great chili, kid. You like chili?"

"Love it," Hayden says.

"You'd better call Shane and let him know we're bringing a guest home," Conor says to his brother.

"Good idea." Mikey takes his cell from his pocket. "He can make sure Liam is all calmed down by the time he gets home. We don't want him getting all stabby."

"Stabby?" Hayden almost chokes on the word.

"He's joking," I lie.

.   .   .

HAYDEN STANDS at the large window in our kitchen with a bottle of Bud in his hand. I walk to stand beside him. Mikey is cooking in the background and Conor sits at the kitchen table watching me and Hayden so intently that I feel his eyes burning into me. Hayden has been here for two hours now and both Mikey and Conor have been perfect hosts. They haven't let either of us out of their sight, but they also gave us a little space to talk privately. Not so private that they wouldn't have heard every single thing that we said, but they have kept their distance and I know how hard it must be for them not to interrogate him because I know they want to.

I have asked questions mostly and Hayden has seemed happy to talk. I know he's only ever lived in New Jersey but he wants to move to New York. He's smart with numbers and was going to major in business before he had to drop out of college to help look after his mom. She was sick for three years before she died. He has no other family. He doesn't have a girlfriend or a boyfriend, and he has worked waiting tables since he was eighteen.

I like him.

"This is some view," Hayden says with a low whistle.

"It sure is," I agree as we look out over the city skyline. "You should see it from the roof terrace."

"You have a roof terrace?" he asks as his eyes widen in excitement.

"Yep, with a pool."

"Wow!" He takes a swig of his beer. "How long have you lived in New York?"

"A few years."

"And before that?"

"All over really," I say with a shrug.

"You're so lucky. I've always wanted to travel," he says with a sigh and I can't help but smile that he thinks my running from a psychopath was traveling.

"No reason why you can't one day," I tell him and he shrugs.

He looks like he's about to say something when the kitchen is filled with the unmistakable sounds of all four Ryan brothers being in the same room. A chorus of 'hey, bro's' ripples around the kitchen.

I spin around and smile at Liam as he stands beside the kitchen island. He smiles back at me but he scowls at Hayden.

"That's Liam," I whisper and Hayden gives him an awkward wave.

Shane walks toward us and as soon as he reaches us, he wraps me in his arms and kisses me. Not a soft peck on the lips, but a full on, passionate Shane Ryan kiss. I gasp for breath when he lets me up for air. That was a blatant display of his possessiveness, but I love that about him so I let it go. "This is Hayden," I say to him and then I turn to Hayden. "And this is Shane."

Shane extends his hand and Hayden takes it gingerly in his.

Oh please, don't crush his fingers, Shane!

But he doesn't. He shakes it gently as he forces a smile. "I hear you're joining us for dinner?"

"Yeah. It smells delicious," Hayden says breathing in the aroma of Mikey's delicious chili.

"It is. You're in for a treat," Shane replies, his hand coasting over my back until he rests it just above my ass. "Shall we sit?" He motions toward the table and the tone of his voice makes it clear this is not a request.

MIKEY AND CONOR have dished out dinner and we are all sitting with a plateful of chili, and we're about to dig in when Shane speaks.

"So, how much debt are you in, Hayden?" he asks matter-of-factly, like he's asking what his favorite soda is.

"U-um," Hayden stammers as he holds his fork halfway between his plate and his mouth.

"Shane!" I frown at him.

"What? Let's not waste time with small talk and discuss the things that are on all of our minds."

"I..." Hayden starts to speak but he is flustered.

"You haven't told him that you already know about his mom's huge medical bills?" Shane arches an eyebrow at me.

"Well, it wasn't part of our opening conversation, Shane," I hiss through gritted teeth.

Shane puts his fork down and rests his huge forearms on the table. "I think it's best that we lay all cards on the table," he glares at Hayden. "Jessie here has a gift. She can find out pretty much anything about anyone. So we already know that you're in debt that you have no hope of repaying. You see the building we're sitting in?" He looks around the room. "The building we own. You can see why my brothers and I might be concerned that you're not looking for a sister at all?"

Hayden nods. "I can see why you might think that, but it's not true. I don't want Jessie's money."

"It's not my money," I say, earning me a withering look from Shane.

"So, how do you intend to pay?" Conor asks.

"I honestly don't know. I pay off what I can, but I don't earn that much," Hayden says quietly. "But that's not why I came looking for Jessic - Jessie," he quickly corrects himself.

"What if I were to offer to pay of all your debts right now?" Shane arches an eyebrow at him and I close my eyes and suck in a breath. I should have known this was coming. This is Shane's test.

"What's the catch?" Hayden whispers.

"You leave here now and never come back. You never mention Jessie or Jessica's name again and you forget that either of them existed. I'll even throw in an extra fifty thousand bucks so you can get back on your feet. What do you say?"

Hayden doesn't speak for a few seconds as he considers Shane's proposal. "I'm not gonna lie and say that's not a tempting offer... But I'm not here for money."

I flash Shane a sarcastic smile and refrain from calling him an asshole in front of our guest, hoping that he knows that's what I'm thinking anyway.

"Then let's eat," Shane says as he picks up his fork again.

Hayden is hesitant at first, no doubt wondering if he is about to be blindsided again. I give him a gentle nudge on the arm. "You'll have to excuse my husbands, they're very overprotective."

"With good reason," Liam snaps before he shovels a forkful of chili into his mouth.

"Well, yeah," I admit with a laugh.

"I don't think I want to know," he says with a shake of his head and a soft smile. "But I guess it's kind of nice to have people looking out for you."

I swallow the ball of emotion that rushes up from my chest and gets lodged in my throat. I remember how it felt to be all alone in the world like he is right now. My possessive, overprotective husbands might be a bit much sometimes, but I wouldn't have them any other way. "It is," I whisper.

AFTER THE STRAINED start to our meal, we end up enjoying the remainder of it and once Hayden has relaxed, he is surprisingly good company. He even makes Mikey laugh when he tells him a story about the chef at the bar where he works getting fired for stealing the owner's spare panties from her purse.

"That *would* make you laugh, being a fellow panty-fiend." I arch an eyebrow at Mikey and he winks at me.

Liam has been quiet throughout the evening and I make a note to speak to him about it later.

Hayden checks his watch as Shane and Liam start clearing the dishes. "I should be going if I'm going to catch the last train."

"We'll have a driver take you home," Shane says.

"If that's not a problem that would be great. I hate taking the train late at night," he says.

"You do?" I squeal. "I love the train at night. Not that I ever take it any more."

Hayden shudders, making me laugh. "It's full of scary people."

"No wonder you like it, Red," Mikey says, pressing a soft kiss on my forehead. "You're a magnet for scary people."

"Like you?" I narrow my eyes at him.

"Oh, definitely me," he whispers in my ear.

"This has been great though. Thank you so much," Hayden says as he pushes back his chair. "I'd love to see you again, Jessie."

Neither of us miss the exchange of looks, grins and arched eyebrows that bounce across the room between the brothers.

"I mean, like..." Hayden stammers again, his cheeks turning bright red as he thinks of the right words. Then he throws his hands up in the air. "She's my damn sister, guys. I didn't mean..." He shakes his head and everyone except Liam laughs.

"Is she?" Shane asks as he comes up beside me and wraps an arm around my waist. "Because this has been nice, but we don't really know that you two are even related."

"So how do we find out?" Hayden asks. "A DNA test?"

"No," Liam snaps and Shane shoots him a warning look.

"That seems the quickest and easiest way to prove it one way or another," I say with a shrug.

"Then it's fine by me," Hayden replies. "So what do we do? Get one online or something?"

"No," Shane says with a shake of his head. "You don't need to do anything. We'll be in touch."

"Okay," Hayden replies with a frown and I give him a reassuring smile. "I'll wait for you to call me then?"

"Yeah," I say.

"I'll walk you downstairs," Shane says.

Hayden stands awkwardly for a second until I break the tension and give him a hug. He seems reluctant to hug me back at first and I have no doubt he has four pairs of eyes burning into his skin. But then he wraps his arms around me. "It was great to meet you, Jessie," he whispers.

CHAPTER 21
SHANE

When I walk back into the kitchen after getting one of our men to drive Hayden home, the atmosphere is tense. Liam leans against the kitchen island while Mikey and Conor sit at the table and Jessie hovers by the window.

"What's going on?" I ask.

"Liam doesn't want me to have the DNA test done," Jessie snaps.

I frown at him. "Why not?"

"Because I don't trust that guy, that's why."

"Why not? He was perfectly nice," Jessie says with a shake of her head.

I walk toward my younger brother and lean beside him. "Whether you trust him or not, the only way to know if he is Jessie's half-brother is if they do the DNA test. Nobody is asking you to trust him just yet."

"I don't see why we can't just pay him to back off," Liam snarls.

"Shane just tried that and it didn't work. He's not interested in money..." Jessie says.

"Of course he is," Liam interrupts her. "Why are you so quick to believe everything this guy says?"

"Why are you so quick to doubt him? He could be my family, Liam."

That seems to flick some kind of switch in my usually placid, at least around her, youngest brother. "We are your fucking family, Jessie!"

"I know that, but he might be my family too, and if he is..."

"And if he is, he's likely to be a lying psychopath like the rest of them were."

Fuck kid!

The change in Jessie's face is instant. I rub a hand over my jaw as I wait for her to tear him a new one.

"My family were not lying psychopaths," she shouts, her body trembling with suppressed rage.

"Really?" Liam takes a step toward her, his fists balled at his sides and his breathing getting faster and harder. "Your mom didn't steal you from your real father and lie to you from the minute you were born? And your dad wasn't an evil, murderous prick?"

"My parents did what they did to protect me," she shrieks. "And are you forgetting about my little brothers?" She's crying now and tears run down her cheeks. I watch her unravel and know I can't stop it because she needs to say her piece. "They were children. Innocent children. They never hurt anybody in their whole damn lives until they were slaughtered right in front of me. Do you know what it's like to listen to your little brothers screaming for help as a madman slits their throats? And you talk about *my* father being an evil psychopath!"

Liam shrinks back from her words, as though she's sliced him wide open with a knife, and I suppose she has, not that he didn't have it coming.

I have never seen Jessie so angry or Liam so unreasonably

stubborn and I don't know how to fix it. I also know that I can't - they have to fix this themselves.

We all watch as Jessie storms out of the room like a tiny tornado, full of anger and tears and frustration.

"What the fuck was that?" I ask Liam.

He opens his mouth to reply but no sound comes out and then he closes it again, shaking his head as he sits on a stool at the kitchen island.

Mikey and Conor look at me and then him, and then the door, no doubt wondering if our irate wife is about to come flying back through it to carry on the argument. She won't though. She was too upset.

I walk to my youngest brother and place my hand on the back of his neck. "What is up with you, son?"

He shakes his head again and refuses to look me in the eye.

"You need to go apologize to her."

His head snaps up then and he glares at me. "She brought up the fact that my dad was..." He doesn't finish the sentence. It has taken a long time for him to come to terms with who his biological father was.

"Yeah, after you called her entire family a bunch of liars and psychopaths. That was out of line and you know it. So man the fuck up and go and make it right."

"Fine," he snaps as he jumps off the stool. "But don't blame me if she sets me on fire or something."

"I'm sure you can handle her," I smile at him and he skulks off out of the kitchen and me and my two remaining brothers sit down at the island.

Mikey glances at the doorway. "You think I should go check on them? I mean she was pretty pissed?"

"No. Let him handle it."

Conor gives our younger brother a nudge on the arm. "Don't take this away from him."

Mikey frowns "Take what away?"

I chuckle to myself because I know exactly what Conor is talking about.

"He's about to have make-up sex with Jessie for the first time ever," Conor replies with a wink.

"Fuck!" Mikey breathes. "They've never had a fight before really."

"Nope," Conor shakes his head. "Liam is about to see the light, brother, so leave him the fuck alone."

Mikey nods and takes a seat beside the breakfast bar beside Conor and I pour us each a mug of coffee and join them. "Make-up sex," Mikey says with a wistful sigh. "I can't remember the last time I pissed Jessie off enough for that."

"Mine was two weeks ago when I wouldn't let her win at poker and I took all of her chips and ate them in front of her," Conor laughs and Mikey and I join him. Potato chips are the only kind worth playing Jessie for because she doesn't give a damn about money.

"That's cold, bro," Mikey says with a shake of his head.

"*Fuck!*" Conor has stopped laughing but he is still smiling at the memory. "She had to come to the office to get something. She was so pissed at me. I fucked her over my desk and came so hard, I almost passed out."

Mikey laughs again while I remain quiet. It was only days ago when I made her pissed on purpose so that she'd act like a brat and I could spank her incredible ass. I can spank her ass without her acting like a brat of course, but it's always better for both of us if I have a reason.

"What about you, Shane?" Mikey asks.

"Can't recall," I lie.

"That's because all sex with you two is make-up sex," Conor says with a flash of his eyebrows. "I mean I make her pissed at stupid stuff, but you do it like it's an Olympic sport."

"Asshole," I smile at him.

"Poor Jessie," Conor says with a grin. "Once Liam realizes how good make-up fucking is, he's gonna start being an asshole to Jessie too."

"No, he wouldn't do that," I shake my head. "He hates conflict too much, even fake conflict."

"True," Mikey agrees.

"Any idea what's going on with him?" I ask Mikey, who understandably knows his twin better than any of us. "I've never seen him like that with her before."

Mikey sucks in a breath. "He's still struggling with finding her in Paul's basement."

"Really?" I frown. I had no idea and I'm usually in tune with my brothers.

"Yeah. You know he keeps shit to himself and he tries to forget about it, but he's been having fucked up dreams about it all."

"For real?" Conor frowns too.

"Yup. If he's not sleeping with Jessie, he freaks out when he wakes up and she's not there."

"Why hasn't he said anything?" I ask.

"It doesn't happen all the time and you know he doesn't like to worry anyone. But he thought she was dead when he found her, you know?" Mikey says with a sigh.

"So the thought of anyone taking her..." I start to say but I don't need to finish the sentence.

"Yup," Mikey says before taking a drink of his coffee.

"No wonder he freaked out then." Conor flashes his eyebrows.

"What do you both think of Hayden?" I take a swig of my coffee.

"Don't trust him one little bit," Conor replies first.

"Me neither," Mikey adds.

"Neither do I, but I wouldn't trust anyone when it comes to her. Jessie seems pretty open to this guy being her half-brother, though," I say.

"Yup," Mikey nods his agreement. "And if we don't support her just because we can't stand the idea of sharing her with anyone else, then we're assholes."

"Kinda," Conor sighs. "But that still doesn't mean we have to trust a single thing that comes out of this guy's mouth."

"True."

Conor arches an eyebrow at me. "You gonna ask Jax to look into him?"

Jackson Decker is one of the best hackers in the world. He's a buddy of ours and he looked into Jessie for me when we first met her and had no idea who she really was. And while Jax is good at what he does, my wife is better. "Are you kidding me? Jessie would lose her shit for real if I did that. She's perfectly capable of looking into this guy on her own."

"What if she..." Conor shakes his head and stares at his coffee.

I frown at him. "What if she what?"

He runs a hand over his jaw. "You know that thing where people are having a debate or something, and they only look for the evidence that will support their argument?"

"You think she won't be objective?" I ask.

"Do you? You saw how she reacted in there. How she smiled when he talked about how they both have a sweet tooth and love baseball."

"She's the best at what she does, Con. We ask Jax to look into this guy for us and it's telling her we don't trust her. She'll never go for it."

"Do we have to tell her?" Mikey asks with a shrug.

"Yes!" Conor and I reply in unison.

"Okay. Just a thought."

"Let's see if there is anything else she can dig up and if Hayden gives us any reason to, I'll broach the subject of Jax taking a look into him too. Okay?"

"Okay," Mikey and Conor agree.

CHAPTER 22
LIAM

I walk into Jessie's bedroom to find her lying on the bed.

"Go away!" she snaps when I walk into the room.

I ignore her and close the door behind me. She's been crying and I hate to see her upset, especially when I'm the cause of it, but that doesn't stop the anger burning through my veins. She is one of the smartest people I know, so how can she be so fucking naïve when it comes to trusting people?

After everything she's been through, she still sees the best in everyone. I know that makes me a complete hypocrite, because that used to be one of the things I loved about her – the fact that she sees the positives in everything and everyone. But now it just terrifies me, ever since I found her in that basement back in Ireland and for a few horrible seconds, I thought she was dead and I'd lost her forever. I can't get that image out of my head. Try as I might, I can't forget that feeling and the complete despair I felt in that moment. I'm not sure I would survive losing her.

"I don't want to talk to you, Liam," she says with a sigh as I approach the bed.

"Then just listen."

She rolls her eyes and it stirs something in me that I've never felt before with her. I want to spank her ass until she's begging me to stop.

"I don't want to listen to you either, because you're an asshole!"

I clench my fists into balls. "An asshole?"

She turns her head so she can glare at me. "Yes! I expect that kind of crap from Shane, and even Conor, but not you!" She pushes herself off the bed and stalks toward the bathroom and I am hot on her heels.

I grab hold of her arm and turn her to face me. "So, everyone else gets to speak their mind, but not me? Is that it?" I snarl at her as every nerve in my body burns with a pent-up rage that I haven't felt in a long time. I have never felt it with her before and I don't know what to do with it.

"That's not what I said," she glares at me defiantly.

"Then what is it, Jessie? Why does everyone else get to be an asshole to you but not me?" I challenge her.

She blinks at me and my heart constricts in my chest as I wait for her to answer me. Is this where she tells me that I'm just the added extra? That she could do without me as long as she has my three brothers? That they give her everything I can't?

"I..." She shakes her head. "Forget about it!"

She turns and goes to walk away from me but I keep hold of her arm and stop her in her tracks. "Don't turn your fucking back on me, Jessie!" I hiss as I pull her toward me until our bodies are just inches apart.

"Liam!" She gasps at the harshness in my tone, but her eyes darken with heat.

I'm holding tightly to her wrist and her pulse thrums against my skin. It's racing, just like mine is. She glares at me, her eyes full of fire and anger. Fury radiates from both of us like heat from a raging inferno. She gasps in a stuttered breath that makes her tits rise and fall and suddenly my cock is throbbing as hard as the blood in my veins.

I stare at her, my jaw clenched so tight that my teeth are grinding together. I need to do something with this anger that is burning through me, so I do the only thing that comes to mind. I am going to fucking bury myself in her cunt until she screams my name.

I pick her up and wrap her legs around my waist before carrying her to the dresser a few feet away. I throw her onto it, causing the small bottle of perfume she has on there to fall off onto the floor. The glass shatters and the fresh citrus smell fills my senses. It smells so much like her that it makes my cock throb painfully.

Her body is trembling but she winds her arms around my neck as she keeps her legs wrapped around my waist. I pull my cock free from my sweatpants before reaching between her thighs and tugging her panties to the side. My knuckles brush over her folds and I realize she's not quite wet enough for this, but I'm going to fuck her anyway. I'm going to fuck her until I feel better.

I drive my cock into her tight pussy and her walls squeeze around me.

She hisses out a breath as she claws at my neck. "Liam!" she half-groans, half-shouts.

I pull her closer to me with my arms around her waist until there isn't a millimeter of space between. "Is this what you want?" I growl as I rail into her.

"Fuck! Yes!" she pants as she pulls me deeper, her nails scratching my skin.

I fuck her harder than I have ever fucked anyone in my life, my thighs smacking against the drawers and the dresser banging loudly against the wall behind us.

"Liam!" she shouts as I drive harder and the whole dresser starts to rattle as the drawers slide in and out and it bounces off the wall. It's going to fall to pieces if I don't let up but I don't care. I'll buy her a dozen new dressers if I need to. My fingers dig into the soft flesh of her hips as I tilt her back and go deeper, making her groan loudly.

I bury my face against her neck and bite on the tender spot beneath her ear and she starts to whimper, rocking her hips against mine as though she can't get enough even as I'm giving every single fucking thing I have. My balls draw up into my stomach as I'm overcome with a need to claim her. She is fucking mine and I will never let anyone take her from me.

"Fuck! I will never get enough of you," I growl in her ear.

"Liam, I need you," she groans as she pulls at my hair and suddenly all the not feeling good enough disappears. She wants this as much as I do.

I pick her up from the dresser and carry her to the bed instead. When I pull out of her, she groans in frustration.

"I just want you naked, baby," I pant as I reach for her dress and peel it off over her head. Then I pull her panties off too and toss them onto the floor before I settle back between her thighs and she wraps her arms and legs around me again. Her skin is soft and hot against mine. Her nipples are hard against my chest as she pulls me close. When I sink into her smooth, wet heat she moans my name so fucking loudly it makes me feel like I'm going to blow my load in her right now.

"I love fucking you, Jessie," I breathe in her ear.

"I love it too."

I rail into her harder than before, nailing her into the mattress. Every thrust. Every scratch of her nails on my skin.

Every whimper and moan that I pull from her body makes the rage inside me ebb away.

When she finally comes, squeezing and dripping all over my cock, she screams my name so loudly that I think everyone on this block must have heard. The feeling of her hot pussy milking me as she does tips me over the edge too and by the time we're both done, we're panting for breath, our bodies completely spent.

I lie on top of her, my head resting on her chest as she curls her fingers through my hair.

"I'm sorry about what I said," she whispers.

"I know, baby," I whisper back. "Me too."

"Why are you so upset about Hayden?"

I push myself up and roll onto my side, bringing her with me so that we can lie facing each other. "I don't trust him."

"I get that," she frowns at me. "I'm pretty sure your brothers don't either, but this is about more than that, Liam."

I nod at her. It's about so much more, but how do I tell her that I can't stop thinking about her in that basement back in Ireland?

She places her hand on my chest, right over my heart. "What is it?" she whispers. "Please tell me."

"When I saw you chained to that bed in Paul's basement, Jessie, I thought you were dead."

She blinks at me.

"It was the worst few moments of my entire life. I..." I suck in a breath and she shuffles closer to me, draping her leg over mine until our bodies are flush together.

"I didn't know that," she whispers.

"You were so cold and still. I thought I was never going to see your smile or your eyes, or feel your warm skin on mine. I dream about it all the time and when I wake up and you're not there..."

"Liam." She presses a soft kiss on my lips. "I'm not going anywhere."

"But what if he's not who he says he is, Jessie? What if he wants something more from you?"

"I know you think I'm being naïve, but I'm not stupid, Liam. There is a chance Hayden is lying or has an ulterior motive, but by the same token, there is also a chance that he's not. I don't want to be the kind of person who always assumes the worst of people. I'm sorry, but I can't be that, not even for you."

"I don't want you to change who you are, Jessie," I tuck her hair behind her ear. "I just want you to be careful."

"I will be." She smiles at me and my cock twitches to life again.

"What were you going to say before?"

Her beautiful face pulls into a frown. "When?"

I don't want to argue with her again, but I have to know the answer. "When I asked you why everyone but me gets to be an asshole to you?"

She blushes and her eyelids flutter. "I... It's silly," she whispers.

"Not to me."

She looks into my eyes and bites on her lip.

"Stop chewing your lip and answer me."

"I do like this bossy side of you," she purrs.

"Then answer the damn question, Jessie!"

"You remember you were the first to kiss me?" she breathes and I wonder if she's answering the question or trying to distract me.

"Of course I do. I think about that night all the damn time." It was the night all of our lives changed. One minute, me, her and Mikey were watching movies on the couch and the next thing I was kissing her. A few moments later, I tasted her pussy for the first time and I've been addicted to her from that moment. Mikey and I fucked her together shortly afterward and we've been fucking her every chance we get since.

"I do too," she smiles at me. "You were the first man I kissed that I ever really wanted to kiss, Liam."

"What?" I blink at her. How can that be true? She was twenty-six when we met.

"I kissed a boy when I was fifteen and I wanted that," she adds. "But he was just a boy."

"Jessie, I don't understand." I shake my head.

"I had sex with plenty of guys, and not always through choice," she says it so matter-of-factly that it makes me want to kill every man who has ever laid a finger on her. "Some were through choice, of course, but usually as a means to an end. Because I needed information, or a place to stay or something." She shrugs. "And occasionally just to scratch an itch, but they could have been anyone and I never kissed them. I mean our lips may have touched briefly, but we weren't kissing. No tongues or open mouths."

I realize I must be looking at her funny now because she starts to babble. "It's not that all of the others forced me, and I even enjoyed it sometimes..." Her cheeks redden further.

"You don't have to explain yourself to me, Jessie."

"I know." She takes a deep breath. "I'm just trying to tell you that I never really wanted to kiss anyone before I met you and your brothers."

"Fuck! Really?"

"Really."

"But what does that have to do with me being an asshole?"

"I kind of always saw you as..." She chews on her lip again and my heart stops beating. What the fuck does she see me as?

"As what?"

"My ride or die. The one who'll always have my back, even when I'm being an asshole too," she finally says and my heart starts beating again and I feel like a complete jackass for thinking that she thought any less of me than she does my brothers. "Conor and Shane kind of have that, and obviously you and Mikey do. I just thought... Like I said, I'm being silly."

"I have always got your back, baby. One hundred percent."

"I know," she smiles.

"I can't keep quiet when I think you're in danger though. That's having your back too."

"I know that, but sometimes I feel like it's the four of you, and then me."

"Jessie!" I roll on top of her, pinning her to the mattress again. "It is never like that. There is no us and you, just us. Tell me that you believe that?"

"I do most of the time," she breathes. "I think I'm just feeling emotional right now for some reason. Maybe it's thinking about my little brothers and my mom and dad."

"Maybe." I kiss her softly and she opens her mouth, allowing me to slide my tongue inside. My cock is already hard again and she rocks her hips against me, grinding herself on me. I pull back from our kiss, leaving her gasping for breath. "You're insatiable, you know that?"

"Says the guy with the huge boner?" She arches an eyebrow at me.

I rub my nose along the column of her throat. She smells so fucking good. "Shall I fuck you again, baby?"

"Yes."

"Properly this time." I arch an eyebrow at her.

"What do you mean?" she purrs.

"Before wasn't the way I usually fuck you, was it?"

"No," she giggles, "but it was hot."

"You liked it, huh?"

"Couldn't you tell?"

"Well, your pussy was gripping me like it was never gonna let me go." I grin at her.

"That's because I never want to let you go, Liam Ryan." She smiles at me as she wraps her arms around my neck and pulls me closer, and I'm pretty sure there is no man on this earth who is happier than me right now.

CHAPTER 23
SHANE

I fasten my Breitling onto my wrist as I walk into the kitchen. Jessie is sitting on the breakfast bar, with Liam standing between her thighs as he kisses her. He didn't leave her bedroom last night after he went after her, so Conor, Mikey and I left them to it.

"Haven't you two had enough of each other by now?" I ask as I sit beside them and pour myself a fresh coffee. "I mean we all heard you make-up fucking all last night."

Jessie blushes even though there is no way she can't have known we didn't hear them. At one point we were worried they were killing each other until we heard her coming – loudly.

"Never," Liam says with a grin as he pulls back from her and turns to me. "You want a protein shake? I was just gonna make one."

I arch an eyebrow at him. "I'd rather have scrambled eggs."

"Fine." He rolls his eyes and walks to the refrigerator.

"Did you sleep okay?" Jessie asks as she shuffles along the counter until she's sitting in front of me.

"Not really. I never sleep well when you're not with me."

"Sorry," she whispers.

I slide my arms around her waist. "You don't need to apologize. It's just a fact."

"A fact that you can't function without me?" She grins at me.

"I can function without you," I say, bending my head and dropping a soft kiss on her bare thigh, "but I don't want to."

She runs her fingers through my hair and my cock twitches to life. Fuck, I wish I had time to take her back to bed. Even just to lie next to her for a while. I'm so fucking tired, but there are never enough hours in the day. I need to cut back on work, but every time I try, something seems to go wrong.

I look up at her and she gives me the sweetest smile. Sometimes I think about leaving everything behind and running away with her and my brothers. Living in our lake house, with a few kids running around and no shit to deal with.

"You look tired," she whispers.

"I'm fine."

"You're working too hard." She tugs gently on my hair, tilting my head back so she can stare into my eyes and right into my goddamn soul.

I wrap my arms tighter around her waist. "Come here." I pull her to me until her thighs are wrapped around me. Grabbing a fistful of her hair, I pull her lips to mine and kiss her and she moans softly into my mouth. "Fuck, Jessie," I groan as I pull away from her. "I need to stop before I take you to bed and barricade us in for the rest of the week."

"That sounds good to me."

"Not a chance." Liam appears with a plate of scrambled egg and two slices of toast.

Jessie scoots down off the counter and sits beside me. "I need you with me today," I say to Liam before I take a bite of my food.

"Why? We having more problems?" He frowns.

"What problems?" Jessie asks.

I swallow before I answer them. "It's nothing we can't handle. More of an annoyance than anything else," I say to Jessie. "But yeah, someone has been upsetting some of our customers again. I just need to smooth some things over but it won't hurt to taken some muscle along."

"Is there anything I can do to help?" Jessie asks.

"No, sweetheart. We got it."

"Okay, but let me know if I can do anything, especially if it keeps happening. I mean I know you say it's just an annoyance but if it's happened before then someone is deliberately targeting you, right?"

I hate that she said you and not us but I let it go. "But they're such minor issues though. I mean if someone wanted to seriously target us, they'd make more of a move. At least that's how it's always been in the past."

"You say it's minor but it's got two of you dealing with it."

"Only because it involves some of our best customers," I tell her. Usually I would let some of our employees sort minor disputes but this security contract is one of our biggest and the director can get a little antsy if he doesn't speak to me or Conor.

"It could be a distraction," Jessie says with a shrug. "Just don't dismiss the idea that it's something bigger is all I'm saying."

"She has a point," Liam chips in.

"Hmm." I rub a hand over my jaw. She does.

Two hours later, Liam and I are on our way to Connecticut to meet with Brad Sawyer, the director of Sawyer Transport. We provide security for him amongst other things.

"You and Jessie sort your differences then?" I ask Liam

"We did," he says as a smile flickers over his lips.

"I've never seen you so worked up like that with her before. There something else going on, son?"

He sucks in a breath. "I know I've been a dumbass over this Hayden guy..."

"But?"

"But I don't trust him and I'm terrified that someone is gonna take her from us, Shane. I mean every time we think her past is behind her, it comes back and bites us all on the ass. I couldn't handle it if we lost her again."

"I know. None of us could, but you have to stop living every day thinking you're going to lose her. You'll drive yourself and her crazy if you don't."

"I keep seeing her in that basement, Shane. I keep dreaming about it, only in my dream, she's dead. Then I wake up and I think it's real and I relive the most horrible moment of my life over and over again."

I reach over and put my hand on the back of his neck. "You've been through a lot this past year. Maybe—"

"I don't want to talk to no shrink," he interrupts me.

"Okay. But just talk to us then. Stop keeping it all bottled in until you explode like you did last night."

"Okay," he says with a soft sigh.

We're quiet for a while and when I turn to look at him, he's got a goofy smile on his face.

"Making up was that good, huh?" I chuckle.

"It was fucking epic." He laughs too. "I can see why you argue with her all the time."

"Not all the time." I shake my head.

"Not as much as you used to, no, but still..."

I arch an eyebrow at him. "Well, you said yourself, fucking epic."

"You're definitely less tightly wound than you used to be, bro," Liam goes on. "Our girl is good for us."

I roll my shoulders and flex my neck. I don't feel less tightly wound today, but I do agree that she's good for us. In fact, Jessie Ryan is the best thing that's ever happened to the Ryan family.

CHAPTER 24
JESSIE

I wrap my arms around Mikey's neck and press a soft kiss against his throat. "I wish you didn't have to work tonight," I whisper in his ear.

"So do I, Red," he chuckles as he slides his arms around my waist. "But Conor is downstairs on his own, so I gotta go."

"I know," I say with a sigh. Conor manages the brothers' nightclub and the twins manage the security side. They all work there at least four nights a week in a pair so one of them is always home with me and Shane. They used to work there almost every night, but since we got married, all of the brothers spend less time working and more time in the apartment. It took some time, but all of us have found a better work-life balance between us, even Shane who is still something of a workaholic, but less than he was.

"Why don't you come with me?" Mikey asks with a flash of his eyebrows. "It will sure make my night more interesting to have you doing the rounds with me."

"Won't I distract you?"

"I sure fucking hope so," he replies with a chuckle. "Especially as you're going to wear those crotchless panties for me."

"I can't wear them to the club," I protest, even as the thought sends shivers of pleasure skittering up my spine.

He bends his head and grazes his teeth over the delicate skin of my neck before he replies, "You can, because I won't let you out of my sight for even a second. Now go change!" He slaps my ass, making me giggle and then he sits on my bed and waits for me to get dressed.

As MIKEY and I work our way through the club, he holds onto my hand tightly. People greet him as we pass. Even though he's with me, I don't miss the admiring glances he draws from both men and women alike, but I suppose he is the perfect package. Tall. Handsome. Powerful. He turns to me and winks and I smile back at him, feeling like the luckiest woman in the world that I get to call him and his brothers mine.

We just left Conor in his office. He spends most of his time in there while he's at the club, while Mikey and Liam prefer to stay out where the customers are, keeping an eye out for any potential trouble. They have an amazing security team, but they much prefer to be in the midst of any action rather than behind a desk. I suppose that's why the brothers work so well together. Each of them has their own role which they're happy with.

When we reach the downstairs VIP area, Mikey leads us to a quieter corner of the room.

I know you want me by Pitbull comes on and I grin at him because it's one of our favorite songs and he sings it to me all the time. Wrapping his arms around my waist, he presses his mouth against my ear. "You want to dance, Red?"

"Hmm." I chew on my lip as though I'm considering his proposal even though there is only one answer to his question. "Yes." I snake my arms around his neck and he pulls me closer as we move to the music.

His hands roam over my back and ass and I suck in a breath as warmth floods my core. His solid chest is pressed up against me, making my nipples harden as our bodies grind against each other.

"I can't stop thinking about what you're wearing under this dress," he groans softly in my ear as he rocks his hips against mine.

"I can tell," I giggle as his hard cock presses against my abdomen.

"Have you ever come in public before, Red?" he growls as his lips dust over my ear making me shiver in anticipation.

"Once. In a restaurant in Ireland with Shane."

"Really?" he murmurs as he trails soft kisses over my throat.

"Yes," I say against his ear so he can hear me over the loud music. "But it was dark and quiet, and we couldn't really be seen."

"Well, it's dark in here," he chuckles.

I look around at the sea of other bodies surrounding us. Some so close they are almost touching. "But there are people all around us." I gasp as his hand slides to my ass and he squeezes hard.

"I won't let anyone see what I'm doing. Promise," he says, his breath dusting over the shell of my ear. "But I need to take advantage of those damn panties."

I pull my head back and stare into his eyes. They are full of mischief and trouble, but they are also dark with lust. Damn, he is so freaking hot. How am I supposed to resist him? And I trust him. If he says he won't let anybody see, then... "Okay," I breathe and he grins in response.

He steps forward, pushing me back slightly until we're standing near one of the large pillars in the basement of the club. "You think you can keep a straight face while I'm making you come?" he chuckles in my ear.

"No," I admit with a shake of my head and he laughs loudly.

"That's okay. I got you." He flashes his eyebrows at me as he presses me back against the pillar, one hand on my ass while the other slides to my front, down to the edge of my mini dress before slipping between my thighs. "Open a little wider, Red," he whispers and I obey, allowing him easier access to my pussy. He circles the tip of one finger over my clit and I suck in a breath as I wrap my arms around his neck. "Fuck! I'm gonna make you wear these damn panties every day, Red. Such easy access to this sweet pussy."

"Mikey!" I whimper. I'm not so sure about this now. Everyone around us is going to know what we're doing.

"It's okay, Red," he soothes in my ear. Then with his free hand, he presses my face into his neck. "Just keep your head right here and you'll be fine. I promise that I'll stop if anyone gets too close or sees us. Okay?"

"Okay," I murmur as I press my lips against his throat and inhale his intoxicating smell. Then his hand is back on my ass as he holds me tight to him while he starts to toy with my clit again.

"So fucking wet," he whispers in my ear. "I'm gonna make you come all over my fingers in the middle of our club, Red."

I bite on my lip to stop myself from moaning loudly because even the way he talks to me has me needy and desperate to grind myself on his fingers.

He teases me slowly, his fingers barely moving as we keep on swaying to the music. I tell myself that anyone who does look our way will just see us dancing closely, but if he keeps this maddening teasing up much longer then I'll be so desperate for him, I'm pretty sure I wouldn't care if he pinned me against the pillar and fucked me in full view of everyone.

"Mikey, I need more," I groan into his ear.

"Soon, Red," he murmurs. "You're so fucking greedy for me."

I press a soft kiss on the base of his throat and rock my hips against his hand and my clit pulses at the slight increase in friction.

"Fuck!" he hisses, but it has the desired affect and he glides his hand further up my dress until one of his fingers slides to where I want him. He presses the tip against me, swirling gently at my wet entrance, taunting me with the promise of more. I try to move to take him inside me but he holds me in place with his huge frame.

"This what you want?" he growls as he pushes the tip in a fraction.

"Yes!" I gasp, my face still pressed against his neck.

"Yes what?"

"Please, Mikey?"

"I love making you beg, Red," he groans as he pushes his finger all the way inside me and my walls squeeze him tightly as I coat him in a rush of slick heat.

"Ah!" I moan into his ear and he rewards me by adding a second digit. He moves them slowly in and out of me and my knuckles turn white as I grip the collar of his suit jacket. My legs tremble as delicious waves of pleasure pulse through my body along with the heavy bass of the music from the club.

"This is what you want, right?" he chuckles as he drives in further and I gasp against his skin. "Your tight little pussy is so needy, Red," he breathes in my ear. "I love how much my girl loves a finger-fucking. You can't get enough of me, can you?"

"Mikey," I groan as he maintains a steady rhythm with his fingers while the palm of his hand nudges my clit. I am teetering on the precipice of oblivion and if he doesn't stop with the filthy talk I'm going to mount him in full view of all these people.

"You gonna come for me like my good girl?" he chuckles and my knees almost buckle. Dammit he's onto my praise kink now too. As if him and his brothers didn't already drive me crazy enough with the things they do to me. "You think I didn't notice that the other night? When I was fucking you while Conor was in your ass and he called you his good girl. How tight this pussy squeezed me?"

I whimper into his neck as my walls squeeze him, proving his point.

"Well are you?" he hisses as he drives his fingers deeper, curling the tips inside me so he can press on that spot that makes me come apart.

I squeeze my thighs together as my orgasm threatens to burst out of me but he pulls his fingers out slightly and it ebbs away.

"You're not playing fair," I murmur in his ear.

"Well, I learned from the best, Red," he says softly and I'm pretty sure he's talking about his oldest brother.

But I learned a lot from him too. I slide one of my hands down Mikey's back and then beneath his suit jacket. Then I rub his back, dragging my fingernails up and down his spine, because it drives him crazy. His muscles flex beneath his soft cotton shirt and he starts to work his fingers harder.

"I thought no one was supposed to see us, Red?" he hisses in my ear as he pushes his body further against mine until I'm pinned to the pillar.

I breathe deeply as I try to focus on maintaining at least some modicum of decency. But I'm overwhelmed by everything that's happening. The loud music and his soft groans in my ear as he tries to maintain control. The feel of his lips at my neck. His groin pressed against mine and his hard cock digging into me as though to remind me what I have in store later. His soft, kisses. His powerful hands, one squeezing my ass as he pulls me to him while the fingers of his other one drive in and out of me.

"You're dripping all over me," he hisses in my ear. "I'm gonna make you scream my name in front of all these people, Red."

"No, I can't," I mumble as I press my mouth against the hot skin of his throat. I part my lips as I kiss him softly, darting out my tongue and licking a trail over his damp skin. He tastes so good, I could lick him from head to toe.

A low growl rumbles in his throat. "If you don't stop that, I'm gonna fuck you right here," he snarls in my ear and I feel a rush of wet heat as I get closer and closer to that edge.

I look down and seeing Mikey's hand beneath my dress, I imagine the muscles on his huge forearm flexing as he thrusts his fingers inside me and I come undone.

"Mikey, I'm gonna..." I can't even finish my sentence as my orgasm crashes into my body like a subway train. As it does, Mikey's free hand moves to the back of my head, and he keeps my face pressed into the crook of his neck, muffling my groans as the tremors roll through my core.

"God, you make me want to bury my cock in you so fucking bad," he whispers as he rubs my clit softly while I cling to him, my entire body shaking as I come down from the epic high he's just given me.

CHAPTER 25
CONOR

I stare at the image on the computer screen with my mouth hanging open in shock and my cock straining against the zipper of my suit pants as I watch my deviant little brother making my wife come in the middle of our fucking nightclub. At first I wasn't sure that was what he was doing. They could have just been slow dancing, but as soon as he pressed her face against his neck I knew.

I should have run down there and told him to stop, but I was rooted to the fucking spot. Anger burns through my veins that he would do that while people stood just inches away from her. That someone might see is bad enough. But somebody could have accidentally brushed up against her while he was making her come. Felt her trembling in that way that's only for us. Heard her fucking soft, moans and whimpers. Got even the slightest scent of her hot, wet pussy.

If I had gone down there I might have punched him in the mouth, or even worse I might have joined in on the action - either way, I would have caused a huge fucking scene and none of us want that.

If I needed any further proof of what the two of them have

just done, watching Mikey put two fingers in his mouth and suck them clean just gave it to me.

God, I am going to fucking kill him.

I walk to my office door and stick my head out. "Chester!" I shout to our head bouncer standing nearby.

"Yes, Boss?" He jogs over to me.

"Go find Mikey and my wife in the VIP area and tell them to meet me in the apartment. Now!" I bark.

"Yes, Boss," Chester says with a nod before he disappears into the crowd.

I STAND in Shane's office as I wait for my asshole younger brother and my horny wife to get up to the apartment. I hear her giggling in the hallway and it makes the rage burn in my chest. I hold onto the back of Shane's office chair, my knuckles turning white as I will myself to calm the fuck down before I say something I'm going to regret.

The two of them stroll into the room with smiles on their faces, her cheeks flushed pink still after she just came in a room full of complete strangers.

"Everything okay, Con?" Mikey asks.

"No it's fucking not okay, you fucking selfish asshole!" I snarl.

"What the fuck?" he snarls back while Jessie stands beside him, blinking at me in shock.

"You just finger-fucked my wife in the middle of my fucking nightclub!" I shout.

Jessie's cheeks redden further while Mikey scowls at me.

"No, I finger-fucked *my* wife, in *my* nightclub, jackass!"

"Hey!" Jessie tries to interrupt us but I ignore her and focus on him, because it's easier to be mad at him than her.

"She is *our* wife, which means you don't just get to do whatever the hell you want with her, Mikey."

"What?" he walks toward me, squaring his shoulders as he approaches. "So, I'm supposed to ask your permission before I make my own wife come now, is that it?"

"You were in a room full of fucking strangers!" I shout, remaining behind the chair because if I step toward him too, I might just knock him on his ass.

"Nobody saw a thing," he says with a shrug.

"I saw *every* fucking thing!" I shout louder. "She is not some random that you picked up at the bar, so don't fucking treat her like one."

"Conor," Jessie shouts now too and I turn and blink at her. The hurt on her face is obvious, but I'm too pissed at the two of them to back down.

"What is the big fucking deal, Con?" Mikey asks. "We were just having a little fun."

I push the chair aside and march over to him, bringing my face close to his. "The big deal is that I would have to fucking kill any man who watched my wife come, you fucking selfish little prick."

Mikey scowls at me, the tension in his shoulders matching mine. My fists are clenched by my sides as I wait for his apology.

"What the fuck is going on?" Shane's voice cuts through the tension in the room but it is Liam's hands I feel on my shoulders and his voice I hear in my ear. "Calm down, Con," he says softly. I remain glaring at his twin for a few seconds before I step back.

"Mikey fucked Jessie in the VIP room downstairs."

"I didn't," Mikey snarls.

"He did not!" Jessie adds.

Shane and Liam look at the three of us in confusion.

"I finger-fucked her," Mikey adds with a shake of his head.

"Oh my God," Jessie hisses as her cheeks flame with heat

and shame, and a part of me feels guilty for making her feel bad about herself. But the anger overrides it.

"Mikey," Shane says with a sigh. "Why the fuck would you do that?"

"Really, Shane? You of all people are asking me that?" Mikey frowns at our oldest brother.

"That was different, nobody could see us," Shane replies and I shake my head in disbelief.

"You too?" I snap. "Is there anyone in this room who hasn't made my wife come in front of a room full of strangers?"

"What?" Jessie gasps in the background.

"For a start, she wasn't your wife at the time. Secondly, we were in a private booth in a quiet restaurant," Shane says quietly as he makes his way toward me. He keeps his voice calm and controlled but I know he's on the verge of losing his shit too. "But most importantly, Con, it was a mutual fucking decision between two consenting adults. And right now you are being very disrespectful to one of those people, so calm the fuck down and we'll talk about this."

"He let people watch her come, Shane." I shake my head in disbelief that I'm the only one who has an issue with this.

"You're an asshole, Conor Ryan," Jessie says and I hear the crack in her voice and it breaks my heart. I look at her and consider apologizing for making her feel bad but she turns on her heel and walks out of the door.

"Nice work, dumbass," Mikey snarls at me as he goes to walk after her.

"Stay!" Shane orders him and Mikey does as he's told.

"Fuck, we've only been gone a few hours," Liam says with a soft sigh and a shake of his head.

"What the fuck were you thinking, Mikey?" Shane asks. "You know how he is about people seeing her like that."

Mikey looks between me and Shane. I do have major issues

with anyone seeing Jessie undone that way. I've never been like that with anyone before and I wasn't always like that with her either, but since she became my wife, I don't know what changed. My possessive side has completely taken over. It's why I refuse to go to one of our sex clubs on a date with her, even though she and my brothers all want to go.

"I didn't think he'd be watching," Mikey says.

"He's always watching her," Shane reminds him.

"I'm sorry, Con," Mikey finally says with a sigh. "I know you don't like the public thing, but I swear no one saw anything. I didn't even let them hear her. I wouldn't do that."

I stare at my brothers. The anger slipping away and leaving a bitter taste of guilt in my mouth instead. "I just hate anyone seeing her like that. I can't help it. It drives me crazy."

"I know and I want to say it won't happen again, Con, but..." Mikey shrugs.

"But what?" I frown at him.

"But it's something you're going to have to work on with her, bro, because it was fucking hot. I loved it and more importantly, Jessie loved it too. You know that he's into the voyeur thing." Mikey indicates his head toward Shane. "It's only a matter of time before he actually fucks her in public."

I look at Shane and frown, wanting him to tell me this will never happen. "I won't until you're okay with it," Shane assures me.

"But you do want to?" I ask.

"Fuck, yeah," he nods in response.

"Fuck!" I hold my head in my hands and sink onto Shane's chair. "Was I just a complete asshole to Jessie?"

"Yup," Mikey replies without missing a beat.

I shake my head. My brothers and I have lived together our whole lives and obviously we piss each other off occasionally. We can have huge fights but they're forgotten moments later because we all know that each of us would do anything for the other. But Jessie is different. I would die for her just as much as I would my brothers, but she doesn't fully get that yet and so it breaks my heart knowing that I've hurt her.

"Go make sure she's okay," Shane says to Mikey and Liam and they both go after her.

"Fuck!" I say again under my breath.

"You okay?" Shane sits on the edge of the desk next to me.

"I almost fucking punched him in the face, Shane," I say with a shake of my head but my older brother laughs softly and it makes me smile.

"Well, it wouldn't be the first time either of us has felt like punching the little miscreant. But at least you didn't." He arches an eyebrow at me.

"I need to work on this thing though, right?"

"Yes," he says with a nod, "but not for me or Mikey. For her, because she's into it, Con. And she would love to explore it with you too."

"You think?"

He shakes his head. "I know."

"Yeah," I agree feeling even more guilty now that I upset her.

"You know how wet she gets when you spank her?" he grins at me.

"Yeah." My cock twitches just at the thought.

"The public thing gets her just the same." He punches me on the arm before he stands. "I'm having an early night for a change."

"With Jessie?"

"Nope. I figured you'd want her to yourself after what you just did."

"Thanks, bro."

"Any time, dumbass."

CHAPTER 26
JESSIE

I open the door to Shane's office and see Conor sitting in a chair in the darkness. Flipping on the light switch, the room is quickly bathed in bright light and he blinks at me. "It's late," I say.

"I know," he whispers. "I came to find you earlier but you were with Liam and Mikey."

Walking over to him I perch on the desk beside him. I'm still wearing my dress from the club and his eyes roam over my body appreciatively.

"You know you made me feel really cheap earlier," I whisper.

"I know, Angel," he reaches for my hand and laces his fingers through mine. "I have no excuse for making you feel like that. You have more class and elegance in your little toe than I do in my entire body. And I'm so fucking sorry."

"I understand why it made you mad though."

"Still, I was a jackass. Can you forgive me?"

"Hmm." I chew on my lip. "Maybe?"

"Maybe?"

"Yep. Maybe I should punish you first though?"

His Adam's apple bobs in his throat as he swallows. "Punish me how?"

"For a start..." I open one of the desk drawers and pull out two lengths of rope that Shane keeps in here. I've been tied up with them plenty of times before, by both him and Conor, but I've never used them on anyone else. "I think I should tie you up for a change."

He arches an eyebrow at me. "You want to tie me up?"

This is not how we play. This is not our relationship. He is dominant and I am completely submissive to him when it comes to sex. But I have no intention of changing that dynamic; he just doesn't know it yet.

"Uh-huh." I pull the length of rope through my fingers.

He narrows his eyes at me now, his curiosity well and truly piqued. "And then what?" he growls.

"Well, you'll just have to wait and see, big guy." I grin at him. "So are you up for the challenge or not?"

"Careful, Angel," he warns as he reaches out and grabs my wrist. "Or you'll be the one tied up in here."

I shake my head and sigh dramatically. "So, you can give it but you can't take it, Conor Ryan. That's such a disappointment."

"Fuck!" he hisses with a shake of his head. Then he holds out his wrists and my heart starts to hammer against my chest. I don't even know if he's going to like this, or if I can even do it right.

I take a deep breath and channel my inner Shane Ryan – bossy alpha-hole extraordinaire. "Hands on the armrests," I command and he glares at me but he does as I instruct. I run my hand along his muscular forearm before I wrap the rope around his right wrist, securing it to the chair.

"That's kind of tight."

"What can I say, I learned it all from you." I straddle him

and press a soft kiss on his throat and he growls his appreciation. I remain on his lap while I secure his left wrist, pulling tight until the rope bites his skin. He narrows those deep brown eyes at me but he doesn't flinch.

"You all safe and secure there, big guy?" I ask.

He pulls at his restraints. "Seems like."

"Good," I purr in his ear as I pepper soft kisses over the skin of his throat. Those ropes are thick and I tied them as tightly as I could. He's most definitely restrained, but he's more than capable of escaping if he wants it badly enough. And that's the Conor I want. The tiger, not the pussycat.

"Now what?" he whispers in my ear.

"What do you think?" I catch his earlobe between my teeth and tug gently.

"You're going to take out my cock and ride me like a good girl," he offers.

"Well, that wouldn't be much of a punishment now, would it?" I flash my eyebrows at him as I climb off him and he watches every single move I make.

Pressing my foot on the small brake on the base of the chair, I lock it in place to stop the wheels from being able to move.

"What are you doing?" he breathes as I take a step back from him.

"Punishing you," I whisper. "I already told you that."

He swallows hard, his breathing growing louder and faster.

"Showing you what you could have had tonight if you hadn't been such a possessive asshole today," I say as I reach for the edge of my dress and start to pull it up, working it slowly over my thighs.

"You love it when I'm a possessive asshole," he growls and I smile because it's true.

"Maybe," I purr as I lift the dress high enough to expose the top of my sheer stockings.

"Fuck, Jessie," he hisses.

"You like these?" I breathe as I lift the dress higher until my tiny black lace panties are exposed too. "And what about these?"

"You know I do," he growls.

"Such a shame you can't peel them off me yourself." I catch my lip between my teeth and he narrows his eyes in warning.

"Then untie me, Angel and I will."

"I can't do that, big guy. Sorry," I whisper as I pull the dress off over my head and toss it onto the floor until I'm standing in my underwear. My bra is sheer and my pebbled nipples protrude through the fabric. His eyes roam over my body and he pulls at his restraints.

I edge closer, leaning toward him so that my breasts are inches from his face. He lunges forward, his mouth open as he tries to take a bite but I'm too fast and his teeth clamp together with a soft click, making me chuckle.

"You've made your point, Jessie. Now untie me."

"Made my point?" I shake my head at him. "I haven't even started yet."

I take a few more steps back as I reach behind me and unhook my bra, letting it drop to the floor. Sliding my hands over my skin, I palm my breasts, kneading each of them in my hands and wishing it was him doing this instead of me.

He sucks in a breath at the sight. "Fuck, Jessie, that's enough. Let me out of these." He pulls at the ropes again, making the chair rattle.

"You know I'd love to, but..." I purr as I tug on my nipples. "I'm having way too much fun seeing you squirm."

"The longer you leave me tied up like this, the more I'm going to make you beg for my cock!" he hisses.

"Oh, I think you'll be the one doing the begging, big guy." I grin at him and then I look at his cock straining at the zipper of his trousers. "Because that looks super-painful."

"It is," he growls. "Untie me, Angel. I said I'm sorry."

"Nope." I step back toward the sofa and sit down. Then I lean back, spreading my legs wide and planting a foot either side of me until I'm revealing that my tiny panties are crotchless too.

"Fuck!" he snarls, pulling harder at the ropes until the chair starts rocking violently.

A shudder runs down my spine as I watch him growing increasingly agitated but I can't stop now. This is his punishment, right?

I run my hand over my breasts and my stomach before dipping between my thighs and sliding two fingers through my slick folds.

"Jesus, Conor, I'm soaking wet," I hiss as I circle my clit. Closing my eyes, I let my head hang back as the soft waves of pleasure roll through my body.

"I can fucking see that," he snaps, still pulling on the ropes. "Come here and let me taste that pussy." I ignore him and he rattles the chair again as he pulls at his restraints. "Come untie me and I'll take care of you. This is your last chance."

I lift my head until I can look into his eyes and they blaze with fire and fury. The veins in his neck bulge as he struggles against the ropes. I give myself a virtual pat on the back for tying those knots so well. Shane's office chair is sturdy. It kind of has to be given all the fucking we do on it, but any moment now, Conor is going to tear it to pieces to break free.

"My last chance for what?" I tease him.

"Jessie! Untie me. Now!" he barks.

This is it. The turning point. So, am I all in or not?

I take a deep breath. "Not a chance," I say, maintaining eye contact as I sink two fingers inside my pussy and groan in pleasure.

That tips him over the edge and he struggles some more before he lets out a roar of frustration and rips the armrests clean off the chair.

I swallow a gulp of air as he stands, two huge pieces of metal dangling from his arms as he works quickly to untie the ropes now that he can reach them.

All I can do is watch him. I'm frozen still. My heart pounding in my chest as I wait for him to make his way over to me. He looks like he's been possessed by a demon – but he has never looked hotter. He is about to fuck me into oblivion and I am totally here for it.

Just as he's loosening the last of the rope he looks up at me, his eyes burning into me so fiercely I feel like I might melt.

"You'd better run, Angel," he says as he licks his lips and I realize he is not playing.

I spring up from the sofa and run straight for the door. My stockinged feet don't have the best grip and I can't move as fast as I'd like to.

I run straight into the hallway. My heart beats wildly in my chest. Adrenaline pulses through my veins giving me a surge of energy as I race toward the other end of the apartment.

My rational brain knows I'm not in any real danger, but that doesn't stop the fight or flight response from completely overtaking my body.

When I hear Conor running behind me, I pump my arms faster, trying to get a grip on the solid wooden floor as my feet slide back slightly every time I take a step, losing me vital seconds. I mean as if Conor being a foot taller than me didn't already give him enough of an advantage. I gasp for breath as I hear him closing in behind me, getting closer with each second no matter how fast I run.

I sense him before I feel him and I yelp in terror right before he body-slams me into the wall, shaking the breath from my lungs. I tremble beneath the weight of him as he pins me against the cool plaster.

His hot breath dances over the skin of my neck, making me shiver. "You should have run faster," he growls in my ear and I almost pass out from terror, anticipation and excitement. Then his hands are pulling at the waistband of my panties. He tears them off me in one swift move, causing the fabric to dig into my delicate flesh. "And you should have called for help when you had the chance," he chuckles darkly before he shoves my balled up panties into my mouth.

All I can do is whimper, the sound muffled by the damp material. He pulls my hands behind me, binding my wrists tightly together with the same rope I just used on him. I try to wrench from his grip but he pulls the rope tighter until it pinches my skin and I moan softly as tears run down my cheeks and wet heat pools between my thighs.

When he's done, he lifts me over his shoulder, slaps me on the ass and carries me to his bedroom like a caveman claiming his prize.

As soon as we reach his room, Conor kicks the door closed behind him and tosses me face-down onto middle of the bed as though I'm as light as a feather. Then he grabs the rope binding my wrists, pulling me up until I'm on my knees on the end of the bed, my ankles hanging over the edge and my face pressed against the mattress.

"Do not move a fucking inch," he orders and I swallow hard. I want to look behind me to see what he's doing, but I don't dare disobey him.

I strain to listen instead but the only sounds I hear are my heavy breathing and my heartbeat thumping in my ears. I figure he must be getting undressed because he isn't touching me. Then I hear his footsteps on the wooden floor as he pads into the bathroom and the sound of the faucet being turned on makes fear and pleasure skitter along my spine. A few seconds later he is behind me and the warm water being poured over my ass makes me flinch.

Fuck!

I love that he is an expert when it comes to causing pain.

"Don't move!" he repeats and I stay still as the water drips off me, onto the bed and the floor.

I mumble his name, the sound muffled my panty-stuffed mouth.

"Still think I'm going to be the one doing the begging, Angel?" he chuckles as he rubs a wet hand over my ass cheeks. I tense my muscles involuntarily. A spanking on wet skin is always much more painful.

"You need to relax," he growls. "This is what you wanted, right?" He slaps my ass hard and it stings like a bitch.

I give a muffled cry and he slaps me again.

"Do you have any idea how fucking hard you make me?" he growls as he spanks me harder, making tears prick at my eyes. But despite the pain, wet heat sears between my thighs and my pussy throbs in anticipation. "How fucking torturous it was to have to watch you touching yourself and not being able to get to you?"

"No," I whimper but the word isn't even audible so I shake my head.

"Will you ever do that to me again?"

Dear God, yes!

"I asked you a question," he snarls as he spanks me again.

I lie and shake my head.

He rewards me by sliding two thick fingers into my pussy

and I groan loudly as I coat him in a rush of slick heat. He spanks me as he finger-fucks me and pain and pleasure fight for control of my body. Just as pleasure is about to win out, he pulls his fingers out of me and I cry in frustration.

Then he leans over me, tracing his tongue over the shell of my ear. "You smell so fucking sweet," he growls. "I'd eat your pussy right now if I didn't think it would tip you over the edge."

I try to beg him to have a little mercy on me, but my words are drowned by my damn panties.

"Because you're on the edge, aren't you, Jessie?"

"Hmm." I nod.

"It's a shame bad girls don't deserve to come, isn't it?" he laughs as he pushes back up.

Asshole!

"And you're so desperate to come, aren't you, Angel?" he says as he grabs hold of my hips, his fingertips digging into my soft flesh. "Because your cream is dripping down your thighs."

His words alone stoke the growing fire in me and the ripples of pleasure roll through my body. When he pushes the tip of his cock against my entrance, I moan loudly through my makeshift gag.

"You want this?" he chuckles as he edges slightly further, stretching me open so painfully slowly.

"Hmm," I whimper.

"Only good girls get my cock," he whispers as he pulls out of me and I close my eyes, my body pulsing with need and frustration. "And you're not my good girl, are you?"

If I could talk I would tell him that I am and I always will be. Instead, I lie in silence as the tears roll down my cheeks. Every part of my body craves his touch, but more than that, my heart and soul crave his approval.

He spanks my ass again and a rush of wetness sears between

my thighs, making me moan softly. "Being spanked isn't really a punishment for you, is it, Jessie?" he growls. "You love my hands on you, don't you? You love my belt. And the flogger. Anything that turns this pretty ass red?" He lands another hard slap in exactly the same place as before and it makes me gasp for breath.

"Maybe I should just fuck this ass instead? Leave your pussy dripping while I come in your tight little hole?" he growls and my stomach muscles contract.

I mean I'd take him fucking me anywhere with anything right now. I hear a soft sucking sound just before he slides his thumb into my ass and my thighs tremble.

"You think you could come just from having your ass fucked?" he breathes as he works his thumb in and out of me. "Or you need this too?" he adds as he thrusts two fingers inside my pussy again and starts to fuck both of my holes until I feel like I'm about to pass out.

"Hmm, my girl needs both, right?" he says as pulls his fingers out of my pussy and the wet sucking sound reverberates around the room making my cheeks flush with heat. "You hear how wet you are for me?" he hisses.

I mumble incoherently because even if my mouth wasn't full of crotchless panties, I can barely form a rational thought. When he pushes the tip of his cock into me again, my knees buckle and I fall flat to the mattress, my entire body trembling with the need for release that he withholds.

"We're not done, Angel." He chuckles darkly as he grabs my hips and lifts me back up onto shaky knees.

I don't know how much more I can take and as he rubs a warm hand over my ass cheeks, I brace myself for another spanking on my poor throbbing ass, but he grabs my ankles and flips me over instead, until I'm lying on my back, with my wrists still bound behind me.

To my relief, he pulls my panties out of my mouth and I suck in a deep breath.

"You have any idea how much I need to be inside you all the fucking time?" he growls as he crawls on top of me, wrapping one hand around my throat as he pins one of my thighs flat to the bed with the other. His hard cock nudges at my opening and wet heat surges between my thighs.

"Yes," I croak.

"No you don't, Jessie, because if you did, you wouldn't have teased me like that in Shane's office. You would know how dangerous it is to rile me up like that."

"I..." I start to speak but he drives into me so hard that he steals the breath from my lungs and all I can do is gasp for air.

"You never keep this body from me, you got that?" he grunts as he drives into me again, fucking me so hard I feel like I'm going to slip into unconsciousness. "You are *mine!*"

"Yes." I gasp out the word as I wrap my legs around him, trying to pull him closer and deeper even as I know it's not possible because there is not even a millimeter of space between us. He bites my neck and shoulders, causing the blood to bloom beneath my skin. These aren't the tiny, delicious bites I'm used to. They are hard. Feral. Driven by his need to mark me as his own.

"You're mine too. You got that?" I gasp, because he doesn't get to be the only possessive one here.

"Always, Angel," he grunts before he bites down on me again and suckles my skin.

I'm going to have a huge bruise there tomorrow but I don't care.

He releases his grip on my throat and pushes himself up onto his hands. "Sit up," he barks and I silently obey.

He reaches for my wrists and unties me, working quickly so that my hands are free and I sigh in relief as I stretch my aching limbs. Then he wraps both of his arms around me, lying us back down and squeezing me tight as he rails into me.

I rake my nails down his back as my walls clench around him.

"Your cunt is so fucking desperate for me," he hisses.

Our breathing is hard and fast, matching breath for breath as we try to take everything we can from each other.

"Conor," I whimper as my legs tremble and my body screams for some release.

"I told you I'd make you beg," he groans as he slams into me one last time and we both come hard, me roaring his name and him whispering obscenities in my ear.

When the final tremors of our climax have ebbed away, we lie together, him still inside me and our foreheads pressed together.

"Wow!" I whisper.

"I know," he breathes. "Fuck, Jessie. You just turned me into some kind of demon."

"A super-hot demon," I giggle. "I thought you were going to lose your mind."

"I almost did," he groans as he trails soft kisses over the places where he bit me. "I need to put some arnica on these. Did I hurt you?"

"No." I place my hand under his chin, lifting his head so I can look at him. "You know you could never hurt me like that."

He narrows his eyes at me before pressing a soft kiss on my forehead.

"Conor?" I whisper.

"Yeah?"

"I am your good girl, right?" I ask, the words getting caught up in the emotion that wells in my throat. I enjoy being Shane's brat but that's not mine and Conor's dynamic.

"Every second of every day, Angel."

"Okay." I smile at him.

"You are going to kill me one of these days though. Like I'm going to have a fucking heart attack from coming so hard."

"You will not. If anyone is going to die from an orgasm, I think it will be me. But what a way to go," I sigh contentedly and he laughs. "You might die when Shane sees what you did to his chair though. He's going to lose his shit."

"I'll just tell him it was your fault."

"Hey!" I swat at his chest. "Don't I get in enough trouble with him without you blaming me for you hulking out on his chair?"

"Speaking of trouble." He pushes himself up, pulling out of me as he looks down at where our bodies were just joined. He traces his fingertips over the top of my stockings. "I'm gonna need you to wear these way more often."

"You like them?" I purr.

"Like them? I damn near came in my pants when I saw you standing there in them, and those fucking panties too," he growls and his cock twitches against me.

"Then I'll wear them whenever you want me to."

"Yeah, you will. Because you're mine."

"Yours."

CHAPTER 27
JESSIE

I wake up with Conor's huge arms wrapped around me. When I squirm a little his eyelids flutter open.

"What is it, Angel?" he asks, his voice even deeper than usual in his half-awake state.

"Nothing. I'm just stretching," I say as I free myself from his arms and stretch my limbs. As soon as I have, he pulls me back to him and buries his face against my neck, tickling me with his beard and making me giggle.

"How is that ass?" he asks.

"Hot and a little sore."

"Sorry." He laughs too.

"Don't be. You know I love it."

"Hmm," he nuzzles my neck and I wiggle my ass against his semi-hard cock. "Stop that or I'll tie you up again."

"Is that supposed to be a deterrent?" I arch one eyebrow at him. "Because you know it's not, right?"

He pushes himself up onto one elbow and takes one of my hands in his, turning it over and inspecting my wrist where he tied me with rope. There is a slight pink mark and he rubs the pad of his thumb over it. "You're a deviant, Jessie Ryan."

"But you love it?"

"Fuck, yes," he groans. "But no more fucking this morning."

"Aw." I pout and he smiles at me.

"I fucked you so hard last night, Angel, and I'm gonna need you to be able to walk to breakfast this morning or my brothers will be pissed at me."

My pussy throbs at the memory of him last night – feral and unrestrained. "I'll be able to walk. Promise," I whisper as I wrap my arms around his neck and pull his face close to mine. "As long as you're gentle. You can do that, right?" I arch an eyebrow at him.

He rolls on top of me, settling between my thighs as I spread them wider for him. "With you I can,,," he whispers.

"Then fuck me, Conor Ryan," I giggle.

"No." he shakes his head and starts to trail kisses over my throat, over my shoulders and breasts, peppering feather light kisses over all of the places where he marked me last night.

"Please," I plead as I squirm with delight beneath his touch.

"No fucking," he repeats as he moves lower, trailing his teeth, lips and tongue over my breasts and stomach. "But I will make you come."

He moves lower until his head is between my thighs and I'm panting for breath. "Conor," I gasp loudly, running my fingers through his hair as he runs his tongue the length of my pussy lips.

"Relax, Angel. Let me take care of you," he whispers and then his head dips low and he sucks my clit into his mouth. I press my head back against the pillow and concentrate only on him and his magical tongue.

AFTER CONOR TOOK care of me twice with his incredible mouth, we threw on some clothes and are now wandering down the hallway toward the kitchen where the delicious smell of bacon and pancakes is wafting from the kitchen.

"Mmm." I lick my lips as my stomach growls. "Smells like Mikey is up."

"Yup," Conor agrees as he squeezes my hand and together we walk into the kitchen to find his three brothers already in there. Mikey is cooking as usual, with a dish towel slung over his shoulder while he whistles the tune of *You know you want me,* and the memory of us dancing in the club last night makes me smile. Liam is pouring coffee and Shane is sitting at the breakfast bar flicking through his cell phone. Never off duty!

"Morning," I say with a smile, making them all look toward me and Conor.

"Morning you two," Liam replies with a wink.

"Morning," Mikey says gruffly and I suspect he's still a little pissed at Conor about last night. Shane places his cell on the counter and smiles at us both. Then he holds out his hand and I walk over to him, allowing him to pull me between his thighs before he gives me a soft kiss. "Morning," he says softly. "I missed you."

I wrap my arms around his neck. "I missed you too."

"Coffee?" Liam interrupts us, sliding his hand around my waist and giving me a kiss on the cheek as he slides a mug of coffee onto the island in front of me.

"Thank you," I whisper. Shane and Liam release me and I pull out a stool and hop on, wincing as I sit on the hard plastic.

Liam has already walked back over to the coffee but Shane notices my discomfort. He narrows his eyes at me. "You okay?" he asks quietly so his brothers won't hear.

"Yeah. Just a little tender this morning." My cheeks flush with warmth as I think about the incredible spanking Conor gave me. How hot it was to see him lose a little of the self-control he works so hard to maintain.

"Come here." Shane pats his thighs. "It's a softer seat."

"I'm not sure I'd describe anything about you as soft." I arch an eyebrow at him but I take his hand and he lifts me onto his lap. I lean against his chest and smile as he runs his hand over the top of my ass cheeks.

We both watch Conor and Mikey at the kitchen counter. Conor has his hand on Mikey's shoulder and the two of them talk quietly. When Mikey laughs loudly, Conor wraps his arm around his shoulder and kisses the top of his younger brother's head before walking to the kitchen island to join Shane and me. Shane smiles at me because we both know their fight from last night is completely dealt with.

When Conor is seated, Liam hands him a mug of coffee too before taking a seat beside him.

"You need any help there, bro?" Conor shouts to Mikey.

"No," he replies with a vigorous shake of his head. "I got it."

"So, Con," Shane says, wrapping his arm tightly around my waist. "Why is that Jessie here has a sore ass when you were supposed to be apologizing to her?" He arches an eyebrow in amusement making Conor rolls his eyes while Liam chuckles softly beside him.

"You want to tell them, Angel?" Conor asks me with a tilt of his head.

"No." I blush.

"What did you do, Red?" Mikey wanders over now and leans his elbows on the counter, resting his chin on his hands.

"You been in your office yet?" Conor asks Shane.

"No. Why?" Shane frowns.

"Jessie tied me to your chair," he replies and both Liam and Mikey start to laugh.

"You tied him up?" Shane asks me.

"Yeah," I whisper. "It was his punishment."

"I would pay good money to see that," Mickey chuckles.

"That wasn't really the punishment though, was it?" Conor narrows his eyes at me.

"No."

"What else did you do, Red?" Mikey asks with a devilish grin.

I look at Conor, too embarrassed to describe what happened next myself.

"She gave me a fucking strip tease," he says with a smile.

"Fuck!" Shane whispers as his hand grips my waist.

"Now that I would definitely pay good money to see." Mikey grins at me.

"That doesn't sound like a punishment to be honest, Con," Liam says with a shake of his head.

"I was tied up, Liam," he reminds his little brother. "She was standing there in stockings and black lace underwear, peeling it off and I couldn't fucking touch her."

"Evil genius," Shane whispers in my ear making me shiver.

"And that wasn't all," Conor goes on.

"Conor," I say, blushing to the roots of my hair.

"I can't stop the story now, I'm getting to the best bit," he replies.

"Which is?" Mikey urges him to finish.

"She sat on the sofa right in front of me and started playing with her pussy," he says matter-of-factly and his brothers let out a collective groan. "I begged her to untie me and she wouldn't. So that's why she got the spanking of a lifetime."

My ass throbs deliciously at the memory.

"So how did you get out?" Shane asks.

"He hulked out on your new chair," I say with a grin. "It's currently in pieces on your office floor." That makes Liam and Mikey erupt into a fit of laughter. "He was standing there with parts of a chair still tied to him, stomping around like a giant who had just trampled a tiny village." I snigger and the twins laugh harder.

Liam rests his head on the kitchen island as he giggles uncontrollably while Mikey holds onto his stomach as the tears roll down his face.

"A... fucking...stomping..." Mikey gasps through his tears and Conor shakes his head as he watches the two of them before turning to me. I have to bite down on the inside of my cheek from laughing too hard along with them.

"Sorry," I mouth.

"Careful or you'll be getting another spanking later." He winks at me.

Shane seems completely immune to the hilarity going on around him and is instead focused on the demise of his beloved chair. "For fuck's sake," he grumbles. "That chair was custom-made."

"Yeah, we all know it was, and why, you fucking deviant," Conor laughs now too and the twins start off again. Shane had an extra wide and reinforced office chair made to accommodate all of the fucking he and I do in his office. We work together almost all day, at least four days a week and there is only so long I can spend in a room with this man before I jump his bones.

"It will take weeks to get a new one," Shane adds.

I run my fingers through his hair. "We'll just have to use the sofa for a while. And we can fit on the other chair too," I remind him.

His hand skims over my ass again and I shiver at his touch. "Well, just to be sure, I think we'd better test your theory this afternoon."

"Sounds fun." I smile at him.

Mikey wipes the tears from his eyes. "That was the funniest thing I've heard for a long time," he says as he straightens up.

"I'm not surprised you got an ass whooping, Red." He winks at me before he goes back to his cooking.

I sigh contentedly as I look around the room at my four hot husbands. Nobody is mad at anyone else right now and the world feels right again.

"So, about this DNA test?" Shane says, abruptly changing the subject and making me groan inwardly. I should have known the calm wouldn't last.

"I definitely want one," I say firmly before any of them have a chance to disagree. "I think we need to know one way or another whether Hayden is my half-brother."

"I agree," Shane says with a nod and Mikey and Conor voice their agreement too.

"Liam?" I say quietly.

"I know, baby," he says with a slight nod of his head. "You have to find out."

I heave a sigh of relief. "Good. I thought we could ask Dr. Lisa to do the tests. Then we know for sure there will be no tampering or anything."

"Want me to call her?" Shane asks.

"No, it's okay. I'll speak to her after breakfast."

As if by magic, Mikey places a huge plate of bacon and eggs on the breakfast bar in front of us all and my stomach growls noisily, but the sound is masked by Conor and Liam's loud grunts of appreciation.

"You want me to sit on my own stool?" I ask Shane.

"No, you're fine right where you are," he says before bending his head and placing a soft, sweet kiss on the nape of my neck that makes me shiver.

CHAPTER 28
JESSIE

I sit on my bed as I dial Dr. Lisa's number, keeping my eyes on the door in case one of my overprotective husbands walks in while I'm having this conversation, as it's one I don't particularly want them to hear. After a few seconds, Lisa answers the call and I tell her all about Hayden and the tests I'd like her to run. To my delight, she tells me she can squeeze me in this afternoon. That means less anxious waiting because I need answers and fast.

THE ELEVATOR DOORS open as Shane and I stand in the apartment hallway and we're greeted by Dr. Lisa's smiling face.

"Hey," I almost squeal as she steps out, holding my arms open for a hug. I don't get a lot of female company around here and she and I get along so well that I love a visit from her, even if it is going to involve some needles, which I despise.

"Hi, Jessie," she says as she hugs me with one arm, holding her medical bag in the other.

"Here, let me take that," Shane offers and she hands it to him before wrapping both her arms around me.

"I'm so glad you could do this," I say quietly in her ear.

"Anything for you guys, you know that," she says as we release each other.

"You need anything, Doc?" Shane asks.

"Hmm, a coffee would be nice," she replies with a smile.

"Sure, I'll get Mikey to bring us some. He's got a new machine he loves to impress people with. We can use my office," he says as he slides an arm around my waist and we all start heading down the hallway. I glance sideways at Lisa. I have a feeling Shane isn't going to let me out of his sight and it makes me groan inwardly.

As we pass the kitchen, Mikey is in the doorway and we stop to talk to him.

"Hey, Doc," he says with a smile. Lisa saved his life not long after the brothers first came to New York and they all have a genuine affection for her, and she for them.

"Hi, trouble," she replies.

"Could you bring us some coffees?" Shane asks.

"Sure thing," Mikey replies.

"Can I have some peppermint tea instead please?" I smile sweetly.

"Of course. You feeling okay, Red?" he asks, his eyes narrowed in concern.

"Yeah." I rub a hand over my stomach. "Just feeling a little queasy. I think it's the thought of the needles," I say with a shudder.

"You don't have to do this," Shane says, his hand gripping my hip tighter. "A cheek swab will do, won't it?"

"Yes, but you want to be one hundred percent sure, right? There is no way to falsify a blood test. Cheek swabs can be contaminated more easily. I took the blood directly from Hayden's arm myself. I just assumed I'd take Jessie's the same way so I don't have any swab tests with me. Sorry," Lisa replies.

"Let's just get this over with as quickly as possible then," I say.

"If that's what you want, sweetheart," Shane says and then we leave Mikey to make our drinks while the three of us walk to Shane's office.

Once we're inside, I take a seat while Lisa starts pulling her equipment from her bag.

"What did you think of Hayden then?" I ask her.

"He seems like a nice enough kid," she says with a shrug. "He didn't talk much though. Seemed a little jumpy."

Shane frowns and I see the cogs in his brain ticking over.

"Maybe he's scared of needles too," I offer with a faint smile as I try to diffuse the tension in the room and settle my growing anxiety.

I can't stop looking at the sharp needles that Lisa is pulling out of her bag and each time I see one it makes me feel a little more nauseous.

Sensing my discomfort, Shane perches himself on the desk directly in front of me so I can no longer see Lisa's torture devices and instead I'm looking up at his handsome face.

"It will be over in a few seconds," he says with a wink. "And I'll be right here."

"I'm fine," I say trying to keep my voice as calm and steady as possible because I need to convince him that I'm fine. Preferably, I need him to leave and if I start trembling and sweating like an idiot, he's not going to. "Really. It's no big deal." Even as I say the words I feel an urge to throw up right into his lap.

"That's my girl." He brushes his fingertips over my cheek and my heart starts racing as Lisa moves around the desk with a needle in her hand.

"Can you see where Mikey is with that tea?" I say with a swallow.

"As soon as this is done," he nods.

Fuck!

"You ready, Jessie?" Lisa asks. Her voice is so soft and calm that it should be soothing, but it's not and my breathing comes faster.

Why the hell am I doing this to myself?

Because I need answers and a few moments of discomfort will be worth it for the outcome. My needle anxiety is rooted in the fear of someone drugging and kidnapping me again – and there is no way in hell that Lisa would do that, and even less chance that Shane would let her. I'm completely safe here.

I take a deep breath. "Do it. Just get it all over with quickly."

"Okay," she says softly. The next thing I feel is her warm soft hand on my arm.

I stare into Shane's eyes and he smiles at me. I need to keep his attention only on my face. If I can do that then maybe we'll pull this off.

"So, you doing anything later?" I stammer, my voice trembling as I try to distract the two of us.

"Apart from you?" he arches an eyebrow at me.

Lisa half-groans, half-chuckles and my cheeks turn pink.

"Yes," I whisper aware that Lisa's grip on my arm is tightening signaling she is about to stick me with her giant needle.

"Just a scratch, Jessie," she says softly as the metal pierces my skin, and I flinch but she holds me steady.

"Almost over, sweetheart," Shane says as he takes my free hand and squeezes it in his.

"It's no big deal." I pant out a breath. "So, later? A movie?"

"Maybe." He narrows his eyes at me as I start to babble about the new Fast and Furious movie. I don't look at Lisa taking blood from my arm but I feel a slight tug and a sharp sting and I know she's filled her first vial.

I wince as Shane turns to her and takes a hold of her wrist as she is attaching the second vial to fill.

"Why do you need more blood?" he asks with a frown.

"I need to attach this right now." She looks down at the small plastic tube in her hand. "She's still bleeding."

Shane loosens his grip but he doesn't let go, and she attaches the second tube to the needle in my arm.

"Extra just in case," I say, trying to distract him.

Shane doesn't look at me and instead continues to glare at Lisa who glares right back. "Why?" he asks again. "And don't make me ask for a third time."

Lisa looks between him and me, her jaw ticking as she wrestles with what to tell him. She would never breach my confidence but I know she doesn't want to lie to his face. I also know that he is not stupid and he is so damn overprotective, he's not going to let this go.

"I asked Lisa to run a few additional tests for me, is all," I answer for her and he releases his grip on her wrist and turns his fierce gaze and all his attention to me.

"What kind of tests?"

I suck in a breath as I glance between Lisa and him. "Just to make sure everything is working okay," I whisper.

"Is this about a baby?" he growls.

"Yes!" I snap as I sit up straighter in my chair.

"We discussed this, Jessie!"

"No, you gave me an order and I obeyed like an obedient little puppy." I see the hurt flash across his eyes momentarily but he continues glaring at me. "But now that Lisa is here taking blood, what's the harm in taking a little extra and running a few tests?"

"So you two planned this behind my back?" he snarls as he looks between Lisa and me now.

"It's my body, Shane!" I shout.

"There is nothing fucking wrong with you!" he shouts back while Lisa rolls her eyes in frustration at the two of us.

"You're not having any tests. It is perfectly normal not to get pregnant straightaway. Tell her," he barks to Lisa.

She shakes her head. "I am not getting in between you two, but if Jessie wants the tests then I'm her doctor."

"Then I'll find her a new one," he barks.

"Shane! Stop being such an asshole!"

He turns back to me, his nostrils flaring in temper. "Lisa, can you give us a minute, please?"

She takes the filled second vial and the needle from my arm and places a small piece of gauze over it, fixing it with some tape.

"Sure. I'm just outside when you want me to take the rest of that blood, Jessie." She winks at me. She knows I'll win this argument. Shane is grumpy and unreasonable, but I can wrap him around my little finger and she knows it. He knows it too.

"Why are you so convinced that something is wrong with you?" he says, glaring at me.

"I'm not, but I just want to know, Shane. Why can't you understand that?"

"Why are you putting so much pressure on this, Jessie? You're driving yourself fucking crazy. You're driving me crazy!"

I swallow as tears prick at my eyes. "I'm scared I'll miss my window," I whisper.

"Your window? You're only twenty-seven years old."

"I mean with you," I admit.

"With me?" he frowns.

"What if this gets too hard and you change your mind? What if you decide that having kids isn't for you after all?"

I see his Adam's apple bob as he swallows hard. "That you went behind my back and conspired with Lisa to have tests run without any of us knowing is bad enough, Jessie, but the fact that you honestly believe I'm such a coldhearted bastard that I would do something like that..." He shakes his head as he trails off.

"Shane." I reach for his hand but he pulls it away.

"Do whatever the fuck you want," he snaps and then he walks out of the door leaving me sitting alone. A fat tear runs down my cheek and I swipe it away with my hand. Why am I so goddamn emotional all the time?

A few seconds later, Lisa walks back into the room. "Everything okay?" she asks.

"Yeah," I sniff as I hold out my arm. "Let's get this over with."

CHAPTER 29
JESSIE

The door to Shane's office is closed over which is a sure sign he's still in a bad mood. Lisa left three hours ago and I've been sitting in my room since. Conor and the twins are working, leaving Shane and me alone in the apartment. We haven't spoken to each other since this afternoon and I can't get our fight out of my head.

I push his door open and walk inside. He has his head bent as he frowns at the computer screen. I don't know if he's too distracted to have heard me, or he's trying his best to ignore me, but I pad barefoot across the room. He doesn't glance up even as I reach him.

Trying his best to ignore me then!

I perch on the edge of his desk and begin to shuffle in front of his screen, until I am squeezing myself between him and his desk and he's forced to push his chair back slightly to allow me some room. I lift my legs over his and plant them back down between his thighs.

"Jessie!" he sighs deeply. "I'm busy."

"Are you, or are you just avoiding me?"

"I'm busy!" he meets my eyes for the first time since I came into the room. My heart starts to beat a little faster and warmth pools in my core. Damn. No man has any right looking this fine when he's pissed at me.

"I'm sorry," I whisper.

"What for?" He arches an eyebrow at me.

"For hurting you. What I said about you changing your mind about a baby, Shane, that is my deepest fear, but it's not because I think you're a coldhearted bastard. It's because I want it so damn much. I convinced myself that I didn't but now that I know it's a possibility, it's all I can think about. You always put everyone before yourself. I suppose a part of me was worried that you agreed to a baby for the rest of us and not really for you," I whisper.

He swallows and looks back down at where his computer screen would be if I wasn't blocking his view. "Like I said, I'm busy."

Damn! Time to try a different tactic.

"Well, I won't take up much of your time," I breathe as I slide forward and straddle him.

He keeps one hand on the desk and one by his side. His knuckles flex and his jaw ticks with the effort of not touching me. This man knows how to push every single one of my buttons, but I can do the same to him. I roll my hips over him as I settle into a comfortable position and his cock is already hardening against my bare pussy.

"Are you wearing any underwear at all?" He glances at my pebbled nipples as they protrude through the thin fabric of the t-shirt I'm wearing, which happens to be one of his.

"No." I bite on my lip.

"That's a cheap shot." He arches one eyebrow at me. "You think I'm that easy that all you have to do is roll that hot pussy over me and I'll forget about this afternoon?"

Yes!

"No," I say instead with a flutter of my eyelashes, "but I just got out of the shower and I'm heading to bed, so what would be the point in getting dressed?"

He checks his watch. It's the one I bought him for his birthday and it's the only one he ever wears now, despite having an extensive collection of incredibly expensive timepieces. "You're heading to bed at seven p.m.?"

"Yup. I'm tired." I fake a yawn although I actually do feel pretty beat. Then I stretch my arms high so that the t-shirt lifts, giving him a glimpse of my pussy and thighs. "And I don't want to go to bed with you still mad at me, so I thought I'd come in here and apologize to you. I also wanted to see if you've had time to reflect on how unreasonable you were today," I purr as I run my hands through his hair and grind my pussy against his cock.

A growl rumbles through his chest and I clamp my lips together to stop myself from smiling.

"Unreasonable? Me?"

"Kinda," I say with a shrug.

"Are you looking to get your ass spanked again today? Is that it?" He frowns at me but there is an unmistakable glint in his eye.

"If that will make you feel better."

"Hmm." He rubs a hand over his jaw and his wedding ring catches the light as he does. Suddenly I'm overwhelmed with a rush of emotion as I think about how much I love him and his brothers and how much I want to give them a child. I choke down an unexpected sob and blink away a tear as I rest my forehead against his.

"What is it, sweetheart?" He frowns as he rests his hands on my hips, sending warm pleasure coursing through my body.

"I just want to be able to give you all everything you want, just like you do for me," I whisper. "If there is something wrong, then isn't it better that we know sooner rather than later?"

"Jessie!" He sighs again. "You are everything we want. You are everything we need."

"I just want to know, Shane. Why can't you understand that?"

He leans back and stares at me. "I do understand, but you went to Lisa behind my back and asked her to run some tests. What if I hadn't found out, Jessie? When would you have told us?"

"I don't know," I admit as my cheeks flush pink. Lying is the one thing that Shane hates more than anything in the world.

"We don't keep secrets from each other, do we?" He frowns at me.

"No," I whisper.

"So why didn't you tell us about your little plan with Lisa?"

"Because I knew you would try and talk me out of it, Shane. In fact, you *would* have talked me out of it. You have this way of making me agree to anything. You tie me up in knots and sometimes it's easier to ask for your forgiveness than for your permission."

His tongue darts out and he runs it along his bottom lip as he continues to glare at me, My pussy walls contract as I think about his magical tongue on me instead. *Focus, Jessie!*

"I swear I never meant to lie to you. But it is my body, Shane, and I have every right to know if there's a part of it not working right."

"No." He shakes his head.

"What?" I blink at him in confusion.

He reaches for the edge of my t-shirt and lifts it and I raise my arms in compliance, allowing him to pull it over my head. Then his warm hands run over my back as he pulls me closer. "This body is mine, Jessie."

Wet heat surges between my thighs. "Really?" I breathe.

"Yes," he growls as he slides his hand between my thighs and he thrusts two thick fingers inside me, making me gasp as I grind against him. "This belongs to me and don't ever forget it."

"God, Shane," I pant as my walls clench around him and the pleasure starts to spread through my core.

"Jesus!" he hisses as he curls the tips of his fingers. "You're fucking soaking, sweetheart." Then he looks down at his suit pants. "You have any idea how much my dry cleaning bill has increased since you moved in here?"

I look down too and blush as I see the stain of my arousal on the expensive dark fabric. I run my hands over his chest and onto his biceps, feeling his powerful muscles flexing beneath my palms. "Well, you will insist on wearing these incredibly expensive tailored suits all the time."

"You think I should start walking around here in just my sweatpants like Mikey and Liam?" He arches an eyebrow at me as he presses his fingers deep inside.

I suck in a breath as specks of light begin to flicker behind my eyelids. Damn this man can do things to me that should be illegal. The thought of him in just his grey sweatpants is certainly appealing enough, but I love the way he fills a suit.

"I love your suits," I purr, "the way your muscles stretch the fabric." I lean closer and plant a soft kiss on his throat. "The way you look so polished and respectable on the outside." I kiss him again and a soft groan escapes his lips as he continues finger-fucking me. "How the soft, expensive fabric hides all of that ink on your hard muscles."

"Jessie," he groans as my kisses grow hungrier.

I graze the soft skin of his throat with my teeth and he shudders, making me smile against his skin. When I trail my tongue from the base of his neck, along the thick column of his throat, tasting the sweet saltiness of his skin, his soft groans turn into animalistic grunts as he drives his fingers deeper and harder. I ride them, sinking my hips low enough that I feel his hard cock straining against his zipper.

"You're so hard for me," I purr against his ear and that's when he loses all control. Pulling his fingers out of me, he hisses out a breath before standing and sitting me on the desk in front of him.

"You want to feel how hard I am for you?" he growls as he unfastens his belt and zipper.

I reach for him, squeezing his cock in my hand and making him growl deeper before he takes my hands and pins them behind my back, reminding me exactly who is in control here — who is always in control.

I pant for breath as I wait for him. My body desperate to feel him inside me and sate the constant need that he stirs in me whenever I'm around him. Holding my two wrists in one of his large hands, he wraps his other hand around my throat as he pushes the tip of his cock inside me.

"This is what you want, right? What you always want?" he says, his fiery green eyes burning into mine.

I lick my lips as I stare back at him. His jaw clenched and his fingers flexing as he maintains a firm grip on my hands and throat. He is on the edge just as much as I am, desperate to drive himself inside me just as much as I want him to.

"Tell me what you want, Jessie." He grinds out the words as though it pains him to say them.

"You inside me," I breathe and he rewards me by filling me with his huge cock.

I gasp loudly and he tightens his grip on my wrists while the hand on my throat slides to the back of my head where it fists in my hair so he can pull me closer as he nails me on his desk.

He kisses me as he fucks me, claiming my mouth with the

same intensity he claims the rest of me and my head spins from the rush of endorphins and euphoria flying around my body. I wrap my legs around his waist, pulling him tighter and deeper as I try to take everything he can give me.

Eventually, he releases my wrists and circles his arm around my waist instead. I snake my arms around his neck until we are pressed so tightly together, I feel his heart beating wildly against my chest.

"You gonna come hard for me, sweetheart?" He groans into my mouth as he tilts my hips back slightly, driving against that sweet spot deep inside me. My legs tremble and my core feels like it's become liquid chocolate as my orgasm rolls through my body while he keeps on kissing and fucking me until he finds his own.

I cling to him even as he pulls out of me, desperate to maintain the contact between our bodies. He presses his damp forehead against mine, keeping the connection that he knows I need from him.

"I love you," I whisper.

"I know."

CHAPTER 30
JESSIE

I t's been almost twenty-four hours since my blood tests and as each minute ticks by, I get more and more anxious. Lisa said a day to get the results and I'm holding her to it. I curl a strand of Conor's hair around my fingertip as I sit on his lap watching a movie. Mikey and Liam sit on the sofa next to our armchair while Shane sits opposite.

I spoke to Hayden earlier and he is anxious to get the results of the tests as much as I am. I know that the brothers are worried he can't be trusted, but I kind of like him. And although I've tried to convince myself that I'd be happy with either result, I am secretly hoping that he is my half-brother.

Apart from my husbands, I have no family of my own and sometimes I think about my younger brothers and what they would have been like. I know they would have grown into fine young men and I miss the relationship we should have had as adults – the one that was stolen from us by the psychopath who murdered them when they were just twelve years old. The fact that I have no siblings is even more pronounced because I spend my life with four brothers who would literally die for each other.

So I am feeling anxious too and I know my boys know it, which is why they've all taken time out of their schedules to watch movies with me this afternoon. I wonder if they are anxious to find out the result too. If Hayden is my half-brother then it impacts their lives as much as mine.

When my cell starts to ring they all look at me expectantly. I don't get many calls so we all know this is probably the one I'm waiting on. Conor reaches for it and hands it to me. I see Lisa's name on the screen and my stomach flutters with excitement. I climb off Conor's lap and walk to the side of the room. It's not that I want privacy, but I want a second to process the news before I tell them and Conor would hear every word if I stay sitting on his lap.

"Hi, Lisa," I say when I answer.

"Hi, Jessie. I have your results."

I suck in a deep breath. "Yep?"

"Yours and Hayden's DNA is a significant match. You are half-siblings," she says matter-of-factly.

"Oh? Wow!" I say as four pairs of eyes watch me intently. "Have you told him?"

"Not yet. I wanted to tell you first."

"Can I tell him?" I ask her.

"Are your husbands with you?" she asks.

"Yeah," I reply with a frown.

"Then it might be better if I tell him. I have a feeling you're going to be busy talking about something else."

"What is it?" I ask as my heart starts to race, but Lisa sounds happy, so it can't be something bad, right?

"I have the results of your blood work too..."

"Already?" I interrupt her because she told me they would take a few days.

"Well, the first test I did was a very straightforward one."

She laughs softly and I feel my heart racing faster. "You're pregnant, Jessie."

I reach for the wall, placing my hand flat on its surface for support.

"W-what?" I stammer. "But I had a period three weeks ago."

"Was it lighter than normal?"

"Yes. Quite a bit," I recall my period at the lake house.

"Probably implantation bleeding. You are definitely very pregnant."

By this point, the brothers are surrounding me as I take deep breaths. Is she mistaken? Because this feels like everything I've ever wanted and that doesn't happen to people like me, does it?

"How long?" I whisper and a warm strong hand grips my shoulder but I don't look around to see who it belongs to.

"Well, here's the thing," Lisa says with a soft sigh. "Your HCG levels are higher than I'd expect based on your dates that you gave me."

"What does that mean?" I daren't look up at my husbands but I feel their eyes burning into my skin anyway.

"It means you're either further along than I thought..." she pauses.

"Or?" Dammit, Lisa. You're killing me here.

"Or you're about five weeks pregnant with multiple babies."

"Multiple?" I whisper.

"Well, you both have twins in the family," she chuckles. "Congratulations, Jessie. I'll set you up an appointment with an OB-GYN I know, Dr. Stein. She's amazing."

"Thank you," I whisper as my stomach flutters with so much nervous excitement, I feel like I might throw up.

She ends the call and I stare at my cell phone wondering if I just imagined that conversation. No. It was real. She said it. It must be true.

"What is it, Angel?" Conor asks and I look up to see it's him with a hand on my shoulder. I look between his and his brothers' expectant faces.

"I'm pregnant," I whisper.

"I knew it! Peppermint tea!" Mikey yells with delight as he and Liam press me into a twin sandwich and they plant kisses all over my face and head, making me giggle.

"Careful, assholes," Conor warns them good-naturedly and a few seconds later, the twins release me from their hug.

"I'm so proud of you, baby," Liam whispers in my ear. When they step aside, Conor pulls me into his arms.

"Lisa thinks it might be twins too," I say, still in a state of shock.

"Yes!" Mikey and Liam say together.

"You're fucking incredible, Angel," Conor says as he presses a soft kiss on my forehead. "And you just made us the happiest men alive, you know that right?"

"Yes," I nod before I press my face against his chest and breathe in the scent of him.

A moment later, he releases me too and steps back to allow his oldest brother to take his place. Of all of them his is the reaction I'm most worried about because I've been so worried that he's going to regret our decision. He slides his arms around my waist and pulls me tight to him.

"I love you so fucking much, sweetheart," he says as he rests his cheek on the top of my head. "I can't believe you just made us all a dad," he chuckles softly and the sound rumbles through his chest.

I look up at him and smile. "I did, didn't I?"

I lean against him and smile, becoming a mom and a sister again in the same day! I am the luckiest girl in the world.

CHAPTER 31

JESSIE

I lie on the bed in the small examination room. I suppose that it's not actually that small, but it's currently filled with four giant Ryan brothers, and their excitement and nervous energy is making me feel giddy. In a few moments we will see our babies on a screen and only then will this feel real to me.

Since Lisa gave me the news of my pregnancy yesterday I've been in something of a daze. I woke this morning to five missed calls from Hayden and two text messages. Lisa gave him our DNA results yesterday and he was so excited when I finally called him back. He wanted to come over today but I don't want to share my other news with him just yet. I want to keep this just between us for now, and besides, until I see those babies on that screen, I can't believe it's true. I invited him for brunch tomorrow instead so we can talk through everything properly.

News of my pregnancy has obviously overshadowed the discovery that I have a half-brother, and so far my husbands haven't spoken about it other than to agree to my brunch invite to Hayden.

As promised, Lisa set me up an appointment with an OB-

GYN, Dr. Stein, today and after being shown in by her receptionist, we are waiting for her to join us.

"You okay, baby?" Liam asks as he takes my hand and brushes the pad of his thumb over my knuckles.

"Yeah, just a little nervous," I smile.

"You're not the only one," Shane smiles at me reassuringly. "We all are. Especially Conor." He indicates his head to his younger brother standing at the back of the room chewing on his thumbnail.

"He looks like he's about to throw up," I whisper.

"I know," Shane whispers back.

I've never seen Conor looking so nervous before and I'm about to call him over to me but we're interrupted by the door opening and a woman with honey blonde hair and a huge smile practically bounces into the room.

"Jessie?" she says to me.

"Yeah," I reply with a smile because her joy is infectious.

She closes the door behind her and then makes her way straight to me, holding out her hand. "I'm Dr. Stein. But you can call me Brooke."

"Hi, Brooke." I take her offered hand. "Thank you for squeezing us in today."

"Well, Lisa is my homegirl, so I'm always happy to help her out," she says with a smile. Then she looks around the room at the brothers. "And these must be your husbands?" she asks and I heave a sigh of relief that Lisa has explained our situation. It's not that I feel any shame about our set up, but it can be hard to explain to people sometimes, particularly if they don't have an open mind about this kind of stuff.

"Yes we are," Liam answers first and then each of my husbands introduces themselves in turn. As soon as he has, Conor goes back to chewing on his thumbnail and frowning.

Brooke chats away to me while she sets up her equipment

ready for the ultrasound. I remove my panties when she asks and Mikey holds onto them for me, a devious look in his eyes as he takes them from my hand.

I lie back on the bed and when Brooke picks up the wand-shaped object, Liam can't help himself from shouting out. "What the fuck is that?"

"It's a trans-vaginal wand," Brooke replies calmly as she starts to roll a condom over it before covering it with lube.

"The babies are too small to see on a normal ultrasound yet," Mikey adds confidently and his level of research makes me smile.

"Usually I'd have one of my ultrasound technicians do this, but given the unique nature of your case, I'll handle all of your care," Brooke says.

"You mean because I have four baby daddies?" I ask with a smile.

"I was thinking more because you're married to the Irish Mafia, but yeah that too," she says as though she's just called them lawyers or something.

"Oh," I giggle as Shane frowns.

"Of course that information would never leave this room," Brooke says with a flash of her eyebrows and I have already decided that I love her.

"So you're gonna put that thing...?" Liam uses his index finger to point upwards.

"That's the idea." Brooke laughs softly before she gives me her full attention. "You ready, Jessie?"

"Yep." I nod as my eyes dart to the screen beside me.

That's where we'll see our babies. That's where they'll be if everything is okay.

The screen flickers with grainy images as Brooke inserts the wand and we all stare at it. I'm vaguely aware of Conor moving closer, his soft breathing beside me as he reaches the edge of the bed.

I hold my breath as I stare at the small monitor because right now that is where our world begins and ends.

Brooke is quiet as she presses the wand deeper inside me. She presses a few buttons on the keyboard and I keep holding my breath as I wait for her to tell me that I have a baby, or babies growing inside me and this wasn't just a huge misunderstanding.

"Is everything okay?" I whisper.

Brooke doesn't nod or smile. Her face is completely unreadable. "It sometimes takes a few moments," is all she says.

Conor reaches for my hand and squeezes it in his.

"There they are," Brooke exclaims with a smile and the collective sigh of relief ripples around the room. She points at the screen and I squint until I see the tiny dots that she is pointing at.

"They?" Mikey asks. "How many, Doc?"

"Two," she says as she turns to him and smiles.

"And everything looks good?" Conor asks.

"Perfect," Brooke replies.

Conor leans over and kisses my abdomen softly. "Thank fuck." He swallows hard, his voice thick with emotion. "I thought..."

I run my hands through his hair and can't believe I didn't realize why he's been looking so anxious since we got the news from Lisa.

He stands straight again and lets out a long slow breath.

"Can you tell how far she is?" Mikey asks as he peers at the screen.

"Five weeks and three days," Brooke replies confidently.

"Wow!" Liam gasps. "You can be that specific?"

"Sure can," she says, giving me a smile before she pulls the wand from between my thighs.

She removes the condom and wipes the wand with some tissue before she stands. "I'll let you clean up a little and then I'll pop back in and we can talk through your care and appointments."

"Thank you," I say with a smile as my heart feels like it's going to burst with happiness. *I'm pregnant! With twins!*

"You're welcome." She snaps off her rubber gloves and then she leaves her office.

As soon as she is gone, Conor leans over me and kisses my cheek. "I was so worried, Angel," he breathes. "I was too rough with you the other night."

I place my hand on his cheek. "You weren't. We didn't know."

"No more spankings for you, sweetheart," Shane says with a chuckle as he sits on the bed.

"What?" I open my mouth, feigning my indignation. "That seems so unfair."

"Just until the babies are born," he adds with a wicked grin before he leans down and presses a soft kiss on my stomach.

"We're having twins," Liam says, shaking his head as though he's still in shock.

"Looks like." I smile at him and he nudges Conor out of the way.

Cupping my face in his hands he bends his head and kisses me softly. "I love you."

"Love you too."

"You're fucking amazing, Red. Right now the babies are just the size of a strawberry seed but next week they'll be the size of a baked bean," Mikey says as he muscles his way in between his brothers.

"Are you going to be a pain in the ass with your research this entire pregnancy, Dr. Mikey?" Shane asks with a grin, teasing him good-naturedly.

"Yes!" Mikey replies.

CHAPTER 32
JESSIE

I sit on the sofa with my feet up while Liam rubs them softly. We got back from the doctor's office six hours ago but the excitement still hasn't worn off. Mikey made us all a beautiful turkey dinner, with six different kinds of vegetables, all of which he insisted I eat because it's good for the babies. And he was so sweet and went to so much trouble, how could I refuse? He also made chocolate brownies for dessert and served them with fresh strawberries and ice cream.

All four of my boys have taken the day and night off work and I have to say I am loving being spoiled by them. I could sure get used to another eight months of this. A wave of tiredness washes over me and I yawn loudly just as Shane and Conor walk into the room.

"Bedtime for you, sweetheart," Shane says with a smile.

"No. I'm watching the movie."

He looks at the TV screen and sees *Fast and Furious 4* is on. "You have seen every one of these movies at least two hundred times." He holds out his hand as he reaches me. "Bed. Now."

"You can't order me to bed just because I'm pregnant." I

pretend to pout but I love being looked after by him. "Besides, it's early and I'll get lonely."

"Since when do you ever go to bed alone, Hacker?" he growls and my insides melt like butter. He doesn't often call me that any more but it still does something to me, reminding me of all the angst and tension there used to be between us, and how we dealt with it by having lots of hot sex.

"I'm kind of tired too," Liam says with a grin as he stands and switches off the TV.

"Looks like we're all having an early night then?" Conor winks at me.

"Where's Mikey?" I ask.

"In the shower in your bathroom," Shane replies as he slides an arm around my waist and we all make our way to my bedroom. Well, it used to be mine but now it's kind of everyone's. The bed is large enough for all five of us to sleep in and it is a rare night that there is less than three of us in it.

"We can watch the end of the movie in bed if you like," Shane says as we walk down the hallway.

"I can think of better things to do," I breathe.

"Haven't we all had enough excitement for one day, Angel?" Conor says with a wink.

"But..." I protest but nothing else comes out.

"She's fucking insatiable," Conor chuckles.

"Mikey told me some pregnant women get super-horny," Liam adds.

"Fuck. We're all done for," Shane says with a sigh and I nudge him in the ribs.

"I just refuse to believe that we're all going to bed before ten p.m. and we're not going to do anything more than watch a movie is all," I say.

"If you haven't fallen asleep by the end of the movie, we'll make you come."

"If I do fall asleep then you know I'll just wake you all up in the night," I say with a shrug.

"We'd expect nothing less, sweetheart."

MIKEY CRAWLS onto the bed and I spread my legs wider so he can lie between them. Like he usually does, he takes a pillow and rests it between my thighs before lying on his back so he can watch the movie with us.

"I'm not hurting you, am I, Red?" he asks.

"Nope." I reach down and run my fingers through his hair. "I'm only pregnant you know. I'm not made of glass."

He takes my hand and kisses my fingertips. "Let me know if you get uncomfortable anyway. You have more pressure in your abdomen and increased blood flow can make things more sensitive."

I bite my lip and stifle a giggle. I love how much he has researched pregnancy.

His three brothers laugh though.

"What's so funny? It's true. It's why it can make orgasms more intense too," he goes on.

That certainly gets my attention. "Oh?" I sit up.

"Fuck!" Shane hisses and Conor and Liam laugh louder.

"I'm not sure we can handle Jessie coming any harder than she already does," Liam says and then even Mikey joins in with the laughing.

"You're all arrogant assholes, you know that?" I sigh as I lean back against the pillows and watch the movie.

"Aw, Angel, we're just teasing you," Conor says as he wraps an arm around me and kisses my forehead.

"Are you saying we don't make you come hard, though?" Shane arches an eyebrow at me, a wicked grin on his face.

"I don't remember." I sniff. "It's been so long."

"Yeah. A whole fucking twelve hours. We should be ashamed of ourselves," he replies.

"You should," I agree. "I mean I'm pregnant and everything. I'm growing two human beings as we speak. I need taking care of."

Mikey jumps up and spins around until he's on all fours. "I have no idea why we're not fucking our wife right now. I came out here and you were all watching a movie so I thought that was the vibe, but seems like our girl wants to be fucked and I'm all about that." He arches an eyebrow at me.

"For fuck's sake," Shane sighs but then he climbs off the bed and starts taking off his clothes, swiftly followed by Conor and Liam.

"You wanna be reminded how hard we make you come, sweetheart?" Shane growls as he pulls down his boxers revealing his cock, already hard.

I swallow. Why do I feel like I just poked four very angry bears?

"Well?" he arches an eyebrow at me.

"Yes," I whisper. I am no longer even the slightest bit tired.

"You think we need to make some new rules?" Mikey asks as he crawls over me.

"Rules?" I whisper.

"Yeah, 'cause you're pregnant, Red."

"No spanking," Conor says as he pulls off his boxers too.

"Aw!" I pout. Shane already said that earlier and it felt unfair then too. "None at all?"

"An occasional slap on the ass is fine," Shane says and Conor nods his agreement. They are the only ones who spank me anyway.

"No double stuffing the Oreo," Mikey says with a flash of his eyebrows and I don't know whether to laugh or shout at him for being so crass.

"What the fuck does that even mean, Mikey?" Conor slaps him around the back of the head as he climbs onto the bed beside him.

"No DVP," Mikey snaps as though his analogy was the most obvious thing in the world.

"Then no," they all agree.

"Can we do other double stuff though?" Liam asks.

"What about ass in general?"

I lie back against the pillows with a smile on my face as I watch them, witnessing another of my husbands' conversations about my body that they don't include me in.

"Ass is fine, right?" Shane asks and they all look at me now.

"Oh, you want my opinion now?" I grin at them.

"Sorry, Angel," Conor leans over me and kisses my stomach. "You know we'd never do anything you weren't happy with."

"I know." I smile at him.

"So butt stuff?" Mikey asks.

"Jesus!" Shane hisses.

"It's good with me," I say.

"Although pregnant women are more prone to hemorrhoids so we probably need to be a little more careful," Mikey adds.

"Mikey!" we all shout.

"What?" He holds his hands up in surrender. "Just a heads up. I'm just looking out for you, Red," he says with a wink.

"I need to taste some pussy to get the word hemorrhoid out of my head." Conor chuckles as he trails kisses over my abdomen while Mikey starts removing my panties.

Liam starts unbuttoning my shirt while Shane lies beside me; cupping my chin in his hand, he turns my head so he can kiss me. As his tongue slides into my mouth, Conor's slides over my clit while Liam sucks on one of my hard nipples.

I moan softly as their hands roam over my skin and when Mikey sinks two fingers inside me, I try to wrench my lips from

Shane's but he holds me in place, swallowing my cries of pleasure. When my cries turn to soft whimpers again, he pulls back and I suck in a breath. "No, we don't make you come hard at all, do we, sweetheart?" he teases me.

I bite on my lip and thread my fingers through his hair before I pull him back for another kiss.

CHAPTER 33
JESSIE

The smell of freshly baked croissants is making me feel hungry and I rub a hand over my stomach, smiling to myself as I remember there are two babies inside there.

"Have something to eat, Red," Mikey says as he comes up behind me, pressing a soft kiss on my shoulder as he places two pots of jelly onto the table.

"No, I'll wait for Hayden," I say as I shift from one foot to the other. "He should be here by now."

"He'll be here soon," Shane says as he looks up from his cell phone.

"Maybe he is here and Conor is interrogating him in one of those rooms downstairs," Liam chuckles darkly.

"What?" I gasp.

"Liam!" Shane warns his younger brother before he turns to me. "He's not going to do anything but bring him straight up here, sweetheart."

"Okay," I whisper, fidgeting with the hem of my tank-top.

"Why are you so nervous, Jessie? It's not like this guy is anyone special," Liam grunts.

"Liam!" Shane warns again.

"Maybe one day he might be special to me," I say as I blink away a tear. Pregnancy has me so damn emotional. I know he's still struggling with the possibility of allowing someone else into our family unit, but he doesn't get to be a complete jackass because of it.

"I'm sorry, baby," he whispers as he reaches for my hand and squeezes.

"I know you don't trust him, Liam, but can you at least give him a chance? For me?"

"For you," he says with a sigh. "We're not telling him about the babies though, are we?"

"No. Not yet," I agree.

The sound of footsteps and muffled voices in the hallway makes us all look to the door. My heart starts to beat a little faster as excitement and nerves flutter in my stomach. A mild ripple of nausea rolls through my stomach.

I'm just excited and I need to eat.

Hayden walks into the room and he has a huge smile on his face when he does which tells me that Conor has been perfectly well behaved while he's been escorting him from the basement where he's been waiting for him for the past twenty minutes.

I smile when I see him. I can't help it. He looks so happy. He looks a little like me. He is really my half-brother.

"Hey," he says giving me an awkward wave and I figure he's just as nervous as I am.

"Hey," I wave back and Conor smiles at me, his face full of amusement.

"Come in and sit down, kid. Me and Jessie have made enough pastries to feed a platoon of Marines so I hope you're hungry," Mikey says.

"Yeah," Hayden replies as he walks into the room and then suddenly he is standing right in front of me and I feel like I might cry. Jeez! Am I going to be this emotional this whole pregnancy?

"Hi," he says again.

I laugh at his nervousness and hold out my arms. He laughs too and then suddenly we're hugging. And everything is perfect – until it's not.

I don't know what the lingering aroma is on Hayden's jacket – maybe oregano? But it is suddenly the most offensive thing I've ever smelled in my life. I'm hit by a huge wave of nausea and I push him away and bolt to the kitchen sink where I retch.

Concerned voices chatter around me and then a warm hand is on my back, rubbing softly. "You okay, Angel?" Conor asks.

"Urgh!" I groan as I retch again but nothing comes up. The feeling passes as quickly as it arrived and I stand straight. Conor hands me some paper towels and I wipe my mouth. When I turn around Hayden is staring at me with a look of shock on his face.

"You okay?" he asks.

"She's had stomach flu, haven't you, baby?" Liam says.

"Yeah," I nod.

"Shit!" Hayden shakes his head.

"It's not catching," Mikey adds quickly. "I mean we're all okay, so..."

"Shall we eat?" Shane says and indicates the table.

"Um, sure," Hayden says as he heads to the table, a little uncertain now, understandably when he thinks the food has been prepared by someone with the stomach flu.

As I walk back to the table, Hayden waits for me. "Are you sure you're okay?" he asks as he puts a hand on my shoulder and as he lifts his arm I get another whiff of the smell.

"Fuck!" I hiss as I run back to the sink.

"Maybe I should go?" Hayden offers.

"No," I shout as I hang my head over the sink again. "It's just your jacket. Can you take off your jacket?"

"My jacket?" he frowns.

"Give me the jacket, kid," Shane says.

"B-but...I..." Hayden stammers.

I stand straight again. "Sorry. It just smells a little..."

Hayden's mouth opens in horror as he sniffs his jacket. "Do I stink or something?"

"No," I shake my head. Oh God, he thinks I think he smells. "It just smells of something," I say with a smile.

He shrugs it off and passes it to Shane. "Does it? I didn't even notice. I mean it hasn't been washed in a week or two but... Have I been walking around stinking?"

Shane sniffs the jacket too and the look on his face tells me he doesn't smell anything even remotely offensive but he pretends anyway. "Yeah. Stinks," he agrees and Hayden's cheeks turn red.

"Shane. It doesn't stink," I say. "Don't make him feel bad."

"What does it smell like? BO or something?" Hayden sniffs his armpits now and suddenly Mikey is pressing his lips together to stop himself from laughing and Shane is looking at me so I can tell him what it smells of.

"No. Not BO," I say quickly. "Like oregano maybe?"

"Maybe. It was hanging in the kitchen in work last night. We do a lot of Italian stuff."

"That explains it," I say with a smile.

"Oregano made you want to hurl?" he asks with a frown.

"Yes. I hate the stuff."

"Oh." He shakes his head and then he takes a seat at the table as Shane takes the jacket out into the hallway.

I take a seat next to Hayden and smile at him. Poor kid looks so embarrassed and I want to hug him again – so I do. Big mistake.

"I can still..." I bolt again as nausea washes over me like a tidal wave. I have never experienced anything like it in my life.

"Fuck, Jessie, you're gonna give the poor kid a heart attack if you keep doing this," Mikey chuckles.

"Do I really stink or something?" Hayden asks innocently and I feel so bad for him.

"We have to tell him," I groan as I stand upright again.

"No." Liam shakes his head.

"Liam. The kid thinks he has a body odor problem so bad that he's making people spontaneously hurl," Shane says.

"What is going on?" Hayden asks.

"It's not you, kid," Shane pats him on the back and he and Mikey and Conor start to laugh.

"Then what?" he asks as I walk back to the table and take a seat opposite him instead, in between Liam and Conor.

"She's just developed a severe aversion to oregano," Mikey chuckles.

Conor takes my hand and squeezes it gently. "You okay?"

"Yes. Fine now," I say. "But oregano is banned for the next eight months. Okay?"

"Eight months?" Hayden smiles at me. "Wait! Are you...?"

"Yes. I'm so sorry, Hayden. This wasn't how I imagined today going at all."

"Wow! A baby." He beams at me. "That's amazing, Jessie. I'm so happy for you."

"Babies actually. We're having twins. And thank you."

"Twins!" he laughs softly and then he looks around the table. "Who is..."

"Don't even finish that sentence, kid," Shane warns him. "We all are and that's all you need to know."

"Okay. I'm sorry if I offended you," he swallows.

"Don't worry about it," I tell him as I shoot Shane a look. "Our set up is quite unique."

"Is someone gonna eat some of these pastries I've been slaving over?" Mikey says, breaking the tension.

"Yes! I'm starving," I reply as I take one from the giant pile in the center of the table.

AFTER OUR INCREDIBLY AWKWARD START, we ended up having a lovely brunch. Hayden is funny and sweet. Even Liam joined in the conversation after a while, unable to keep quiet when Hayden mentioned his aversion to tequila following an experience during his first semester of college when he passed out at a party and woke up with no eyebrows and a mustache drawn in permanent marker that took him days to wash off.

It's late afternoon by the time Hayden is leaving, and that's only because he has a shift at work to get to. Shane and Conor have agreed to drive him home and I have made them promise to behave themselves.

"You think we can risk a quick hug?" Hayden asks me as he stands outside the elevator. Conor and Shane have gone ahead and Liam and Mikey are in the kitchen clearing up, allowing the two of us to speak alone for the first time.

"I'll hold my breath," I say with a smile, doing exactly that as I embrace him quickly.

"Today has been amazing, Jessie," he whispers in my ear. "I'm so glad I found you."

I pull back from him. "Me too," I say with a smile.

"I was feeling so lost since my mom died," he says as a tear escapes and he quickly wipes it away. "I know you don't really know me yet, but I hope that we can do lots more of this and maybe I can be a part of your life in some way."

"Of course, Hayden. I would love that," I admit.

"Can I see you again soon?"

"Sure. How about Saturday?" I offer.

"I have to work Saturday, sorry. How is Friday?"

Friday is date night, but I suppose I could see him in the afternoon? "Sure. We could have lunch?"

"Great. Where shall we meet?"

"Um." I bite on my lip. The brothers won't like me leaving the apartment without them and I'm not sure any of them have the time to take the afternoon off with me, especially as they won't be working in the night. "Are you okay to come here?"

"Sure. I love it here," he says with a grin.

"Perfect!" I reply.

And that was how Hayden Chambers came to be an almost daily afternoon visitor to our apartment.

CHAPTER 34

JESSIE

THREE MONTHS LATER

My stomach rumbles and I check my watch. Right on cue! Every day at two p.m. I get ravenously hungry and crave ice cream, specifically butterscotch and pistachio mixed together in the same bowl. I've convinced myself that it's a pregnancy craving, though the truth is I've always loved that flavor combo. But now I get to indulge in it every single day without feeling even the slightest hint of guilt.

"You want a snack?" I say to Hayden with a pop of one eyebrow.

"Ice cream time?" he grins at me.

"Of course. Come on." I stand and walk out of the den and to the kitchen with him following me. Opening the door to our huge freezer, I reach in and pull out the two tubs of ice cream. They feel suspiciously light.

Placing them on the counter, I pull off the lids to find both tubs almost empty.

I frown as my stomach growls in protest. "That's so strange."

"What is?" Hayden says as he comes to stand beside me.

"There's none left." I hold up the empty cartons as proof.

"Maybe one of the guys ate it?" he offers with a shrug.

"No." I shake my head. "They're not huge ice cream fans and even if they were, they're not mean, or stupid enough, to take the last of it from their pregnant, hormonal wife. They wouldn't have put the empty tubs back either."

"Maybe you ate it and you forgot?"

"Hey!" I nudge him in the ribs. "I don't eat that much of the stuff."

He chuckles. "I didn't mean that. Anyway, it's no big deal. Let me take you out for some ice cream instead. It's a beautiful day and I could do with some fresh air."

I look at him. The brothers are upstate signing some paperwork. They'll be back in a few hours. They won't like me going out with Hayden alone. He's been here almost every day for the past three months and he spends time with all of my husbands as well as me but they still don't fully trust him, and I don't know if I do either.

My stomach growls again. I'm not a prisoner here. I don't need my husbands' permission to go out. I can take care of myself and my babies. "Daisy's is just a few blocks. We could go there?" I suggest.

"Perfect!" Hayden says with a vigorous nod of his head. "Let me just use the bathroom before we go."

"Sure," I smile at him. "I'll wait by the elevator."

Hayden turns on his heel and walks out of the room and I grab my purse. Taking out my cell, I type out a quick text to our group chat to tell the boys where I'm going.

A walk in the sunshine will do me good. Not to mention the delicious ice cream reward at the end.

FORTY-FIVE MINUTES LATER, Hayden and I are sitting at my usual table in Daisy's ice cream parlor. I know it's probably bad that this is my usual table and it speaks volumes about my sweet tooth and current ice cream addiction, but this place is near to mine and Mikey's jogging route too, and we often stop in for a coffee. The place is quiet today but it often is at this time of day, just before the local schools let out.

Hayden is quieter than usual, and he pushes his raspberry swirl around his bowl with his spoon.

"Everything okay?" I ask.

He glances at his watch and it's not the first time he's done that since we sat down ten minutes earlier. The hairs on the back of my neck start to tingle unexpectedly.

"Hayden?" I snap.

"What?" He blinks at me. "Oh, yeah. Everything's fine."

I narrow my eyes at him. He's lying. "Do you have somewhere else to be?"

"No. Of course not," he says with a shake of his head.

The sound of the bell jingling when the door opens makes us both look up. Two huge men dressed in black walk through it and my heart starts beating faster.

"Jessie," Hayden says and I turn my gaze on him. He swallows hard. "I didn't know this was what was going to happen."

I drag my eyes back to the two men who have just walked through the door. They have tattoos on their necks that look vaguely familiar to me. My pulse is racing now too. The bowl of ice cream I just about inhaled is threatening to make a reappearance.

When one of the men starts shouting at the other customers to get out in a thick Russian accent, the bile surges up my gullet, burning the back of my throat as I swallow it down.

"What have you done?" I hiss to Hayden as the customers run out of the door.

"I'm sorry, Jessie. I didn't know they wanted to hurt you," he sobs. "They said they were going to kill me."

I suck in a breath, glaring at the two Russians as they approach our table.

"Miss Ivanov," the taller one snarls as he holds up a syringe full of fluid.

Damn! I hate needles! Why do people insist on sticking me with those things and freaking kidnapping me?

"It's Mrs. Ryan, actually," I snarl back.

I glance sideways and see that Daisy has disappeared and in place of the petite woman with the purple pixie cut and elfin face, stands a tall former Navy SEAL.

Without turning around, I know that another former SEAL is walking out of the back room. At the same time, two men with arms as big as boulders, armed with semi-automatics are coming through the front door. One reaches up as he opens it, taking hold of the bell so it doesn't make a sound as he and his colleague walk silently into the parlor and make their way toward us.

I keep my eyes on the Russians. "Who sent you?" I snap.

"Please don't hurt her. I'll do whatever you want," Hayden snivels.

"She is what we want," the tall one snarls as he reaches out his hand to grab my arm.

CHAPTER 35

SHANE

I glance at my brothers as they sip macchiatos and laugh amongst themselves while we wait for our lawyers to finalize some paperwork. We are about to add Jessie's name to the deeds of every property and legal business that we own and it requires all four of our signatures. Jessie doesn't know yet and she would no doubt try and talk us out of it if she did because she has no desire for money or material things.

We got a new team of lawyers in after I fired our previous one, which was headed by my ex-fiancée, Erin McGrath. She made it clear on more than one occasion how much she hated my new wife and our lifestyle and so I couldn't have her working for us any longer. I stopped trusting her and I need to trust my lawyer. This new one came highly recommended but they work for the same firm as Erin, so I'm waiting to see if they can prove themselves trustworthy enough to handle all of our business affairs.

It's not often my brothers and I get out like this these days, at least not for business, but our signatures need to be witnessed by two lawyers, so we have left Jessie to spend some time with her newly found half-brother. The kid seems to adore his big sister, not that I can blame him; she is pretty fucking adorable. I'm still not one hundred percent sure about him but I'm not sure I ever will be.

I am anxious to get back to her, and I know my brothers will be too. We've always been over-protective when it comes to her, but now that she's carrying our babies too, well it just made my irrational desire to never let her leave the apartment ever again increase one hundred fold. The fact that she has left the apartment to get ice cream with Hayden makes me paranoid and suspicious, but according to Jessie, I'm always paranoid and suspicious and I need to learn to trust people more.

I go back to looking out the window as my cell starts ringing. I take it out and frown as I see Chester's name flashing on the screen. He's one of our most trusted and experienced security personnel, but as such, it's usually Conor or the twins who deal with him. He is also one of Jessie's personal security detail, so if he's calling me, this isn't a regular work thing, this is a Jessie thing. My heart sinks in my chest as I raise the cell phone to my ear.

"Chester?" I bark when I answer the call.

"Code red, boss. Daisy's ice cream parlor," is all he says before he ends the call because that is what he's been instructed to do.

He protects my wife and I want every single bit of his focus and attention to be on her. Code red is the highest threat level and it's the one that makes the blood freeze in my veins. That's all he has to say because all I need to know is where she is and the fact that she's in danger, and any seconds he's spending telling me what's going on are valuable seconds that he's wasting protecting her. I have our best men watching her everywhere she goes and I have to trust that they will protect her with their lives because I wouldn't be able to function if I didn't.

Adrenaline kicks in and I focus on getting out of this office and getting to her because if I think about what might be happening or the fact that she and our babies are in danger I wouldn't even be able to put one foot in front of the other.

"Boys. We're leaving. Now!" I bark as I walk toward the door.

"What's happened?" Conor asks as the three of them fall into step behind me.

"Code red," I say and I watch as each of their worlds comes simultaneously crashing down around their ears. I can't deal with it right now though. We have to focus. We have to get to her and pray that our team don't let her down.

"I knew that piece of shit was bad news," Liam shouts. "What the fuck, Shane!"

"We should never have let her go anywhere with him," Mikey adds, his voice cracking.

"You are aware that would never work," Conor snaps. "This is Jessie we're talking about. Let's just fucking get to her."

"The team are with her. They'll take care of her." I try to reassure them, wishing with everything single thing that I have that it's true.

"What if something happens...?" Liam says what we're all thinking but he can't even bring himself to finish the sentence.

"She's got six ex-Navy SEALs protecting her. They'll do their jobs," Conor adds as he glances at me and I know that he's feeling just like I am. There is conviction in his words but there is still doubt in his mind.

We walk straight past the elevator and run down the three flights of stairs to the basement to our car. Even if we break every speed limit there is on the way, it will still take us forty-five minutes to get to her and that is way too long. Chester will update me as soon as there is something to update, as is the protocol. And until then all we can do is wait and hope that she is safe. The thought of something happening to her and our babies is too much to contemplate. We have lost her twice and even though we got her back, both times it almost broke us. If we lost all of them, it's not something any of us could come back from. It would be the end of us as we know it.

As Conor drives, my mind races with questions. Who the fuck is she in danger from? Is this something to do with Hayden? Or someone else? Is it someone who's trying to get to us through her? It can't be a coincidence that it happened today when we were out of the city. Who knew that we wouldn't be around?

I hold my cell phone in my hand and have to hold back from dialing Chester's number and asking him what the fuck is going on, because that could be moment that he gets distracted and he loses her. But fuck, it is killing me not to know, just as much as it's killing all of us that we're not there when she needs us.

"We should have heard from him by now," Liam snarls from the back seat.

"He'll call as soon as he can," I remind him, the edge in my voice audible even to me.

"What if..."

"Fucking don't, Liam!" Conor barks. "Don't fucking say it."

"We're all thinking it, bro. You don't have to say it out loud," Mikey says quietly to his twin.

"I just..." I hear the strain in Liam's voice and I reach back and put my hand on his knee.

"I know, son. There is not a chance in hell Chester and his team would let anything happen to her," I assure him.

"No, because they know they're fucking dead men walking if they do," Conor growls, his knuckles white as he grips the wheel.

CHAPTER 36

JESSIE

The giant Russian's fingertips have barely brushed my skin when a bullet whizzes through the air and straight through his neck. He crashes against the table as he drops to the floor. His colleague spins around, but another bullet brings him to the same unfortunate end.

I sit back in my chair as my heart races faster and I gasp for breath. The four guards surround me, worry etched on their faces.

"Get her some water!" one shouts.

"Are you okay, Jessie?" Chester asks as he crouches in front of me, rocking back on his heels as he stares at me with concern. With their attention solely on me, Hayden scrambles to his feet and makes a run for the door. One of the SEALs, whose name I don't know, raises his weapon. These four men have been briefed to shoot to kill when it comes to mine and my babies' safety and I don't want Hayden dead.

I jump up and grab his arm. "No! Don't shoot him. Please?"

He turns to look at me and then at his three colleagues, giving Hayden the opportunity to run out the door. "Should I go after him?"

"No." Chester shakes his head. "We stay with Mrs. Ryan at all times."

He nods his understanding and holsters his weapon, allowing Hayden to run to his freedom, albeit temporary. I'll find the little snake before the week is out.

Someone hands me a glass of cold water and I take a sip as my heart rate starts to return to normal. I'm safe.

"You okay?" Chester asks.

"Yes. Thank you all," I say with a weak smile.

"Any time." Chester winks at me.

"Is Daisy okay?" I ask, looking around the room for any sign of the store owner who I'm on first name terms with thanks to my ongoing addiction.

"She's fine. Unharmed and relieved you're safe. Someone is taking her home," Chester replies.

"Good," I nod, feeling a surge of relief that she wasn't caught up in the crossfire.

Chester looks me over once more before he stands straight, barking orders to his men as they all get to work fast. One of them starts closing up the shop's shutters while another makes a call. I listen intently to the plan he instructs his men to follow. Once I'm safely in the armored car outside, where another two ex-SEALS are waiting, one of Chester's team is going to stay behind to organize the clean-up crew to dispose of the two dead Russians currently bleeding all over the floor.

"You ready to go home?" Chester asks.

"Yes, please," I say with a shaky breath.

"Let's move," Chester barks as he takes hold of my arm and the four men escort me to the SUV outside. "I'll call Shane from the car," he says to me and my stomach drops again.

God, the brothers are going to be so mad!

They never trusted Hayden, and with good reason it seems. Liam was right. How could I have been so damn naïve? I thought Hayden and I had formed a bond. I can't believe he could betray me so easily. I wonder if any of his apparent last minute remorse was even real, or simply an attempt to save his own skin.

I sigh heavily as I rub a hand protectively over my stomach. I'm so relieved the brothers designed their protection system and that I actually remembered to implement it. When we came back to New York from Ireland, they would barely let me out of their sights for more than five minutes. But I hated living like that. I felt stifled and claustrophobic. I mean, it's not like I often spend time without at least one of them, and I like it that way, but I still wanted the choice to be able to come and go whenever I wanted.

My overprotective husbands had other ideas though, and we fought about it for weeks until they devised a system whereby I tell them when I'm going somewhere and I have a very discreet security detail. They're so good, I've never met five of them before today, but I know they are there, and something about that is actually quite comforting. It also stops the brothers giving me a hard time.

I have forgotten a few times and I was subsequently punished for it, which isn't all bad, but something about Hayden was off today. That ice cream not being in the freezer was off. There was no way I was leaving the apartment with him alone. I shudder as I think about the fact I could be on my way to anywhere, unconscious and in the back of some Russian's car. But who the hell wants me now? I thought my past was done with. Will I ever escape the burden of being Alexei Ivanov's daughter?

"Can you ask someone to take some pictures of their neck tattoos?" I ask Chester as we climb into the car.

"Sure," he replies with a nod.

I sit in the SUV as it makes the short trip back to the apartment. I listen to Chester's call to Shane and my heart starts racing again for an entirely different reason. "She's unhurt. Nobody touched her," he repeats for the fourth time. "We're on our way back to the apartment now."

"Does he want to speak to me?" I whisper.

Chester shakes his head and my stomach starts to churn. He must be so mad at me!

"I'll stay with her until you're back. Bye, boss," he says before he ends the call.

"Was he super-mad?" I ask.

"No, he just had a poor signal. He's just relieved you're okay," he says with a wink.

"Chester McFeeney, you are a terrible liar!"

He simply laughs in response.

CHAPTER 37

JESSIE

As soon as we got back to the apartment, I got my laptop and started to do some searching on the tattoos I'd seen on those Russian guys' necks. The bodyguard who stayed behind sent some pictures of them to my phone. Chester made us a fresh pot of decaf coffee and has been sitting opposite me the entire time, but I'm too distracted to even speak to him, so distracted that I don't hear my husbands returning until all four of them are in the kitchen with us.

It's Liam who runs to me first, pulling me from my stool at the kitchen island and into his arms. He squeezes me so tightly, I struggle to breathe.

"Jesus fucking Christ," he sighs.

"Liam," I say as I wriggle in his arms.

He takes a small step back from me. "Are you okay, baby?" he asks as he runs his hands over my arms and my stomach.

"I'm fine."

Then he drops to his knees and presses a soft kiss on my growing bump. "We're going to get you all checked out anyway."

I run my hands through his hair and smile. "They didn't even touch me, Liam. There's nothing to check."

He presses his cheek against my stomach and wraps his arms around the back of my thighs as he whispers something I can't quite hear to my rounded belly.

Mikey is beside me next, wrapping his arms around my top half and squeezing me tightly. "Thank fuck you're okay, Red! I'm going to kill that little fucker with my bare hands when we get hold of him," he snarls.

Then Conor is at my other side. He cups my chin in his hand and turns my head so I can look into his eyes. He narrows his as he glares at me. "You're going to give me a fucking heart attack, Angel."

"I'm sorry," I whisper.

Liam stands up and steps back and Mikey lets me go too, allowing their older brother to hug me instead. I press my head against Conor's chest as he holds onto me and that's when I start to cry. Thinking of what might have happened. Thinking of the pain it would cause them if something had happened to me or our babies. I cling to him as tears roll down my cheeks.

"It's okay. We got you," he whispers as he runs his hands over my hair.

"How the fuck did that little prick get away?" Shane asks Chester.

"Max was going to shoot him but Jessie asked him not to," Chester answers matter-of-factly but I hear the slight tremor in his voice. Shane is going to be pissed at him too, now.

"For fuck's sake," he says with a heavy sigh.

"You said to always follow Jessie's orders, boss," Chester adds as he clears his throat.

"I know," Shane snarls.

I lift my head from Conor's chest and wipe my tear-stained

cheeks. Shane really said that? I don't know why that makes me smile but it does.

"Is there anything else right now?" Shane asks.

"Clean up crew are done. My men didn't recognize either of the Russians but they had the same tattoo on their necks, but Jessie is working on that." He looks to me and gives me a faint smile.

"Good. Then you can go," Shane barks.

"Thank you for today, Chester," Conor says, and Liam and Mikey voice their agreement.

"My pleasure," he says before he starts to walk out of the room.

I watch as Shane follows him, stopping him just before he reaches the doorway. I don't know what he says but Chester is smiling by the time he leaves the room so I assume Shane was expressing his gratitude too.

When he walks back toward us, Conor steps back from me until Shane is standing directly in front of me. My legs tremble in nervous anticipation. I feel like I might throw up again. He's going to shout at me and I'm feeling so emotional and hormonal I might just burst into tears again. But he doesn't shout. He pulls me into his huge arms and kisses the top of my head.

"If anything ever happened to you," he mumbles into my hair.

"I'm sorry," I whimper.

He pulls back and frowns at me. "What for?"

"Aren't you mad?" I whisper.

"I'm pissed as hell, sweetheart, but not at you." He pulls me back to him again and I melt into his arms. "Dr. Stein is on her way here to check you over, just in case."

"But I'm fine..."

"Jessie!" he snaps and I stop talking.

"Okay," I breathe as I snuggle deeper against his chest.

"Good girl," he whispers in my ear and despite the circumstances, wet heat pools in my center. When he eventually lets me go, my cheeks are flushed pink and he gives me a knowing smile before he guides me back to the kitchen island and we all take a seat.

"So do we have any idea what the fuck is going on?" Conor asks, rubbing a hand over his jaw in frustration.

They all look to me for answers, but I can't give many – at least not yet.

"I assume you have a reason for keeping Hayden alive?" Shane adds.

"He can give us answers. We could have got some from the Russians, but..."

"Hard to talk when you have no throat," Mikey says with a flash of his eyebrows. "Chester sent us those photographs too. Those SEALS are good fucking shots."

"It's kind of what they're trained to do, dumbass," Liam adds good-naturedly and Mikey fakes a scowl at him.

"If we could have spoken to one of them though," I say with a sigh. "We may have to rethink your shoot to kill policy."

"No!" all four of them reply before I've even finished speaking.

"But we could have got some vital information."

Conor slides an arm around my waist. "We can get information any time from anywhere, but we can never get you back, Angel."

"Fair point," I admit even though it would be so much easier if we could speak to one of those dead guys and find out who they're working for. Especially as the photographs of their tattoos aren't the clearest given that their throats had been torn open by a bullet. Because the fact that someone wants to kidnap and hurt me is pretty terrifying. I mean, you'd think I'd be used to it by now, right? But it's not only me I have to worry about any longer. I look down and rub a hand over my belly absentmindedly.

Shane places his large hand over mine and gives it a gentle squeeze. "So, Hayden. What happened?"

"We were having our ice cream and he seemed kind of quiet and nervous. He kept checking his watch all the time..."

"So you think he told them where you were headed before you even left the apartment?" Mikey asks.

"I think so. He used the bathroom before we left. Maybe he told them then?"

"Maybe." Shane rubs a hand over the stubble on his jaw. "We weren't sure if you were followed, but Chester and his men didn't spot anything to suggest that either. Then what happened?"

I take a deep breath. "Then these two huge Russian guys came into the parlor and started telling the other customers to leave. That's when Hayden started crying. He said he didn't know this was going to happen. He didn't know they were going to hurt me."

"Anything else?" Conor asks.

"And that they threatened to kill him?"

"But he didn't say who *they* were?" Liam asks.

"No. He didn't get much chance to speak because they walked straight over to us and then everything happened kind of quick."

"What did the Russians say?" Shane asks as he stares at me. This is his process. Firing questions and trying to put all of the pieces together in his head.

"They called me Miss Ivanov and one of them had a hypodermic needle, like he was going to inject me and knock me out, maybe?"

"Anything else?" Shane asks.

I screw my eyes closed, trying to picture the scene from earlier today. I replay the conversation in my head. "I told them my name was Mrs. Ryan," I say and Conor gives my thigh a squeeze, making me turn to him and smile. "But that was it. Then one of your men shot them. They didn't know Hayden was involved and when they were focused on me, he made a run for it. One of the guards was going to shoot him, but I asked him not to. I want to know who threatened him and why. I'll be able to track him down."

"How quickly can you do that?" Shane asks and I wince.

"What?" he asks with a frown.

"I mean, he's just a kid. It will be easy enough..."

"But?" Conor says.

"I kind of taught him how to stay off-grid."

"Jessie!" Liam snaps.

"Well, I didn't know he was going to pull something like this, did I?" I protest, but Liam narrows his eyes at me. Of all of the brothers, he probably trusted Hayden the least. He would have predicted this if I'd have listened. I love the fact that he doesn't say this out loud but instead glares at me so intensely that I squirm in my seat.

"Fuck!" Shane hisses.

"It won't take long for him to make a mistake though. I promise. I mean this whole world is all new to him. And in the meantime, I think these tattoos are the key to finding out who those Russian guys worked for. It's just a pity that the photographs aren't great. You think I could get another look at their bodies?"

The brothers all share a look that makes me feel like I'm missing something here.

"That's not an option, Red," Mikey answers for them. "They're already ash."

I roll my eyes. "Your efficiency at disposing of dead bodies is kinda scary, you know that?"

"You fucking love it," Conor chuckles as he plants a soft kiss on my cheek.

I can't help but smile at him. "There is one man who could help me ID these men," I suggest.

"No Bratva," Liam and Conor say at the same time.

"But we can trust Vlad," I insist.

"This could be something to do with Vlad," Shane says.

"No. Vlad has no reason to want me dead."

"You're the legitimate heir to the Ivanov empire that he now reigns over, Red," Mikey reminds me.

"Still... He could have killed me a long time ago. Why now? It doesn't make sense. At least let me call him. Please?"

Conor and Liam and Mikey shake their heads but Shane speaks. "If you think it could help find out who these guys were working for, then call him."

I lean over and kiss his cheek softly. "Thank you."

"Something about this feels way off," Mikey says loudly with a look of something bordering on disgust on his face.

"Well that's because someone just tried to kidnap me, Mikey. Of course it feels off."

He shakes his head and waves a hand in the direction of me and Shane. "Not that, Red. *This!* You two being on the same page and us being on another one." He shivers dramatically as though something has crawled up his spine. "I don't like it."

"Me neither," Liam frowns.

"Well, there's a first time for everything," Shane says with a grin as he slides an arm around my waist and kisses my bare shoulder.

Conor shakes his head and chuckles softly and I smile as I realize how lucky I am to be so loved and protected by these incredible men. For some reason someone wants me and I have no idea who or why.

CHAPTER 38
CONOR

J essie lies on the bed and we all watch while her OB-GYN, Brooke, rolls the ultrasound machine over her stomach. The black and white screen is fuzzy for a few heart stopping seconds as she tries to get a good angle.

"There they are," she says after what feels like an eternity. She traces her fingertip over the screen. "You see them lying together? Top to tail?"

"Yeah," Liam croaks and Jessie giggles as she watches our babies on the screen.

"Heartbeats are strong," Brooke adds as she turns a dial and the sound of tiny racing hearts fills the room.

"Fuck!" Mikey breathes. "That's so much clearer than the last time."

"Well, they're almost double the size they were since last time. I can tell you the sex if you want to know?"

Jessie looks between us all, her eyes shining with happiness as though she wasn't just betrayed by her half-brother and almost kidnapped this afternoon. "Can we?" she whispers.

"If that's what you want, sweetheart?" Shane replies while Mikey and Liam voice their agreement.

"Either way is fine by me. As long as they're healthy, I don't care," I add with a shrug.

"Well, you're having a boy and a girl and they both look super-healthy to me," Brooke says as she wipes the gel from Jessie's stomach with some tissue paper.

"One of each?" Jessie giggles. "That's perfect."

"Perfect," Shane agrees although we all know anything would have been perfect. She is perfect and so are our kids going to be.

"So, we're gonna have a little Jessie and a little Mikey running around here?" Mikey asks with a flash of his eyebrows.

"God fucking help us," Shane groans.

"Why does it have to be a little Mikey? He might be just like me?" Liam says.

"Or a mini Shane," Mikey adds with a shudder and Liam laughs.

"Remember that I can kick both of your asses," Shane reminds them.

"We're just playing, bro," Liam chuckles. "Besides, I mean we could get a mini Conor."

"Fuck!" Mikey gasps, his mouth open as he stares at me in horror. "Our own mini fire-starter."

"What?" Jessie laughs as she looks at me.

"I went through a little arsonist phase when I was a kid," I say with a shrug.

"You were all fucking nightmares as kids, but you were a fucking tornado of trouble, Mikey Ryan," Shane says as he takes Jessie's hand and kisses her fingertips before he adds, "so let's hope they both turn out like their mom."

I frown at him. "What? Stubborn as hell, argumentative little redheads with a raging sugar addiction who refuse to do as they're told?"

"In that case I'd prefer two Mikeys," Shane says as he shakes his head.

"Hey!" Jessie shrieks but my brothers and even Brooke laugh loudly.

"I'm sorry, Angel. I meant sweet and kind and funny," I say with a wink.

"Whoever they're like, I just can't fucking wait to meet them," Mikey says.

Liam is just smiling so widely that I think his cheeks are going to be hurting later.

"And you're sure you're feeling okay, Jessie?" Brooke took her blood pressure when she first got here and it was perfect. Of course it was – my girl has nerves of fucking steel.

"Yes. Never felt better," she replies with a smile. "Thank you for coming and checking me and the babies over."

"Any time. That's what I'm here for," Brooke smiles back before she stands up and starts to pack her equipment away. While she's doing that, Mikey wraps his arms around her and gives her a kiss on the cheek and then Liam does the same until she finds herself in the middle of a giant man sandwich. She blushes slightly making Jessie laugh.

"Boys," she admonishes them. "Poor Brooke can't breathe!"

"It's fine," she laughs as the twins release her. "I'm used to excited parents-to-be, although usually not so many at once."

"Well, we're kind of unique," Shane says as he helps her with her things.

"You sure are." She reaches for Jessie's hand and gives it a squeeze. "Take good care of yourself and I'll see you in two weeks."

"I will."

As Shane sees Brooke out, I lie on the bed next to my wife. I place my hand on her gently rounded stomach and suck in a deep breath. "If anything had have happened to you today," I breathe. Even thinking about her or our babies being harmed feels like someone has my heart in a vise.

"I know, Conor," she whispers. "I'm so sorry I worried you all."

"You know you're never leaving this apartment without one of us ever again, don't you?" I narrow my eyes at her. If she tries to fight me on this, she will lose.

Liam comes and sits on the bed beside her and nods his agreement.

"Yeah," she mumbles.

"That didn't sound all that convincing, Angel?" I frown at her.

"Yes," she says louder now. "I don't want to go anywhere without you guys." She shudders and Liam wraps his arm around her.

"Good girl," I whisper in her ear and she shivers again, but this time I suspect for an entirely different reason.

"I should get up and start looking for Hayden," she says with a soft sigh.

"Nope," Liam replies.

"Not tonight," I add.

"But the sooner I start looking, the better chance we have of finding out who was behind what happened today," she protests as she tries to sit up.

"You're taking tonight off," I snap.

"The doctor just said I'm totally fine," she sighs loudly.

"Yeah, but maybe we're not," Liam says and she immediately stops struggling.

"Oh," she breathes.

"We're all taking a night off," I growl as I trail soft kisses along the side of her neck.

"Shane won't like that." She squirms in my arms as my beard tickles her throat.

"Shane won't like what?" he barks as he walks back into the room.

"Everyone taking the night off," she purrs.

He stands at the foot of the bed, glaring at her as he pulls off his tie. "You really think any of us would be going to work tonight after we almost lost you today?" He arches an eyebrow at her as Mikey walks up behind him.

I roll onto my back and look at my brothers. I hear Liam chuckling softly and Jessie's breathing grows faster and louder. When Shane unbuckles his belt and slides it off, she gasps so loudly that my cock twitches. I look between her and him as she starts to fidget.

"I think we're going to have to restrain her for this first part," he says as he hands me the belt and I swear I smell her cream already as her body starts trembling.

"What are you doing?" she breathes. "Am I being punished?"

"No, baby," Liam replies, kissing her softly before pulls her t-shirt off and over her head. Then he pushes himself up and starts to unbutton his shirt.

"Of course we're not punishing you, Angel. Now give me your hands." I hold out the belt and she holds them out to me in compliance. Goosebumps visibly prickle along her forearms as I wrap the soft leather around her wrists.

"Then what?" she breathes.

"You'll see." I wink at her before I gently push her back against the pillows as I raise her arms above her head and secure them to the headboard. We had this bed specially made after we got married. It's big enough for all five of us to sleep in. The headboard is made of solid oak. It has a long rectangular piece cut out across the center which is fitted with polished steel bars. Perfect for handcuffs, rope, belts, or anything else we might want to tie our girl up with.

When she is securely restrained, I run my hands down the soft skin on the underside of her arm and she shivers. "What are you all going to do to me?" she whispers.

"What do you think?" Liam chuckles as he sits on the bed beside her.

"Dr. Mikey," I shout to my younger brother who is tossing his clothes into the hamper. "Is there a limit on the number of orgasms a pregnant woman should have?"

"Well." Mikey scrubs a hand over his beard as he looks deep in thought. "You know in all my extensive research I've never come across a limit."

"Really?" I arch an eyebrow at him and Jessie's thighs start trembling with anticipation. Her breath hitches in her throat. "Are you comfortable?" I ask her.

"Yeah," she pants.

"You tell us if your arms start to ache or you need to take a breather, okay?"

"A breather from what?" she asks even though she knows what we plan on doing to her. The skin on her chest and cheeks is pink with heat.

At this point, Shane crawls onto the foot of the bed and reaches for her panties. He pulls them gently down her legs and she lifts her ass to help him.

"Your pussy is already soaking, sweetheart," he chuckles as he tosses her panties onto the floor.

"You still... haven't..." she gasps as he starts to circle her clit with his index finger.

"Haven't you figured it out yet, Red?" Mikey asks as he slides onto the bed beside Liam before he starts trailing soft kisses over her rounded stomach.

"We're all going to make you come, Angel," I say as I dip my head and start to kiss her neck as Liam gets to work on her gorgeous tits. "Then when we're done with that..."

Kiss.

"We're going to untie you and get you some food. Then all get a little sleep."

Kiss.

"Then we're going to wake you up and fuck you."

Kiss.

"Tonight is all about taking care of you, Angel. Because we almost fucking died when we thought someone might hurt you today and we need you to know how much we love you."

"I do know," she whispers.

"Yeah? Well, we're gonna remind you anyway. Just sleeping and eating and fucking and making you come."

"Oh, holy fuck!" she hisses as Mikey's mouth settles over her clit while Shane slides his fingers inside her.

"We're going to take real good care of you, baby," Liam murmurs against her skin.

I rub my hand over her stomach as she squirms, pulling at her restraints. I can't believe we almost lost her today – almost lost all of them. I want to wrap her in my arms and never let her leave my sight again. I want to kiss and lick and touch every millimeter of her body so the taste and the feel of her is burned into my brain until the end of time.

"Oh," she whimpers as the first orgasm hits quickly, her body trembling as Shane holds her thighs open while Mikey carries on eating her pussy.

"You have to let me touch you too," she breathes as she pulls at the belt binding her wrists.

"You're touching all of us, Jessie," Shane says as he pushes a finger inside her and gently finger-fucks her.

"You know what I mean," she pants as she looks down at

him and Mikey worshipping her pussy. I'll be swapping places with one of them in about thirty seconds because I want to worship it myself but before I do, I turn her face to mine and kiss her softly, swallowing her soft moans as she's brought to the brink again.

CHAPTER 39
JESSIE

A large hand reaches for me, clawing at my skin, his fingertips grazing my arm as I shrink back from him, pressing myself back against the damp wall as far as I can. Breathing in as though it will me make me smaller somehow. I want to scream but I'm too afraid. I want my mom. I want my papa.

The giant man curses in Russian as he pushes his arm deeper into the crack of the door and I shrink back further, my eyes wide and my mouth tightly closed as I peer at him through the gap in the cupboard door that he's reaching through. His teeth are bared like a dog, his eyes wild with fury. He turns his head to the side as he grunts his annoyance, changing his angle so he might reach me.

There is a tattoo on the base of his neck. A bird. With black eyes and orange wings. It wears a symbol on its chest. Zhar-ptitsa – a firebird. My papa tells me stories of the firebird and the princess. Of difficult quests and true love.

The man's hand grasps for me again, curling over the fabric of my pajamas and I let out an ear-splitting scream.

Then he is gone.

· · ·

My eyes snap open in the dark room as my heart beats wildly in my chest, just like my eight-year-old self in my dream. Except that was no dream. It was a memory. A long-buried one that had been lost in the jumbled collection of fairytales and nightmares of my childhood. But that was real. It happened. That tattoo was real. And it is the same one I saw yesterday.

There is a hand gripping my waist and I turn to see Conor curled up beside me, a protective arm wrapped around me.

On the other side of me, Mikey and Liam snore softly. Shane isn't here though. I knew he wouldn't be able to resist working even after forbidding me to. I wriggle from Conor's grip, trying to shift from under him without disturbing him.

I fail.

"Where are you going?" he grumbles sleepily.

"I need my computer."

"No. Sleep!" he commands as he pulls me tighter, resting his chin on my shoulder.

"I recognize the tattoo. I've seen it before," I whisper.

He opens his eyes and narrows them at me. "When?"

"When I was little. Some men tried to kidnap me and they had the same tattoo."

Conor sits up and takes my hand and indicates his head toward the door and together we both climb out of the bed without disturbing the twins. He hands me a t-shirt and I pull it over my head while he puts on a pair of sweatpants and then we leave the room and head to Shane's office.

Conor keeps his hand grasped firmly in mine as we walk as though someone might steal me away in the night. I smile up at him. Well, someone might try, but he and his brothers would never let them take me and I have never felt as safe and protected as I do as a part of their family.

"You okay, Angel?" he asks, his brow furrowed in concern.

"Yeah," I whisper as I squeeze his hand.

Shane has his head bent, looking through some paperwork when we walk into his office. He looks up when he hears us. "What are you two doing up?" he asks with a frown.

"What are you doing up when you promised we were all taking the night off?" I ask with a flash of my eyebrows as I pull up a chair beside him and switch on my computer. When I became a permanent resident here, Shane bought a much bigger desk. It's big enough that the two of us can work comfortably at it all day on two separate computers. Its huge size also comes in handy for the various other things we like to do on it. Even the thought makes my insides warm and tingly and I remind myself I came here to work.

Shane leans over and kisses my cheek and my skin warms at his touch. "I couldn't sleep."

"I knew you wouldn't," Conor says with a knowing smile as he sits on the edge of the desk beside me.

"I can't stop my brain from ticking over." He scowls at the paperwork in front of him. "I was wondering if this deal we struck up with Chicago had anything to do with it?" He rubs his temples and frowns at the papers on his desk.

"I think I know who's behind this. Well, kind of," I say and he turns back to me.

"Who?"

I start to pull up some of the records from my hard drive. I have stored everything I have ever found out about my past and my family on here.

"Tell us about the dream, Angel," Conor says.

"Dream?" Shane's frown deepens.

"A memory really," I say as I start to trawl through the files. "I knew I'd seen that tattoo before." I pull up the image of the guy's neck from the ice cream parlor and although it's obscured by his blood and a gaping bullet hole, the image is still recognizable. "It's a firebird. See?" I point to the orangey red feathers on the screen.

"A firebird?" Conor asks as he peers closely at the screen.

"Yeah, like a phoenix, you know?"

Both he and Shane mumble their agreement.

"When I was little, The Firebird and the Princess was one of my favorite fairytales. My father used to tell it to me all the time."

I look between both Shane and Conor as they stare at me in confusion and I realize I'm not making much sense.

"There are lots of variations of the firebird folklore, but the one my father told me was of an archer who finds a firebird feather and presents it to the king in the hopes of reward, instead the greedy king forces the archer to steal a princess. But, the princess didn't want to be stolen and she refuses to marry the king. In traditional variations, the archer marries the princess himself, but in my father's unique spin on it, the princess steals the firebird for herself and escapes to a faraway land." I blink away a tear as I think about my papa and his soft, calming voice.

Conor reaches for my hand and squeezes and I smile at him.

"Anyway, because of that story, I think I forgot about the men who came to take me. The men with the firebird tattoos, or at least I jumbled the memory and the fairytales until I didn't realize that part of it was real."

"So you think these are the same men who tried to take you yesterday?" Shane asks.

"Not the exact same men, because as far as I recall, my father killed all of the men who came for me when I was a child." More memories now of gunfire and shouting fill my head and I shake it to clear my thoughts. "But part of the same brotherhood."

"Brotherhood?" Conor frowns at me.

"Hmm. I saw something about this years ago but because I was so focused on the Wolf I didn't do a lot of research into them specifically." I open a document that contains the information I gathered. "Roughly translated as the brotherhood of the firebird."

"And they are?" Shane asks.

"Well, they used to be the Bratva's most skilled assassins."

"Used to be?" Shane frowns again.

"They haven't been active for over a decade. At least not according to any of the research I did, which is why I never focused on them. They had no connection to the Wolf. In fact, the Wolf kind of put them out of business."

"So why the fuck are they active now and why do they want you?" Conor snarls.

"Who even knows that I exist?" I shake my head as I stare at the screen.

"Vlad," Conor growls and I close my eyes. Vlad and his sons are the only people who know who and where I am. I don't want to believe it of him, but all the signs point straight to him. Still, I can't wrap my head around it. Vlad had plenty of opportunity to kill me

"I'll arrange a meeting with him tomorrow," I whisper.

"The fuck you will," Conor snaps.

"He might not be behind this," I place my hand on Conor's thigh. "And if he's not, he'll be our best chance at finding out who is. If you and your brothers go in there and shoot him in the head first then we may never get to the bottom of this."

"You are not putting yourself or our babies in danger, Jessie," he goes on.

"We won't be in danger. You, Shane, Mikey, and Liam will be right beside me. We'll have the meeting here at the club and have our men here. I won't be at risk at all." I look to Shane who has his brow furrowed. "What do you think?"

He rubs a hand over his jaw and sighs. "I think you're right..."

"Shane!" Conor snaps.

"We can't keep Jessie out of this, Con, as much as we'd like to. And I don't know, this doesn't seem like Vlad's style," he says with a shake of his head.

"The Bratva's elite kill squad try and kidnap our wife and you don't think the head of the fucking Bratva had anything to do with it?"

"But they haven't worked for the Bratva for years, right?" Shane asks me.

"As far as I can tell." I say with a nod of my head. "But I'll admit I haven't looked into them for a long time."

"So, maybe this is some kind of takeover?" Shane offers.

"Then why aren't they going after Vlad? Why do they need Jessie?" Conor asks.

"Maybe they are going after him? And Jessie is the only surviving Ivanov – well except for Hayden now, but it's Jessie who Alexei recognized as his heir. Maybe this brotherhood wants back in power, and what better way to make a power grab than with the true heir?"

"So you think they want Jessie alive?"

I shake my head. "I doubt that," I say with a sigh. "But if they kill me then they will have a genuine claim to the top."

Shane wraps an arm around me and plants a kiss on the top of my head. "They won't get close enough to touch you, sweetheart," he whispers. "Promise."

"I know," I smile at him.

"Hmm." Conor grunts beside us and I squeeze his hand.

"At least we have a starting point now," I say. "In a few hours we'll have some answers, and knowledge is power."

He brushes the hair from my face. "Power is power."

"Well, we have plenty of that too," I remind him.

He rolls his eyes but I know that we've won him over. "You'll make the call on loudspeaker and Shane and I will be in the room with you."

"I wouldn't expect anything less," I say with a smile.

"How do you get me to agree to anything you want?" he says before he kisses me softly.

"She's got the keys to the cookie jar, that's why," Shane says with a soft laugh as he goes back to his paperwork.

"Shane!" I admonish him but he winks at me and I can't help laugh too.

"He kinda has a point, Angel," Conor agrees.

"So when are you calling Vlad?" Shane asks as he checks his watch. He's still wearing the Breitling I bought him for his birthday and it makes me smile.

"Maybe we should wait until the sun comes up?" I suggest. "I'm not sure he'll appreciate a call at five a.m.?"

"Then how about we wake Mikey up and get him to make some banana waffles instead?" Conor suggests.

"We can't," I giggle.

"You can, sweetheart," Shane flashes his eyebrows at me. "Tell him you've got a craving."

Conor laughs loudly as I feign my indignation. "Are you suggesting I use our unborn children to manipulate Mikey into getting up at the ass crack of dawn to make us food we could probably make ourselves if we tried?"

"Yeah," Conor and Shane reply in unison.

"Okay," I say with a nod as I push myself up from my chair. "I just wanted to make sure we're all on the same page."

"Good girl," Shane says, slapping my ass as I walk past him and I smile as I walk out of his office to wake Mikey and Liam. I hear him and Conor talking and know they will be discussing the details of our meeting with Vlad. I hope he agrees to a meeting today, because if he doesn't, then I suspect my husbands will just hunt him down and meet with him whether he likes it or not.

I push open the bedroom door and smile at the sleeping forms of Mikey and Liam. I feel a twinge of guilt that I'm about to wake them from a peaceful sleep, but this isn't just about Mikey's amazing banana waffles, it's also because we need to brief them both on the latest development and they will want to know as soon as possible. I crawl onto the bed, into the middle of my two sleeping giants.

"Hey, baby," Liam mumbles.

"Hey, handsome." I lie between him and his brother and smile as they both snuggle closer to me.

"You need something, Red?" Mikey growls.

"Yes. Your banana waffles," I giggle.

"Right now?" he groans.

"Uh-huh. The babies are hungry too."

"That's a low blow," he says as he plants a kiss on my shoulder blade and pushes himself up.

"I also have an update about who tried to take me in the ice cream shop yesterday," I add and that makes Liam sit up too.

"You know who it was?" he snaps.

"Kind of. Let's go have some breakfast and I'll tell you all about it."

CHAPTER 40
MIKEY

I mix the waffle batter as the sexiest sous chef in the world stands right beside me, chopping bananas. When she is done, she dips her finger into the jar of chocolate sauce and then sucks it clean.

"That is very unhygienic, Red. What would your hero, Carl Paxton, have to say about that?"

"I don't care," she purrs. "Besides, you have all had your tongue in my mouth at some point this morning, I'm pretty sure if I got any cooties you already got them too." She arches an eyebrow at me.

"Hmm," I agree as I lean down and slide my tongue into her mouth again and she moans softly. Fuck, I wish I could take her right here on the counter.

"How are those waffles coming along?" Conor asks as he strolls into the kitchen.

"They would be quicker if your wife wasn't distracting me every five seconds," I tell him.

"Oh, so she's *my* wife when she's causing trouble?" Conor laughs.

"I am not causing trouble!" she protests.

"You're always causing trouble," Shane adds as he walks into the room too. He's standing before us in a few strides and he wraps his arms around her waist, taking her attention from me. He's about to kiss her but the change in her face is instant. She pushes him away from her and steps back at the same time, her hand flying to her mouth as she groans.

"What's up?" he asks with a frown as I stare at her in confusion.

She sucks in a deep breath but then balks loudly, rushing to the sink. "I feel like I'm going to throw up," she groans.

I look at Shane and chuckle. He goes to step toward her but I stand in front of him. "You're making our wife ill, dude. Back off." I hold up my spatula and he frowns at me.

"Jessie, are you okay, sweetheart?" he asks, ignoring me as he steps closer to her but she holds out her hand to stop him.

"Did you put cologne on?" she whispers.

"Yeah. The one I always wear."

She shakes her head and goes back to hanging it over the sink. "I'm sorry, I..." She balks again but she doesn't throw up. "It's making me..."

"Fuck!" Shane rolls his eyes while Liam and I try our best to control our laughter, but we fail miserably.

"He'll kick your asses if you don't stop it," Conor says with a smile as he walks to Jessie and rubs a hand over her back but he's barely holding it together either. I can tell by the look on his face.

We're all used to Jessie's sudden attacks of nausea now. She's not often actually sick, but she turns a deep shade of green until the offending smell is removed. First it was oregano. Then tuna fish. Then hot dogs, quickly followed by whiskey – which I found out to my own detriment one night when I had a glass of the stuff at the end of my work shift but directly before bed. I kissed her and she threw up on me after. But now, the offending smell is Shane, so I'm going to enjoy every second of his misfortune.

"I'm fine," Jessie breathes. "Shane can you...?"

"Fuck me! I guess I'll go shower then," he says with a sigh before he walks out of the room to a chorus of sniggers from me and Liam.

"I'm glad you find my discomfort so amusing," Jessie says as she straightens up, but she arches an eyebrow in that way that lets me know she's not really mad at us.

"Aw, I'm sorry, Red," I say as I walk over and kiss her damp forehead. "But if you didn't have your head in the sink, you would have seen the look on Shane's face and wet yourself from laughing so hard. I'm surprised we kept a lid on it to be honest."

"I usually love his cologne too," she says with a soft chuckle as she leans against my chest.

"Well, looks like he's gonna have to get himself a new one."

It's only fifteen minutes later when Shane comes back into the room as I'm placing a plate laden with fresh waffles onto the kitchen island. His hair is still damp and he's changed his clothes too and is dressed in just a pair of grey sweatpants. He makes his way straight to our girl.

"Better?" he asks with a flash of his eyebrows.

She leans close to him, wrapping her arms around him and nuzzling his neck. "Better," she giggles.

"Thank fuck!" he hisses.

"You worried it was just your general smell that was making her sick, bro?" Liam asks with a snort as he takes a waffle from the plate.

"Asshole," Shane says with a roll of his eyes, but there is a look of relief on his face that tells me there is a grain of truth in Liam's teasing. I mean I can't imagine anything worse than having to keep my distance from our horny, pregnant wife for the next four-and-a-half months.

"Shall we eat and then we can fill the boys in on developments," Conor says as he takes some waffles and piles his plate high. It's been nice being in here with them all and acting like a normal family. Being able to forget for a little while that someone tried to kidnap our girl and our babies yesterday, and how terrifyingly close they came to succeeding.

"Yeah," Jessie says as she pulls out of Shane's embrace.

I CHEW on the last mouthful of my breakfast as I listen to Jessie telling us about some weird fucking brotherhood. I won't lie, it sounds like something out of Harry goddamn Potter to me. The fact that these maniacs have tried to kidnap our girl twice now is enough to make me want to slit their throats right now.

"So, Vlad has to know something about this then," I agree, because how can he not? I also agree with Shane that maybe this is part of some kind of grab for power, but I'm not sure if that's better or worse than Vlad wanting her dead. At least we know who we're dealing with if it's him. A brotherhood sounds all kinds of fucked up.

"Yep. So, let's hope he agrees to meet with us," Jessie replies as she takes her second waffle.

"He will." I reach over and take her hand. "We'll make sure of it."

CHAPTER 41
JESSIE

My hand trembles as I dial Vlad's number. At least it was his number over twelve months ago and I hope he hasn't changed it. I glance at Shane and Conor who sit at the desk opposite me. They are here with me but they have agreed to let me handle this.

He answers after a few rings. "Jessica?"

"Jessie," I remind him.

"Of course. My apologies. Old habits die hard," he says softly. "What can I do for you?"

"What do you know about the brotherhood of the firebird?"

He sucks in a breath and there is a few moments pause before he answers. "As much as you do, I suspect. But why are you asking me this?"

"Because they used to be the Bratva's elite assassins."

"Used to be," he interrupts me.

"And they tried to kidnap me yesterday."

"What?" he snarls and I feel like I have his undivided attention suddenly. He curses in Russian and talks to someone in the room with him, who I assume is one of his sons.

"What do you know about them, Vlad?" I ask again.

"They have been dormant for years..." he says with a sigh.

"But?"

"Recently we have heard rumors that they are active again."

"Active? But they are the Bratva's assassins? And you are the Bratva."

"This is not the kind of conversation I want to have over the telephone, Jessie," he snaps.

"Of course," I say with a shake of my head as Conor and Shane bristle at the change in Vlad's tone, but I understand his reasons. "Neither do I. Can we meet?"

"Yes, I think that would be wise," he says immediately and it makes my stomach drop, because that means he knows something bad is going on.

"Can you come to the club? After what happened yesterday, I don't really feel like leaving the safety of this building."

"I assume your husbands are listening?" he says.

"We are," Shane snarls.

"I know you are a man of your word, Mr. Ryan. Can I have your assurances that we won't be ambushed if I agree to this meeting?"

"You have my word if I have yours that you will come in here unarmed and without your army," Shane replies.

"My sons will be with me and they will carry a weapon each. I can't travel unarmed. But they will not use them unless my life is in danger."

"Fine," Shane snaps. "Can you be here in two hours?"

"Yes," Vlad replies and then he abruptly ends the call.

I lean back in my chair and look between Shane and Conor. "He knows something about the brotherhood to agree to meet us like that."

"Yeah." Conor nods his agreement.

"Let's tell Mikey and Liam and get ready for this meeting

then," Shane says as he pushes himself to his feet. "You'll let me handle it, Jessie?"

"Yes," I reply with a nod. He's much better at this kind of stuff than me. I mean it's kind of what he lives for.

"You know I'm not going to play nice?" He arches an eyebrow at me. "At least not until I know for sure he's not behind what happened yesterday."

"I wouldn't expect any less."

"Good girl." He winks at me and I thank the heavens that I have these four incredible men in my life.

TWO HOURS LATER, I'm sitting in the brother's nightclub, with Conor and Liam on my left and Shane and Mikey on my right as we sit opposite Vlad and his sons. He was true to his word and only his sons are with him. Their armored car is in our basement, signaling that Vlad trusts us too, not that he would admit that yet.

"Who have you told that Jessie is Jessica Ivanov?" Shane snarls as his opening question.

"Nobody," Vlad replies.

"So how the fuck does some kid we've never heard of turn up here, claiming to be Alexei's son, looking for his half-sister?"

"Alexei's son?"

"Yes," Shane snaps.

"I had no idea he had a son." He blinks and he's either a very good actor or he's telling the truth.

"Well he does. And the slippery little fuck set Jessie up yesterday."

"Tell me what happened." Vlad looks to me but Shane goes on talking.

"Two of the Bratva's elite assassins tried to kidnap my wife is what happened," he growls. "Now how the fuck do they even know who she is?"

"They are not working for me." Vlad turns his attention back to Shane. "And we have not told anyone of Jessica's existence. Why would I?"

"Because you want to eradicate any threat to your position of power."

"Jessica is no threat to me," Vlad replies coolly and Shane's fists clench by his side, "because she does not exist. And I have no intention of causing Jessie any harm."

"So who activated this brotherhood again?"

Vlad narrows his eyes at him. "I don't know."

"Sure it wasn't you?"

"Yes, I'm sure," Vlad snaps, the vein in his temple bulging.

"Care to tell me why the fuck I would believe you?"

Vlad leans forward in his chair, his hands on the table in front of him as he stares down Shane Ryan. Shane stares right back and the atmosphere in the room becomes so thick, I swear I can taste it as the two of them face off, each ready to declare war on the other if they have to.

"With respect, Mr. Ryan," he snarls. "If I had wanted Jessie dead, I wouldn't have fucked it up. It would be already done."

The vein in Shane's neck pulses as he clenches his fists tighter. I sense Conor and the twins bristling beside me too and I swallow hard. This is going to turn into a bloodbath if things get any more tense. "Is that so?" Shane snarls.

"Yes," Vlad snarls back. "But as I said, I have no intention of causing her any harm." He turns to me then and gives a slight nod of his head as though to reassure me and I shake my head.

"So why are the brotherhood after me then, Vlad? Any ideas?" I ask, needing to ease the tension before someone gets their face blown off. I see Mikey twitching from the corner of my eye and worry that his trigger finger is going to get just as twitchy if we don't ratchet the tension down at least twenty notches.

He runs a scarred hand over his beard and some of the tension slips from his shoulders as he addresses me. "There have been rumblings of a takeover. We have been trying to deal with it for some time now. It seems that some people believe I am not the rightful head of the Bratva."

"And so who is?" Shane snaps. "Who else knows that Jessie is alive?"

"I have already told you that I don't know. The information of her existence did not come from me or my sons," Vlad barks. "If I wanted…"

Conor cuts him off before he can finish his sentence. "Yeah, if you wanted to cause her harm you would have already. You kinda told us that, but the thing is, no the fuck you wouldn't because I would fucking kill you and every person you have ever so much as spoken to before I would let you harm a single hair on her head. And besides that, I just don't buy it."

Vlad narrows his eyes at Conor.

"If you're so shit hot at what you do, why didn't Alexei send you to find his daughter? He sent the brotherhood and they fucked it up. Then he sent the Wolf, and he didn't exactly cover himself in glory either." Conor leans forward now too. "So if you are so fucking good that you think you could take our girl out if you wanted to, why didn't Alexei ask you to find her?"

"I did find her," Vlad shouts back. "I found her before any of them!"

"What?" I stammer as I look between him and my irate husbands. "You can't have."

"I did, Jessie," he says softly. "About six years after your parents left Russia."

"But…" I blink at him.

"You were living in a trailer park in Idaho. Your trailer had a bright green door. Your mom had a herb garden on her window ledge. And you had a cat called Nugent," he says.

I shake my head in disbelief, but there is no way he could have known that if he wasn't there.

"Why didn't you tell him?" I whisper.

"Because you all seemed so happy. Your parents had the twins by then, and I knew what Alexei would do to them. So, I warned your father and I told Alexei that you could never be found."

"I remember we left that place in a hurry. We even left Nugent behind because he'd gone on one of his wanders and he wasn't there when we were leaving. I cried for days." I swallow hard at the memory.

"Alexei called off the search for two years after that, before the brotherhood persuaded him you could be found," Vlad goes on.

"Why didn't you tell me this before?" I frown at him.

"It was insignificant," he says with a shake of his head.

"Not to me," I whisper.

He nods, his Adam's apple bobbing in his throat as he swallows hard before he turns back to Shane and Conor. "You see, I have no reason to want Jessie dead. I have looked out for her whenever I could and I would do so until my last breath. She is a light in this world of darkness and demons, just like her mother before her."

A sob catches in my throat but I swallow it down.

"Well, I can't argue with that," Shane says as he takes my hand and laces his fingers through mine and suddenly the tension in the room has dissolved and we are all on the same side.

"How can we get hold of this brotherhood?" Conor asks.

"My sons have some leads."

"Hmm," one of them grunts in agreement.

"They will be planning an..." he searches for the right word, "encounter with some of the members very shortly. Perhaps you would like to assist us?"

"Maybe." Conor frowns, still suspicious of Vlad's motives.

"It seems right now they are our common enemy." Vlad raises an eyebrow at Shane who nods his agreement.

"It makes sense. But we want our time with them first. I need to know what they had planned for Jessie and who told them she was even alive."

"Of course." Vlad nods his head.

"Then you can kill them in whatever fashion you desire, preferably the most painful one imaginable," Shane adds and that is met with smiles and grunts of assent from Vlad's sons.

CHAPTER 42

SHANE

I lean back in against the leather bench in the booth of the Black Bear. It's a small, rundown bar in Newark and it's the place where Hayden says he was told of Jessie's existence. It only opened up again a few days ago after the cops closed it down. I have a feeling its renaissance is going to be short-lived. Picking up my glass of Scotch, I swirl the ice and amber liquid around my glass.

"They sure look like they're having fun," Jakob Mikhailov laughs. He is Vlad's oldest son and Conor and I have been working with him and his younger brother, Rudolf, to find the brotherhood.

I look around and smile at the carnage unfolding as Conor and Rudolf embark on a violent rampage through the bar.

"You think we should give them a hand?" he asks with a flash of his eyebrows.

I look again as Conor is using one guy's head as a weapon to beat another guy senseless, while Rudolf has someone crushed under his boot while he punches another in the face.

"Nah. I think they got it," I say as someone is thrown toward our table and lands in a crumpled, unconscious heap.

"They are kindred spirits, our brothers? No?" Jakob laughs and I nod my agreement as I take a sip of my whiskey.

"You know much about this brotherhood?" I ask him. "Because it sounds all kinds of weird and fucked up to me."

Jakob laughs softly. "They aren't as mysterious as they sound. They are like a branch of an army."

"But they haven't operated for years?" I frown at him. "At least not for the Bratva?"

"No." Jakob shakes his head. "But they come from a proud line of soldiers. You don't just become a member of the brotherhood. You are born into it. The strongest son from every family must give his life to the order. They take it very seriously."

"But why do they still exist if they don't work for the Bratva?"

"Ah." Jakob runs a hand over his beard. "It is complicated but I will try to explain. They first fell out of favor when Alexei's father, Viktor, was in charge. They failed him and he demanded they all be hunted and killed so they went underground. When Alexei came to power, he liked the idea of his own army of elite assassins, so he found them again and reinstated them."

"And he sent them to search for his missing daughter?"

"Yes. But they had been out of practice for some years by this time. They did some mercenary work across Europe but it was easy money and nothing that honed their skills the same way."

"They got lazy?" I ask.

"And fat," he says in his thick Russian accent before he starts to laugh.

"So they failed Alexei too?"

"Yes, and so they were forced underground again and we didn't hear of them for many years."

"Until recently?"

"Yes. Shortly after my father became the new head of the

Bratva we discovered they had resurfaced. It seems they do not approve of his appointment."

"Why not though?"

Jakob downs his vodka in one and smacks his lips together. "Because my family are not Russian royalty like the Ivanovs. My great grandfather was a poor farmer and my grandfather was a lowly Bratva foot-soldier."

"But why the fuck does that matter?"

"It matters when there are true Ivanov heirs alive," he says with a tilt of his head. "The brotherhood can claim the throne for themselves if they have an heir."

"So you think they want Jessie alive?"

"No." He shakes his head. "I think they want her dead."

His words are like a knife slicing through my heart. "She's too headstrong and smart for them to manipulate."

"Precisely. She would no doubt disagree, but she is a lot like her father."

"Yeah, well I won't tell her you ever said that."

"But the kid..." Jakob tilts his head again.

"The perfect puppet," I say with a sigh right before another body comes crashing into our table.

"*Otva`li!*" Jakob snarls as he pushes the intruder away with his boot.

I down the last of my cheap Scotch. "Maybe it's time to give them a hand before there's nobody left alive to give us any information?" I suggest.

"Yes." He laughs and together we head into the carnage.

CHAPTER 43
JESSIE

I have a trace on Hayden's credit cards and his bank account as well as eyes on his apartment and the bar where he works. It's been three days since the incident at Daisy's and I haven't seen anything of him yet. I must have taught him to cover his tracks well. A bitter wave of sadness and disappointment washes over me when I think about the time we've spent together in the last three months. Was everything he ever said and did a lie?

I swat away a tear as it rolls down my cheek.

"You okay, baby?" Liam asks as he sits beside me on the sofa in the den.

"No," I whisper. "I feel like an idiot for trusting him."

He pulls me onto his lap, forcing me to put my laptop down. "You are not an idiot. Not even a little bit. He is a fucking cold-hearted snake to do what he did, Jessie."

"You weren't fooled by him though."

"I wouldn't trust anyone around you. I never will. It's not because I'm any more perceptive than you or my brothers."

"You never give yourself credit," I say as I push his hair back from his forehead and look into his deep brown eyes.

"You are one of the most insightful people I've ever met, Liam Ryan."

"You haven't met all that many people then," he chuckles as he pulls me to his chest.

"I miss him, Liam," I whisper as he wraps his arms around me.

"I know, baby," he says softly, pulling me tighter.

We sit like that in silence for a while. My cheek pressed against his hard chest as he smooths my hair with his hand. I listen to the soothing sound of his steady heartbeat and for a few moments I forget that someone out there is trying to hurt me and my babies.

Shane and Conor have been scouring the city looking for anyone connected to the Hayden or the brotherhood. Ironically, they have teamed up with Vlad's sons Rudolf and Jakob – the Irish Mafia and the Bratva working together would have seemed unthinkable once given that they have previously kidnapped both Conor and Liam.

An alert pings on my laptop and I sit up, taking it from the sofa and keying in my passcode.

"Is it him?" Liam asks.

"Yes," I nod. I'm running his image through facial recognition software too and he has been good at hiding his face from view - until now. "He's going into an apartment building in Newark."

"Then let's go get him," he says as he helps me stand.

"Okay," I breathe as my heart starts to race.

"You can stay here if you want to. I can get Chester and the guys to sit up here with you," he offers. I insisted that I go along when we find Hayden. The boys refused at first, but I wouldn't back down. I need to look him in the eye myself and ask him why.

"No. I'm coming."

"Okay. Mikey!" he shouts and a few seconds later Mikey comes running into the room. "Jessie found him," he snarls.

"Then let's go get the piece of shit," Mikey snarls back.

"Where are Shane and Conor?" I ask.

"Out with Rudolf and Jakob. We can call them from the car," Mikey replies.

"Okay," I nod my agreement. "But boys..."

"Yeah?" They both turn and look at me.

"Can you let me handle this? Please?"

They both frown at me.

"Please?" I ask again.

"Okay, Red," Mikey finally agrees. "But he puts one toe out of line and I will tear his head off his shoulders."

"Thank you," I say and then the three of us head to the basement to the armored SUV.

CHAPTER 44

SHANE

A call comes through from Mikey, and Conor presses the button to answer it. Our younger brother's voice fills the car. "We found Hayden."

I glance at Conor beside me in the driver's seat. "Where?"

"Some apartment building in Newark. He must have been hiding out there or something. We're on our way to him now."

"All three of you?" I ask.

"Yeah."

I swallow down the ball of anxiety that forces into my throat. "Be careful," I warn him.

"We will, bro," he says with a sigh.

"I mean it, Mikey. If anything happens to her..."

"You really think we'd let anything happen to her, Shane?" he barks at me and I close my eyes and take a breath. We're all feeling the tension and the frustration of the last three days.

"Sorry," he mumbles. "We'll take good care of them all. Promise, bro."

"I know, son."

"Where are you and Conor anyway?"

"On our way to have a chat with a few members of the brotherhood," Conor replies.

"Fuck! You found them then?"

"Yeah. We finally got a good lead and we're heading to meet Jakob and Rudolf now." Our efforts at the Black Bear were pretty fruitless but then Jakob and Rudolf had plenty of other contacts we could shake down and eventually we found someone who had seen a guy with the firebird tattoo at a motel on the outskirts of the city.

"You two be careful, too," Mikey warns.

"We will, kid," Conor replies.

"Keep us posted," I say.

"Ditto."

"We will. Speak soon."

"Bye," I say and end the call.

"They'll all be okay, right?" Conor asks me with a worried look on his face.

"They all know what they're doing, Con," I remind him but I share his anxiety. I don't believe for one minute Hayden was the mastermind behind all this. It's someone much smarter than him. I think the brotherhood are working with someone else too. They have been content to sit on the sidelines for decades. They are assassins not leaders. But who and why? Hopefully, we'll have some answers soon and I can end every single fucker who thought they could try and take her from me.

"You have any idea who the fuck might have got to Hayden?" he asks, I know he suspects the same as I do because we have done nothing but talk about it for the past three days. "Unless the brotherhood did just suddenly decided to make a power grab?"

"Maybe." I rub a hand over my jaw. "But how do they even know she's still alive? I don't think it came from Vlad or his sons."

"Me too," he agrees.

"And who the fuck else knew?" I shake my head.

"Someone obviously did. So let's go get some names."

Fortunately, it's not often that Conor has cause to let his sadistic side loose and I know he would sooner keep it under lock and key these days, preferring to explore the darker side of himself in a much more controlled way with Jessie. But today, he is ready to do whatever it takes to protect our girl and I almost feel sorry for the poor bastards who are going to be on the receiving end. Almost.

WHEN WE ARRIVE at the motel, Jakob and Rudolf are already waiting for us. Conor rolls our car to a stop and we jump out to meet our new colleagues. It's hard to believe we're working with the Bratva, but Vlad's sons have proven to be smart, ruthless and trustworthy – at least so far. They are exactly the kind of guys I like to work with.

"They in there?" I nod toward the motel.

"Yeah. Room 204," Jakob replies.

"How many?" Conor asks.

"Four of them."

"Perfect. One each," I say with an arch of my eyebrow.

"That's what he said," Jakob laughs as he points to his younger brother who rarely speaks.

"Anyone on either side?" I ask.

"Nope. Place is a shit-hole and it's pretty empty but they each have a room each along that bottom floor, so nobody will hear us as long as we don't make them scream too loudly."

"I find if you cut out their tongues first it really helps keep the noise levels down," Conor says matter-of-factly.

"Yes," Rudolf grunts and smiles at my brother.

"Let's not cut out all of their tongues until one of them has told us what we need to know, eh?" I suggest.

"Shall we?" Conor says with a tilt of his head.

"Let's do this," Jakob replies and we walk toward the motel room.

"These guys are hardcore, Con. It's not going to be easy to make them talk," I say quietly as our Russian colleagues walk ahead.

"I know, bro. Don't worry. I got this."

"I know you do."

CHAPTER 45
CONOR

S tanding straight, I spit the piece of the Russian fucker's nose out of my mouth. The coppery tang of his blood seeps onto my tongue and I spit again.

"You taste like fucking shit!" I snarl as I tower over him. He has his hands pressed over the gaping hole in his face as he cries and begs for his life.

We have been in this tiny shit-box of a room for two hours. We had the element of surprise and we had all four of the brotherhood members overpowered and restrained within five minutes of getting through the door. But Shane was right about them being hardcore. For the first hour, they all refused to speak at all, no matter what we inflicted on them.

We're pretty limited in terms of weapons, but both Shane and I, as well as Jakob and Rudolf know plenty of ways to cause pain. It was when we decided that we only needed one of them alive to get information that the real fun began.

So, we chose this poor fuck as the one who would sit and watch as his three colleagues were tortured to death. Even when they begged to be allowed to talk, we didn't let up. They had their opportunity and they wasted it. So now their mutilated bodies lie scattered around the room.

"Are you ready to tell me why you tried to kidnap my wife and babies?" I snarl at him.

He mumbles something but he nods his head. I grab his blood-matted hair and pull him up from the floor before tossing him onto the bed.

"Who told you that Jessica Ivanov was still alive?" Shane asks him. He was asked this question once before when we first arrived and he told us to go fuck ourselves – in Russian – and earned himself a broken jaw. Now he has a hole in the middle of his face where his nose is supposed to be. His jaw hangs at an odd angle and he chokes from the blood running down his throat, but he will give me answers. I'll make him write them down if I have to.

"She...told...us," he sputters the words.

"*She* told you?" I snarl at him. "Who? Jessie?" I bring my face closer to his.

"She... said... take back power..." he says before he starts choking on his own blood.

I grab his throat and squeeze. "Who is she?" I snarl.

"Conor!" Shane's hand is on my arm and I loosen my grip on our captive's throat as Shane holds his chin up and presses a bottle of water to his lips.

"Drink!" he barks. "It will help."

The Russian looks up at him gratefully as he swallows some of the cool liquid. When he has taken what he needs, Shane takes away the bottle and releases his grip on his chin. "I can end this right now if you tell me what I want to know."

The Russian nods softly.

"Who told you to take back power?"

I watch my oldest brother's face crumple before my eyes as the Russian says her name.

CHAPTER 46

JESSIE

My hands tremble as I knock on the apartment door. Mikey and Liam stand either side of me and I feel anger radiating from their bodies like heat from an open fire. I hope that Hayden's friend doesn't come back any time soon.

We wait for a moment and I knock again.

"He's not going to come to the door," Mikey says.

"Then let's go to him," Liam snarls.

Mikey wraps an arm around my waist and pulls me back from the door while his twin raises his right foot and kicks it open in one swift move.

"You're so fucking good at that," Mikey says appreciatively, but I don't think Liam even hears him as he storms into the apartment. I rush in after him just in time to see Hayden scrambling into what I assume is the bedroom.

Liam and Mikey run in after him, while I try and close the apartment door as best I can given that it's now hanging by one hinge.

A few seconds later, Hayden's high pitched shriek pierces

the air as he is dragged from the room by Liam, who is holding onto him by his hair.

"Shut the fuck up, or I will shut you up," Liam snarls as he throws Hayden roughly onto the sofa. "Just give me a reason to rip your throat out right now."

Hayden holds his hands over his head and pulls his feet up to his chest, curling up in a fetal position as he whimpers.

"For fuck's sake, kid, I'd have expected more balls from someone in league with the Bratva," Mikey snarls as he slaps Hayden across the head before pulling him up into a seated position. "Now sit up straight and look my wife in the eye while she asks you some questions. And if you tell the truth, I won't cut off all your favorite body parts and make you eat them."

Hayden clamps his thighs together as he looks up at me, tears running down his face and his lip trembling. "I'm sorry, Jessie," he whimpers.

I sit on the armchair opposite him. "I'm not interested in your apologies, Hayden. I want answers." I turn to Liam. "Can you watch the door?"

"Why me?" he frowns.

"Because I'm worried you're going to rip his throat out and I need him to talk first," I say with a flash of my eyebrows.

"Fine. Mikey..."

"I'll rip his cock and balls off if he tries anything, bro. Don't worry," Mikey interrupts him.

"I'm not in league with the Bratva," Hayden whispers, drawing my attention back to him.

"I know that, because the head of the Bratva wants you dead as much as my husbands do. But you are working for the brotherhood, right?"

"No." Hayden shakes his head. "I didn't know what they were planning until it was too late. She told me that all I had to do was get close to you..." he wails.

"She?" both Mikey and I say at the same time.

"Yeah. The woman who dragged me into all this," he sniffs, wiping his nose with the back of his hand.

"You'd better start talking, kid," Mikey snarls.

He nods his head vigorously. "She came into the bar one night. I waited on her and then she started talking to me about my father and who he was. How he was this super-rich businessman who had died and left all this money to my half-sister and how she was living this rich extravagant lifestyle while I was working fifty hours a week to live in a shitty one-bed apartment that stinks of piss."

I narrow my eyes at him. "So it *was* all about money?"

"Not just money, Jessie. Do you know how it feels to have to work so hard every damn day and never see an end in sight? Never see a way of paying off your debts and being able to live the life you deserve?"

Mikey slaps him around the back of his head. "You have no idea what it means to struggle, you entitled selfish prick," he snarls.

"Let him finish," I say.

"She lied to me, Jessie. She told me I was entitled to this inheritance but that you had stolen it all, and all I had to do to stake my claim on it was to prove we were related. I didn't know our father was the Russian Mafia until I'd already agreed to do it and by then it was too late to back out. She came up with the story that my mom told me before she died, but I never knew. I saw an easy way to get rid of my debts and finally have some money for once so I went along with her."

"But Shane offered you the money to pay off your debts." I frown at him.

"I know, but the deeper I got in with her the more I realized she was never going to let me go. She introduced me to the brotherhood and told me that the way to get my inheritance was to help them take over, and when I refused they threatened to kill me. I was in way over my head, Jessie. But I never thought they'd hurt you, I swear."

"So, what did you think they were going to do, Hayden?" I snap at him because his sniveling self-pity is starting to annoy me. If he was going to betray me like that, the least he can do is own it.

"She seemed so nice at first. She said she just wanted to talk you into signing over my inheritance to me. What was right-fully mine. By the time I realized she was lying to me it was too late. She had them tie me to a chair and threaten to *rape* me," he whispers the word as though it's an excuse for what he's done.

Mikey grabs him by the throat and squeezes so hard that Hayden's eyes bulge out of their sockets. "And just what do you think they would have done to my wife if they had gotten their hands on her, you pathetic piece of shit?" he snarls.

"Mikey!" I snap. I need him to let Hayden go because we still don't have the most vital piece of information.

Mikey releases Hayden from his grip.

"Who is she?" I direct my question to my half-brother.

"She's some shit-hot lawyer. Erin McGrath."

CHAPTER 47

SHANE

Conor kills the engine and I look up at the house on Long Island. We got ourselves cleaned up in the motel bathroom and left Jakob and Ruldolf to deal with the disposal of the four dead Russians. With the information they got before I put a bullet in the head of the last one standing, they are going to seek out the rest of the brotherhood and put an end to any potential future takeovers. Conor and I have no interest in helping them with their venture and they don't expect us to. I'm satisfied that any threat to Jessie and our children is going to end with what we're about to do now.

It's strange how many times I visited this place as a welcome guest, and yet today, while I may be welcomed, what I'm about to do would have once been unthinkable to me. But that was a long time ago.

"You okay, bro?" Conor asks, snapping me from my thoughts.

"Yeah," I say, the word catching in my throat. "I knew she hated her, Con, but I can't believe she'd do this."

"It's fucked up, bro," he says with a sigh.

"If she'd succeeded..."

"She didn't though, and this is not on you. None of it."

"So why the fuck do I feel so fucking guilty?" I swallow hard.

"Because despite the grumpy asshole exterior that you have going on, which you have down pat by the way, you're really a big pussycat, aren't ya?"

I know he's trying to make me feel better about what I'm about to do and I love him for it. I give him a half-smile. "Asshole," I grumble.

He unclips his seatbelt and together we climb out of the car. I walk up the familiar porch steps while Conor heads to the back of the house in case she makes a run for it.

I ring the doorbell, my heart racing in my chest as I wait to see if she has the front to answer and pretend like she didn't try to have my wife and unborn children kidnapped and murdered.

A familiar shadow at the door confirms my suspicion that she's going to try and front this out. I have no doubt she'll be in tears within five minutes.

She opens the door and I suck in a deep breath.

"Shane?" She blinks at me as though she's surprised by my presence. She's a good actress, I'll give her that. But then she always was adept at lying.

"Erin?" I say as I place my hand on the door. "Can I come in?"

She looks past me, no doubt wondering where my brothers are. I push against the wood with force causing her to stumble backward.

"Shane!" she whines as I step into her house and close the door behind me.

"I didn't realize you were back in the States?"

"I came back last week," she whimpers. "I didn't think you'd want to see me."

"Well, you're right about that," I snarl. "But you're lying

about how long you've been here, Erin. I had a chat to some of your Russian friends earlier."

Her face pales but she stands tall, glaring at me in defiance. "I don't have any Russian friends," she insists.

"Well, you're probably right about that too," I agree, running a hand over my jaw as I enjoy watching her squirm. She is a smart woman and I can almost see the cogs working in her brain as she tries to think of a way out of this. No doubt she has at least half a dozen excuses ready to trip off her tongue. "They threw you under the bus at the first opportunity so I guess to call them your friends is a bit of a stretch. Your acquaintances, then?"

I step closer to her and she backs away from me toward the wall.

"I – I don't know what you're taking about," she stammers.

"Really? You don't know Hayden Chambers either?" I scowl at her.

"No," she shakes her head. "Whoever has told you that I do is lying to you Shane. I don't know what this is about, but I would never do anything to hurt you."

"Liar!" I snarl.

"Shane, please listen to me," she pleads as she places a hand on my arm and I shrug it off.

"I have to admit, I would never have suspected you in a million years. You played it so well. But it all makes perfect sense now. You worked for the Ivanovs years ago. You have the contacts. You also have the know-how to make sure those contracts needed all of our signatures and I have no doubt you used some of your old legal contacts to make sure that meeting with our new lawyers happened on the date and time that was convenient for you."

She glares at me but she doesn't speak so I go on.

"You knew Alexei Ivanov. You found out about his other kid

and saw him as the perfect pawn in your little plan. How did you get him on board? Offer him money? Threaten him?"

The slightest smirk plays on her lips and I have to stop myself from snapping her neck right now.

A sound behind us makes us both turn and I nod to Conor as he makes his way along the hallway toward us. "For someone in bed with the Russians I'd have expected you to have slightly better security," Conor says as he pockets the small knife he uses to pick locks. He's never come across one he couldn't beat.

"Are you going to come with us quietly, or is Conor here going to have to carry you to my car unconscious?" I ask her.

Her lip trembles and right on cue, here come the water-works. "Please, Shane," she wails.

"For fuck's sake." I shake my head at Conor and he steps closer to her, more than ready and willing to knock her out.

"I'll come with you," she shrieks as she shrinks back from Conor. "Don't touch me!"

"Gladly," Conor snarls.

"Let's go then," I say as I nod to the door.

She swallows hard but then she starts to walk to the door. She looks around the house before she leaves and I wonder if she's thinking she's never going to see the place again.

She'd be right.

"Where are you taking me?" she whimpers as we walk toward my car.

"I think my wife and my brothers might have some questions for you, don't you?" I snap as I push her forward. She stumbles on the gravel path, falling to her knees. She looks up at me, tears in her eyes as she waits for me to help her.

"Get up. Now!" I hiss.

"Shane. Why are you doing this to me?" she sniffs as she

pushes herself to a standing position and brushes the dust from her knees.

"Because I finally realized what an evil, selfish bitch you are," I snap. "Now get in the fucking car or I will let Conor break your neck right now and bury you in your own fucking yard."

Suddenly the fake tears are gone and she goes back to glaring at me. "You're making a huge mistake," she hisses.

"We'll see about that."

Once Erin is inside the car, I climb on the back seat beside her and lock the doors. As Conor is pulling the SUV away from the curbside, my cellphone rings. Glancing at the screen I see Jessie's name flashing on the screen and I press the cell to my ear.

"Hello, sweetheart," I answer.

"Shane. It's Erin. She's the one behind it."

"I know. Conor and I have her. Are you with the twins?"

"Yes. We have Hayden. We're bringing him to the basement so we can decide..." She trails off. "He's just a kid, Shane."

"I know," I say as I look at Erin and wonder what promises she made to Hayden – or what threats.

"We'll meet you there."

"Okay. See you soon. I love you."

"Love you too," I reply and don't miss the look of disgust on Erin's face. I end the call and put my cell back into my pocket.

"How did you even find that kid?" I ask her.

"I'm good at my job," she says with a shrug. "You always underestimated me, Shane."

"I obviously did," I say and she smiles, mistaking that for a compliment.

"How long have you known about him?"

"Since I worked for the Russians."

I frown at her. "That was over ten years ago."

"I know. Alexei always knew he had a son, but he had no

interest in him. He was only ever focused on finding that slut of a daughter of his," she cackles.

Conor slams on the brake, bringing the car to a screeching halt as he turns in his seat.

"You ever call her that again and I will cut out your fucking tongue," he snarls.

Erin rolls her eyes and leans back in her seat, giving me a smirk. I take a deep breath and squeeze my fists together. She will pay for every slight against my wife soon enough, but right now I want information and she is so damn arrogant and pleased with herself, she's going to give it.

"So you always knew about Jessie then? Who she really was?"

"Not at first, no." She shakes her head. "Not until you came to my office with her and asked me to start looking into the Ivanovs."

"So it was you who told Alexei where she was?" I snarl at her.

"He already knew anyway. One of his men had recognized her. So bloody careless of her to work against the Bratva when you're supposed to be hiding from them."

"Well, she didn't know she was supposed to be hiding from them," I snarl, unable to stop myself from defending her.

"Hmm," Erin sniffs as she looks out of the window.

"And the brotherhood? What were they getting from all of this?"

"Power, of course. I met one of them while I was doing some work for Alexei and when I told them that there were not one but two Ivanov heirs out there, they were more than happy to help me rid the world of one of them so they could use the other to take over."

"So your grand plan was to replace Vlad with Hayden so

that the brotherhood had someone at the top they could control?"

"I don't care what the Bratva do. Whether Vlad or the brotherhood are in control is of no consequence to me."

"You did all this just to get rid of Jessie?"

"Bingo!" she says with a cackle and I stare at her. She must be having some kind of psychotic episode. "So what is your grand plan now, Shane? Kill me and bury me in an unmarked grave?" she laughs.

"Bingo!" Conor pipes up.

"Shane could never kill someone he loves," she replies coolly.

I swear she is unhinged. "I don't love you, Erin," I remind her.

"But you did. And a part of you always will, Shane. You can't deny that no matter how much you want to." She flutters her eyelashes at me and I shake my head in bewilderment.

CHAPTER 48
JESSIE

After Hayden had told us about Erin's plans to assist the brotherhood to take back control of the Bratva, Mikey and Liam bundled him into the SUV. Liam drove while Mikey sat in the back with my half-brother, because we both agreed that Liam couldn't be trusted not to kill Hayden on route. I have never seen him so angry. He is a ball of pent-up rage and aggression and if his brothers don't get back here soon, then I don't know if Mikey and I will be able to control him.

Liam parks the car in the basement of the apartment building and jumps out, opening the back passenger door and pulling Hayden from the car. He pushes my half-brother toward the far side of the basement while Mikey and I climb out of the car.

Hayden's hands are tied and he stumbles to the floor. He is still crying. He has cried all the way here. At first he kept telling me how sorry he was, how much he came to care for me, how terrified he was that Erin was going to have him killed. I have no doubt that she would have, too. Evil bitch.

I knew something was off about her from the moment I met

her. If everything had gone to plan and the brotherhood had managed to get me that day in the ice cream store, I have no doubt she would have pinned everything on him. He would have been killed anyway, but by the Irish Mafia instead of the Bratva.

My heart hurts a little as I look at him cowering on the floor. He was right when he said this is not his world and while he has no experience of the struggles that I've endured, I am glad about that. If my brothers were still alive, I would want them to live a life free of pain and fear. Hayden was broke and all alone in the world when Erin found him and offered him an easy way out. Who can say what we would do if we were in a position like that? And I do believe he has a good heart in there somewhere.

Hayden is sprawled on the floor. Liam grabs hold of his hair, gripping it tightly as he pulls my half-brother's head back, exposing his neck so that I can see his thick vein pulsing. Snot and tears run down his face.

"No," he whimpers as Liam raises his clenched fist, preparing to bring it crashing down onto Hayden's face.

"Liam!" I shout, about to run to him but Mikey grabs hold of me. I struggle in his grip but he holds me firmly in place.

Liam doesn't hear me, or if he does, he ignores me as he punches Hayden in the face and I hear the sickening crunch of bone.

"Liam. No!" I scream as I try to wrench myself from Mikey's arms.

"I can't let you go over there, Red," Mikey hisses in my ear. "He's lost it. He could hurt you."

I see Liam preparing to punch Hayden again. "Mikey, please. If he kills Hayden, he'll never forgive himself. Please let me go to him?"

Mikey sighs deeply but he lets me go and I run to Liam and my half-brother, with Mikey on my heels.

"Liam!" I shout as I reach him, still holding Hayden in his grip as he pummels him with his fist.

He ignores me, completely lost in the grip of his rage. "Liam, please!" I try again, conscious of Mikey hovering beside us. With no option left, I jump on Liam's back.

"Jessie! What the fuck are you doing?" Mikey roars but I tune him out, wrapping my arms around Liam's neck.

"Liam, please. It wasn't his fault," I say in his ear.

He tries to shake me off but I hold on as Mikey joins us too, trying to pull me off his twin while berating me for acting crazy.

Beneath us, Hayden cowers on the floor, his arms over his head as he tries his best to protect himself from Liam's onslaught.

"Liam, please, baby," I plead with him as tears run down my cheeks. "Please don't do this. I love you so much. Don't kill my little brother."

I cling to him as Mikey tries to wrench me free, but Liam stands straight, dropping his fists to his sides and I'm left dangling from his neck like a soap on a rope. I let go of him and slide to the floor.

He turns around to face me, his handsome face full of anger. "He really means that much to you?" he snarls as he wipes the sweat from his brow.

I blink at him in confusion. He thinks I only did this for Hayden. I place my hand on his cheek and his face softens just a little. "You mean everything to me," I whisper. "You would never forgive yourself if you killed him, because this wasn't his fault. Erin manipulated him."

"He could have gotten you and our babies killed, Jessie!" he snaps.

"I know. But he didn't."

His shoulders drop slightly and I feel the wave of relief

washing over me. I wrap my arms around his neck again and rest my head on his chest as he pulls me into his huge arms.

"Looks like you just got yourself a reprieve, kid," Mikey says to Hayden as he helps him up from the floor.

"Thank you," I whisper to Liam.

"I did it for you, not him," he growls.

"I know you did."

We're interrupted by another SUV pulling into the basement. We stand and watch as Shane and Conor climb out, before Conor reaches onto the back seat and pulls Erin out too. My blood freezes in my veins at the sight of her.

Conor holds onto her arm as they walk toward us. He pushes her onto the floor at my feet when they reach us and she shrieks her disapproval.

Liam releases me from his embrace, but he wraps a protective arm around my waist.

"You okay, Angel?" Conor asks with a frown as he gives me a quick hug.

"Yes. I'm good. And the babies seem good too," I add, skimming my hands over my rounded belly and Conor rests one of his large hands over mine before stepping back and training his glare back on Erin.

"Thank fuck for that," Shane says with a sigh as he hugs me tightly and presses a soft kiss on my forehead. Erin looks up at us and pain is so clearly etched on her face that it almost makes me smile. Nothing that happens from here on in could possibly hurt her more than what Shane just did.

"What happened to him?" Conor indicates his head to Hayden, who is practically held up by Mikey with blood pouring from his mouth and nose.

"Liam almost killed him but Jessie asked him not to," Mikey says matter-of-factly.

Shane and Conor both look at me.

"It wasn't his fault. He had no idea what Erin was really planning. She wanted you to think it was Hayden who was behind it all, so then you two could run off into the sunset." I say that last part to Shane and his face contorts with anger before he looks at Erin who sits on the floor, looking at us all like we're something she just stepped in. Even in defeat she thinks she's better than everyone else.

Shane crouches down so he's at her eye level. "Tell me that this wasn't all just some ploy to get me back," he hisses.

She sits straighter, brushing imaginary dust from her clothes as she looks him straight in the eye. "We belong together, Shane. I can give you babies. Lots of them. And you could guarantee every one of them would be yours," she sneers as she looks at his brothers and me.

Bitch!

Liam winces beside me as though he expects Erin to get a punch in the mouth for what she just said, but Shane would never hit her. He's not that guy. Besides, he knows a much more effective way to cause her pain that involves nothing other than his words.

"I thought I made it clear, back in Ireland, that you mean nothing to me, Erin. Less than nothing. You are insignificant," he spits.

She narrows her eyes at him. "You don't mean that. You love me. We'd still be together if it wasn't for your needy little brothers! I'd have fucked them all too if I'd known that was what it would take."

Liam pulls me tighter as Mikey screws his face up in disgust.

Conor scowls at her. "I wouldn't touch you with a fifty-foot pole, you piece of shit."

Shane laughs. "Nobody in this room wants you, Erin. Nobody likes you. Jessie could be carrying a complete stranger's baby and I'd still love her and her babies more than anything or anyone else in this entire fucking world." He pulls a handgun from the waistband of his suit pants and presses it against her temple.

Her lip trembles. "Shane! You don't have to do this."

"You tried to murder my wife and our children."

"You can't kill me. You loved me once. I know you did. This isn't you," she pleads.

"You have no idea who I am," he snarls at her then he looks up at me. "You want to do this, sweetheart?"

I shake my head. I hate Erin but I don't want to blow her head off.

"She doesn't have the balls to shoot me," Erin spits as she glares at me, her face so full of venom and jealousy that it distorts her once beautiful features. "She's a fucking whore and a slut and I hope her babies are born deformed and screaming in pain because what she does with you all is sick and unnatural."

The anger that ripples through my husbands is so pronounced that I feel it in every fiber of my being. Shane grabs her by the throat and Mikey, Liam and Conor edge forward but their anger pales into insignificance compared to mine. "Stop!" I hiss, holding up my hand and Liam, Mikey and Conor freeze on the spot. "Let her go," I say to Shane.

He releases his grip on her throat and stands straight. Anger bubbles through my chest like a mini volcano just erupted in my gut.

I lean over her. "You are an evil bitch!" I hiss. "Our babies are going to be strong and beautiful. They will be given more love than you can even comprehend. You think I don't have the balls to kill you? I have killed men much bigger, stronger and smarter than you, Erin. I could rip your throat out now and I wouldn't feel a shred of remorse, but I won't. You want to know why?"

She glares at me, her eyes burning into mine as though she's hoping I'll burst into flames just from the heat of her gaze.

"I want you to look into the eyes of the man you love. The same man who despises you and who adores me and our babies, as he ends your pathetic existence."

Her eyes flicker to Shane and the change in her face is instant. Tears roll down her face.

"Shane!" she pleads. "I love you."

She's a smart woman and she knows her best odds are to try and talk her way out of this. To try and reason with the man standing beside her, who indeed did love her once. I reach for Shane's free hand and lace my fingers through his.

He frowns deeply and I see the emotions flicker over Erin's face. The soft sigh escaping her lips as she believes he's going to let her go.

Seems like Shane was right. She doesn't know him at all. The sound of the gunshot rings around the small room and Erin drops to the floor. Blood pools around her head and her lifeless eyes stare up at me accusingly.

I blink at her. I don't feel a shred of remorse. She tried to kill me and my unborn children. She was going to pin the blame on Hayden and I can't even begin to imagine the pain my husbands would have forced him to endure if she had succeeded.

Shane stands and wipes the spatters of Erin's blood from his hand while Conor takes the gun from him.

"Fuck!" I hear Hayden whisper behind me.

"You're definitely one of the family now, kid," Mikey laughs. "Now we've beat you up and made you an accessory to murder."

I turn and glare at him. "Mikey!"

"I'm just playing, Red." He arches an eyebrow at me.

I turn my attention back to Shane who is staring at Erin's lifeless body. I wrap my arms around him. "Are you okay?"

He slides his arms around my waist again, squeezing me tightly as he buries his face in my hair. "Yes, but I'll feel a hell of a lot better once we get you upstairs and checked out properly, so let's move."

"What about me?" Hayden asks as he wipes the blood from his nose.

All four of my husbands look at me. "It's your call," Liam says with a sigh.

"Come upstairs and we'll get you cleaned up. And then we can talk," I say and Hayden nods, giving me a small grateful smile.

"She just saved your fucking life," Liam snarls at him and Hayden flinches making Mikey chuckle.

"I'll call someone to clean this up," Conor says as he takes his cell out of his pocket and dials a number. He walks ahead, barking instructions to someone as I walk between Liam and Shane, each of them with an arm wrapped around my waist while Mikey walks with Hayden to the elevator.

CHAPTER 49
JESSIE

Mikey takes Hayden to the bathroom to fetch the first aid kit and help him get cleaned up while Shane, Conor, Liam and I sit at the kitchen island.

"What the fuck are we going to do about that kid?" Shane asks with a sigh as he looks at the doorway. "He has seen and knows far too much."

"I agree," Liam says.

"You can't kill him," I warn them.

Shane rubs a hand over his jaw. "I know."

"So what then?" Conor asks.

"Can you let me handle it?" I whisper.

The three of them look at me. They are used to making the decisions like this and ordinarily I have no problem with that, but like it or not, Hayden is my family.

Liam lets out a long slow breath and Conor shrugs his shoulders as they wait for Shane's answer. He will always be the head of our family unit.

"Do what you think is best, Jessie," Shane finally agrees and I throw my arms around his neck and kiss him on the lips.

"Thank you," I whisper.

"Hey, we agreed too," Conor says with a laugh and so I pull him and Liam to me too and wrap my arms around all three of them as far as I possibly can.

HAYDEN IS CLEANED up and has some butterfly bandages on the cut above his eye. He is wearing one of the twins' t-shirts and it dwarfs him but at least it's not covered in blood. He sits opposite me at the kitchen table while my husbands hover nearby but they at least give us the illusion of privacy.

"I'm so sorry, Jessie," he says again.

"I know," I reply, placing my hand over his because I do believe that. "You're a good person, Hayden. You don't belong in this world."

He swallows hard. "I want to make it up to you though. I want to be your brother, and an uncle." He looks down at my rounded belly and I rub a hand over it protectively. Maybe if I didn't have these two little babies to think about I would handle this differently, but I do. And they are the most important things in this world to me. I wanted him to be my brother so much. I was desperate for some family I could call my own, but I realized that I already have the best one I could have ever hoped for.

"I can never trust you, Hayden. I know you had your reasons, but you betrayed me."

He chokes down a sob. "Jessie!"

"This is hard for me, too." I wipe a tear from my eye. "But I can't have people I don't trust around my children. They won't allow people they don't trust around their children." I look over at my husbands. "I would never be myself around you, Hayden, and that is not the kind of relationship I want. It would be unfair to all of us."

"But I can prove myself, Jessie. Please let me," he sniffs as tears roll down his cheeks.

"You don't have to prove anything to me, Hayden. I love you just as you are, but I can't have you in my life."

He blinks at me but he nods his understanding.

"I've paid off your mom's medical bills and there is fifty thousand dollars in your bank account."

"What?" he shakes his head. "No. Please don't. I don't deserve that."

I squeeze his hand in mine again. "You deserve a good life without the worry of a debt that should never have been yours. Go do some of that traveling you dreamed about."

"Thank you," he sniffs as he wipes his cheeks.

Conor walks over to us and places a hand on Hayden's shoulder. "Time to go, kid."

"I'm so sorry," he says to me again and I stand up and pull him into a hug.

"I know. I forgive you. Go live your life without any regrets. Okay?"

"Okay." He nods and then he turns and walks away, with Conor escorting him.

"Kid," Shane says as he walks past.

"Yeah?" Hayden stops and looks at him.

"Your sister is the best person you will ever meet. She saved your life today, because every single one of us would prefer to carve you into pieces and toss you into the Hudson."

Hayden swallows hard.

"She is also the smartest person you will ever meet, and make no mistake, if you ever speak her name to anyone, or discuss anything of what happened here, she will find out, and I will kill you."

"I w-won't... e-ever..." Hayden stammers.

"Good. Now have a nice life, kid," Shane smiles at him and then Conor escorts him out of the room.

"You think I did the right thing?" I ask once Conor and Hayden are gone.

"Yes," Shane, Mikey and Liam say in unison.

AFTER HAYDEN LEFT and we all took a shower — separately to my disappointment, we are sitting in the den waiting for our take-out to arrive.

I'm sitting on Liam's lap and he is holding on so tightly to me, I can barely move.

"Liam," I squirm in his grip but I smile at him. "I'm not going anywhere. You can relax a little."

"Sorry, baby," he whispers before he kisses my forehead.

"I think we can all agree, you are never leaving the apartment again without at least one of us, Jessie," Conor says as he flops onto the sofa beside us and his brothers mumble their agreement.

I suppose they expect me to refuse and to assert my independence like I usually would, but I'm kinda over getting kidnapped. Besides, there's not just me to think of now.

"Fine by me," I breathe as I snuggle against Liam's chest.

Mikey snorts laughing while Conor stares at me. "Did you just agree to that with no arguing at all?" he asks with a flash of his eyebrows.

Liam places a hand on my forehead. "She's delirious," he says with a smile and I nudge him in the ribs.

"I am not. I'm just not overly keen on being kidnapped by some psycho again is all. I mean three kidnappings is enough for any woman to take."

"And that's not including the times we kidnapped you," Mikey adds with a chuckle.

"Exactly." I grin at him.

"I've already decided I'm sticking a tracker in your ass," Shane says with a completely straight face.

"The hell you are!" I snap.

"Now, there's our little firecracker," Mikey chuckles.

"Yes, the hell I am, sweetheart," Shane goes on.

I look at Mikey, Conor and Liam and they're nodding their agreement. "Fine! If I'm having a tracker in my ass then so are all of you."

"Fine by me," Liam says.

"Me too," Mikey agrees.

"Seems like a good idea," Conor adds.

"You've already decided this then?" I fold my arms across my chest in feigned indignation but actually a tracker is a great idea.

"Yep," Shane says with a nod.

"And you're getting one too?"

He winks at me. "Yup."

"It's not going in my ass though!"

"I agree. Jessie's ass is like a work of art. What if it causes a lump or something?" Mikey agrees with me.

"Your arm then," Shane says with a shrug. "I don't care where, as long as it is somewhere in that hot little body of yours."

The heat between my thighs makes me squirm in Liam's lap again.

"Careful, Shane," Liam chuckles. "You know it literally takes nothing to have our girl on the edge these days."

"Hmm," Mikey says as he walks behind the sofa and bends down to kiss the top of my head. "Pregnancy makes you even hornier than normal, Red."

"I am not horny," I insist.

"You are," Liam whispers against my ear before he presses a

kiss against the spot on my neck that makes me weak at the knees.

"Well, I am now that you're kissing my neck," I moan softly making him laugh. "You all tease me about being horny but that's because between the four of you walking around here half-naked, the kissing, the filthy talk, the ass grabbing, it's like I'm being constantly edged." I pant, blowing a strand of hair out of my eyes.

"Edged?" Shane arches an eyebrow at me. "You're never kept waiting long enough to be truly edged, sweetheart."

"True," Conor agrees. "We all love making you come too much."

"But if you want to keep complaining about being edged, we can make that happen," Shane adds with a wicked grin.

"No thank you," I whisper. "I'm pretty sure orgasm denial is bad for the babies. Isn't that right, Mikey?" I smile sweetly at him.

"If you say it is, Red, then it is," he winks at me.

"Thank you," I whisper.

"Orgasms in general are good for the babies though, right?" Shane asks.

"Actually, there is some research that suggests the babies experience the positive feelings of an orgasm," Mikey says. "And they can also strengthen the pelvic muscles which is good preparation for labor."

"Fuck! Jessie's pelvic muscles must be strong enough that those babies will just slide out with no effort," Liam chuckles and I give him another nudge in the ribs.

"Where the fuck do you read all this, shit, Mikey?" Conor asks.

"On the internet, dumbass."

"Oh, well it must be true then," Conor replies.

"I don't care where he read it, I'm willing to believe it," Shane chuckles too.

"Are you planning on giving me plenty of orgasms then, Mr. Ryan?" I narrow my eyes at him.

"Not just me." He stands up and walks over to me, cupping my chin in his hand. "We're all taking a week off and going to the lake house. So, you're gonna be on bed-rest, sweetheart."

Warmth and wetness floods my pussy at the thought and I actually gasp out loud making all four of them chuckle.

"We're all taking a week off?" I whisper.

"Yeah, baby," Liam whispers.

"I figure we all need it," Shane says as he straightens up and the sound of the intercom signals our take-out is here.

"I'll get it," Mikey runs toward the door.

"I'm starving," I say as my stomach growls in agreement.

"Me too," Liam groans.

"Food and then bed, Angel," Conor says with a grin.

"Sounds perfect to me," I sigh as I snuggle against Liam's chest again. The events of the day are heavy on my mind and this is the perfect way to deal with them.

Shane strolls to the window and I wonder how he is holding up after what happened with Erin. He always takes care of everyone else so well.

I climb off Liam's lap and walk to stand behind him. Wrapping my arms around his waist, I rest my cheek against the warm skin of his back. "Are you okay?" I whisper.

He turns around and wraps his arms around me too. "Yes," he says before kissing my forehead.

"It's okay if you're not," I remind him.

"I know," he says with a nod. "It's never easy to take someone's life, Jessie." He brushes my hair from my face. "But it was the only decision to make. I cannot have my family put at risk. I am one hundred percent okay with the choices I made today and I would make them every damn day to make sure you and our babies are safe."

I feel a huge kick in my abdomen and to my surprise, Shane looks down at my rounded belly. The babies are constantly kicking me but they haven't been felt by anyone else yet.

"What the fuck?" he whispers.

"Did you feel that?" I giggle.

"Fuck, yeah I did," he laughs, his eyes shining as he steps back and puts his hands on my belly and they kick again, right where he is touching me. He keeps one hand on my stomach and places the other on my cheek, rubbing the pad of his thumb softly over my skin. "I can't believe you're making me a dad, sweetheart."

"I can't believe it either," I breathe.

"I hope you know you are stuck with me for all eternity, because I will love you to the end of this lifetime and into the next. We really are from the same star," he says, his voice cracking with emotion.

I have never seen him so raw and vulnerable and it makes my heart sing. "I love you so much," I say as a tear rolls down my face and he brushes it away.

"Boys," he shouts. "Get your asses over here."

"What?" they shout back as they come running over.

"I felt the babies kicking," he tells them with the biggest smile I have ever seen in my life.

"Fuck! For real?" Mikey asks as he stands beside his older brother.

"Yeah, right here," he takes Mikey's hand and places it on my stomach and then he does the same with Liam's while Conor stands behind me and slides his arms around my waist, resting a hand near his brothers'.

"Hey babies," Mikey shouts. "It's your daddies here."

We wait a few seconds and they kick again and the looks of pure joy on their faces makes me start to cry.

"This will never get old," Liam says as tears fill his eyes too. "Do they do this all the time?"

"Yeah. Kind of," I sniff as I smile at him.

"I'm not gonna be able to keep my hands off you now, Red," Mikey grins at me.

"No change there then," Conor mumbles in my ear.

Shane cups my face in his hands. "You are so fucking beautiful, you know that?"

"You're fucking incredible, baby," Liam adds.

"You fucking are, Red," Mikey agrees.

Conor kisses my neck softly. "I'm so fucking proud of you, Angel."

My cheeks flush red at their praise. I spent so long trying to fade into the background. Trying not to draw attention to myself. Making myself look small and unremarkable. But from the moment these four men laid eyes on me, I have been neither of those things. So when they tell me I am beautiful, or incredible, or any of the other wonderful things they say, I believe them.

"Thank you," I whisper.

CHAPTER 50

JESSIE

4 MONTHS LATER

I grab the tomatoes from the refrigerator and hand them to Mikey. "I wish I could help chop them for you," I chuckle, rubbing a hand over my gigantic pregnant belly. "But it's kinda hard to reach the counter top."

He slides a hand onto my behind. "You just go sit your beautiful ass down and leave dinner to me. Besides, you need to keep up your strength for later. I mean it is date night." He arches an eyebrow at me.

Being heavily pregnant has not dampened my sexual appetite one bit, and in fact pregnancy hormones have made me hornier than ever. Group sex isn't quite as easy or straightforward as it used to be, but I have to give it to my boys, they sure are creative.

"I can't wait," I purr.

He squeezes my ass in his large hand before bending his head and kissing me. The sudden and unexpected splash of water at our feet makes both of us pull back and look down at the floor.

Instinctively, I place a hand on my stomach. "Oh, God!"

"Did you just squirt because of how good my kiss was, or..." Mikey asks, his eyes wide.

I punch him playfully on the chest. "My water broke, dumbass."

"Fuck!" he breathes.

"Come on, Mikey. This is not a drill. You've been in training for this for nine months. What do we do?" I ask, completely forgetting everything in my birthing plan except for the fact that I am not going to hospital. No freaking way!

"Shane!" Mikey hollers and a few seconds later Shane comes running through the door closely followed by Liam and Conor.

"The babies," I say.

"Her water just broke," Mikey adds.

"Call Brooke and get her out here now," Shane say calmly to Conor as he walks over and takes my hand. "Come on, sweetheart. Let's get you somewhere comfortable."

"You think she'll get here in time?" I ask, starting to panic now. We're having a last weekend at the lake house before the babies arrive. We should be in the city for this.

"We got plenty of time," Shane assures me. "You got any contractions yet?"

"I don't think so," I say with a shrug. "I've been having twinges all day but nothing that I'd call a contraction. But I have no idea what one feels like."

"Let's just get you to bed," he says and we walk out of the kitchen with Liam hovering anxiously behind us while Conor calls my OB-GYN and Mikey cleans the kitchen floor.

"No needles, Shane. Promise me," I say as we walk through the house.

"No needles."

"Even if I'm screaming in pain. Do not stick one of those things in me! You got it?"

"I got it," he assures me.

"I will never let you touch me again if you let anyone stick me with a needle."

"I won't," he smirks at me.

"What's so funny?" I ask.

"Just thinking about how much fun I could have teasing you while you tried to keep that promise."

"You're an arrogant asshole, have I ever told you that?" I grin at him.

"Many, many times."

"I love you though." I suck in a breath as a sharp pain slices through my abdomen.

"I know," he says before he sees me wincing and his brows furrow in concern.

"Fuck, that hurt!" I hiss.

"Then that was a contraction, sweetheart. Come here." Before I can protest, he scoops me into his arms and carries me to the bedroom before laying me down on the bed.

"Brooke is on her way," Conor says as he walks into the room.

"Let's meet some freaking babies," Mikey shouts excitedly as he walks in straight behind him.

He high fives Liam and the two of them start to chatter like excited toddlers while Conor comes to sit on the bed beside me.

"You know those two are going to fall to pieces the minute they see me in a little pain, right?" I say to Shane and Conor.

"Yup," Conor nods his agreement.

I'VE BEEN in labor for eight hours now. I'm tired. I'm in pain. I'm hot. And everything anyone does to help cool me down or soothe me just makes me want to rip their head off. Why the hell did I decide on no decent pain relief? Oh, yeah. Needles.

"You're almost fully dilated, Jessie," Brooke says, her voice soft and calm. "I'm going to need you to push soon."

She looks around the room at my four anxious husbands hovering nearby and rolls her eyes.

"Hey, I know this is exciting, but there are kind of too many people right here in the loading dock area, you know what I mean?"

"Sorry, Doc," Mikey mumbles.

"Two of you is perfect. One each side of Jessie to give her what she needs. Okay?" Brooke offers.

"You two take the first one and we'll take the second," Mikey says to Conor and Shane.

"They're babies not taxi-cabs, Mikey!" I hiss as a contraction squeezes my abdomen, and he slopes away from the bed.

"Okay, firecracker," Shane says softly as he brushes my damp hair from my forehead and places a cool cloth there.

"Thank you," I whisper as my contraction subsides. "I'm sorry, Mikey."

"Don't apologize," Brooke admonishes me. "You're about to give birth to two babies, honey, You scream and curse as much as you want to. Right?"

"Right," the boys agree.

I SWEAR, pushing a baby's head out of my vagina is the most intense pain I have ever experienced in my life. I squeeze Shane's and Conor's hands so tightly I worry I might break their fingers, but then it would be nothing compared to squeezing out a giant-headed Ryan baby.

"One final push, Jessie," Brooke says as Shane and Conor tell me how well I'm doing and brush my hair from my sweaty face.

"Argh!" I scream, making a sound I didn't even know I was capable of and then it happens. Our beautiful baby is out.

"It's a girl," Brooke cheers as our daughter takes her first breath and her cries fill the air. Mikey and Liam are there, cutting the cord and helping Brooke clean our baby girl up a little so she can lie on my chest. Conor and Shane stay by my side as tears of pure happiness run down my face.

"Look at her, Momma." Brooke holds up the most beautiful thing I have ever seen in my life and I swear my heart is about to burst out of my chest with pure joy.

She hands her to Mikey who places her on my chest and I wrap my hands around her tiny, perfect body as I stare down at her perfect face.

"Ow!" I hiss as another contraction squeezes my uterus in a vise.

"I got her," Conor says as he lifts our daughter and cradles her in his arms. Shane kisses my forehead before he follows Conor, and Mikey and Liam take their places.

"One more baby and we're all done," Brooke says with a reassuring smile.

"Didn't you say the boy was bigger than the girl?" I swallow as I look at Brooke.

"Uh-huh, but that doesn't mean the birth will be any different."

"Unless he has a giant head," I breathe as the pain starts to subside for a few glorious seconds.

"His head is perfectly proportionate to his body. Now let's do this," Brooke says and I swear she was a cheerleader in high school.

I hang onto Mikey and Liam's hands and scream as another contraction hits.

"Should it really be hurting this much, Doc?" Mikey asks.

"Have you ever tried to push a coconut out of your penis, Michael?" she snaps.

"No." He winces, his free hand instinctively flying to his

crotch.

"Isn't there anything you can give her to stop the pain?" Liam asks.

"No. It's too late for pain relief now," Brooke replies.

"I feel sick," Mikey mumbles.

"I thought you were the one who was all prepared for this birth?" I pant as he turns a strange shade of gray.

"Fuck!" Liam breathes out as he wipes sweat from his brow.

"Yeah, I think we're going to need a rotation," Brooke says, turning to Conor and Shane. "I'm not sure these two are prepared for this next part. Can one of you step back in?"

"Yeah, Shane will take care of you, baby," Liam says, kissing me softly before he and Mikey step away from the bed.

Shane walks back over to me and takes my hand in his while Conor is holding our daughter.

I cling onto him, my fingers digging into his forearm as another wave of pain sears through my body. I'm so damn tired. Every part of my body is screaming in agony.

"It hurts," I whimper.

He brushes my sweaty hair back from my damp forehead. "I know, sweetheart," he says softly. "All the best things do."

I suck in a breath and close my eyes.

"But you are the toughest person in this room and you got this, Jessie." He squeezes my hand in his. "I'm gonna be right here every second. Okay?"

"Yeah," I gasp as another contraction almost floors me.

"It's time to push again, Jessie," Brooke says and I nod my understanding because to speak feels like it would take up far too much energy. A few seconds later, Conor is at my side again and I look up to see Mikey holding our daughter as Liam stares at her adoringly.

"I guess I'll just take the next one," Conor says with a wink.

"Fuck!" I screech as I give another huge push.

EPILOGUE
JESSIE

6 Months Later

It's dark when I wake. My breasts are heavy and tender. I need to feed my babies. I can't believe I haven't heard them crying already. I reach out, expecting to feel one of my boys' hard bodies, but there is nothing but cool cotton sheets.

I sit up, blinking at the clock on the nightstand. It's nine a.m. Damn blackout blinds make me so disoriented sometimes. I switch on the bedside lamp and confirm I'm alone in the huge bed. Pulling the covers back, I climb out of bed and look at the monitor for the camera over the twins' cribs. They are empty. The icy fingers that grip my heart are never far away. They have been there all my life and I suspect they'll never leave.

My babies are fine though. Obviously being taken care of by their adoring daddies. The icy fingers melt away and I change out of my nursing tank top and pull on one of Liam's soft cotton t-shirts instead.

The smell of bacon wafts from the kitchen, making me smile as I wander down the hallway. When I walk into the kitchen the sight makes me stop and stare for a few moments. The rush of pure joy I feel almost overwhelms me.

Mikey is wearing his 'Kiss the Chef' apron while he cooks but Conor stands beside him, holding baby Ella and the two of them are singing to her. The fact they are singing along to a hip hop song and the lyrics are entirely inappropriate doesn't bother our daughter one tiny bit and she giggles at her daddies.

On the other side of the room, Finn is sitting on Shane's lap while Liam feeds him some baby oatmeal. They have just started weaning and I'm relieved I'm no longer their only source of food. Not that my gorgeous husbands haven't done their share of night feeds because I pump every day, too. The twins sleep until six a.m. now though and we've moved them to their own nursery. It has a camera and security system that the White House would be proud of, and for the first week they were in their own room, we all sat up half the night watching them.

"There she is," Mikey says with a grin as he sees me.

Conor turns with Ella in his arms and waves her chubby little hand at me. "There's your beautiful momma, baby."

She giggles and I swear my heart is going to burst.

"Morning, sweetheart," Shane says.

I walk to the breakfast table and sit beside him while he and Liam finish giving Finn his breakfast. Leaning down, I give our son a kiss on his plump cheek and he wipes some oatmeal on my face as a thank you, making us all laugh. "Why didn't you all wake me? I slept so late," I say as I wipe my face.

"You deserved a lie in," Shane says with a shrug.

"Yeah," Liam agrees. "And you were snoring when I woke up so I didn't want to wake you."

"I was not snoring. Was I?"

"Not that I remember," Shane shakes his head. "You sure it wasn't her moaning my name that you heard?"

"Shane!" I admonish him and my cheeks flush pink as I remember him waking me up with his hand in my panties and then five minutes later he was fucking me while his brothers slept around us. It's not an unusual occurrence. We all gave up on the idea of separate rooms and sleep in the same bed every night now. I am often woken by one of them, or sometimes I do the waking. Sometimes another brother will join us, or if I'm very lucky they all will.

"Oh, I heard that too," Liam chuckles softly. "I was planning on joining you both but you took your sweet time making her come, bro. I fell back asleep."

Shane covers Finn's ears. "I took my time on purpose. Asshole!" he whispers and I giggle.

Just then Conor comes over with Ella and I take her from his arms and bury my face in her neck, inhaling her sweet-smelling, baby skin. Conor gives me a quick kiss on the forehead before he goes to help Mikey bring the food over for breakfast. At the sight of the pancakes, Ella squeals and giggles.

"She's sure got her mom's sweet tooth," Mikey chuckles as he slices a small piece off and hands it to her.

"Mikey, she's too young!" I admonish him.

"Relax. It's low sugar. Low salt. She only sucks on it," he says with a shrug.

"Here let me put her in her chair so you can eat," Conor says as he takes her from me again and places her in her high chair next to me. Liam puts Finn in his too and Mikey hands our son a small slice of pancake.

Then we all sit and eat our breakfast, talking about our plans for the day and later tonight. Whether we should take the twins to the park this afternoon or to the zoo. What movie we might watch when they go to sleep and we've all finished work for the day. The twins have brought a sense of balance to our lives. Nobody works at night anymore unless there's an emergency. The brothers have employed managers for the club and their security business. Shane sometimes works for a few hours in his office during the evening, but he's always done by eight p.m.

I look around at my wonderful family and wonder if any person in the entire world has ever been so happy as I am right now.

TWO WEEKS LATER

Pulling the hem of my short dress down over my thighs, I take a final peek at the twins. I stand staring at them, listening to their baby-soft snores and my heart feels like it's about to burst with happiness. Ella frowns in her sleep and when she does she looks just like Shane. When she smiles she looks like Mikey and then there are times when she looks just like Liam or Conor. Finn looks a little more like my side of the family with his bright blue eyes, but I see his daddies in him too.

I tiptoe away with my heels swinging in my hand, slipping them onto my feet once I've closed the door to the nursery. I can hear the sound of muffled voices as I reach the den and when I walk inside I swear I almost melt on the spot. My four husbands stand waiting for me. Every single suit they own is custom-made and fits their bodies perfectly, but there is something extra special about the ones they wear for our date nights.

They are each dressed in a dark navy one and a white dress shirt open at the collar. I have never seen four finer specimens of men. I mean any one of them would be a dream come true and I get all four. Wet heat floods my pussy and I'm beginning to regret my decision not to wear panties.

We've had some date nights since the twins were born, but none with all five of us like this. There is no one we trust enough to leave with our babies – well except for the woman who is standing beside them.

"Jessie, love, you look beautiful," Em says with a smile. She flew in two days ago and is staying with us for a month so she can spend time with her nephews and her new great-niece and nephew.

"Thank you," I whisper as Liam walks toward me. He slides his hands around my waist onto my ass. "You look fucking incredible, baby," he whispers as he pulls me to him. "And that dress is goddamn dangerous."

"I hope so." I grin at him.

"You know where everything is, right?" Shane says to Em as he checks his watch.

"Yes," she replies with a soft sigh and I can only imagine how many times he has gone through everything with her. He's always been overprotective of me and his brothers and the twins' arrival has made him one hundred times worse – or better depending on how you choose to look at it.

He spent so long worrying he'd be an awful father but he is amazing with our children. All of my husbands are and if it were possible, seeing them with our babies has made me fall in love with them even more than I already was.

"Now you lot get out of here and enjoy your date," she says, pushing them toward me and the door.

"They shouldn't wake until about six a.m.," I say as I'm surrounded by my four husbands. The heat from their bodies makes me clench my thighs together. Was I always this horny? "But if they do there's plenty of milk in the fridge."

"Jessie has expressed enough to last the week," Mikey chuckles.

"I'm sure I'll cope until tomorrow. Now go," she says with a smile.

"Thanks, Em," the boys say and we walk out of the room.

"Tomorrow?" I whisper.

"Yeah. We're staying in a hotel suite tonight," Conor replies.

"What?" I blink. "Then I need to grab some clothes."

"It's all taken care of, baby," Liam replies as he squeezes my ass before he looks down at his hand on my behind. "Are you wearing panties?"

"No," I whisper.

"Conor is going to lose his shit when he finds out," he chuckles.

"When I find out what?" Conor growls from behind us.

"That I'm not wearing any panties," I offer. I don't understand why it's an issue because I've done it plenty of times before. Is it because I'm a mom now?

"Shane!" Conor groans.

"It will be fine," Shane replies as he presses the button for the elevator and then he arches an eyebrow at me. "You're a fucking sexual deviant, Mrs. Ryan."

"She *is* a deviant and that's what I'm afraid of," Conor snaps.

"What's going on? Where are we even going?" I ask, confused by Conor's reaction. Ordinarily he would love me not wearing underwear.

"The Peacock Club," Conor replies.

"What?" I turn and blink at him.

"Yes, Angel. So you want to go put some panties on?"

Before I can reply, the elevator doors open. "Too late," Shane says as he steps inside and holds the door.

As soon as we're inside the elevator I'm surrounded by the four, hard, hot bodies of my husbands. Heat pools in my core as I think about the place we're going to and all of the possibilities that may lie before us. Conor is standing behind me and he slides a hand beneath my dress. "Fuck, Jessie," he growls as he skims my bare ass. "Why the hell aren't you wearing panties?"

"I thought it would be fun. I didn't realize we were going to The Peacock."

"And if you had?" Shane turns and grins at me.

"Stop it," I whisper. But he knows me so well, I still wouldn't have worn panties.

"Are you sure you're okay with this?" I ask Conor.

"Are you excited to go?" he breathes in my ear.

"Yes," I whimper as his fingertip grazes my pussy.

"Then, yes, I'm okay with it."

"That's if we make it out of the limo," Shane chuckles.

"That's if we make it out of the damn elevator," Mikey adds.

The limo is nearing the club and I finish the last of my champagne. I can't drink too much because it makes me giddy and I'm already overexcited at the thought of going to a sex club with the four sexiest and most attentive men on the entire planet.

Liam takes my glass from me as Mikey slides a hand between my thighs. "I love that you're not wearing panties," he breathes as he presses a soft kiss on my throat and I giggle.

"Enough," Conor warns him. "Don't have her on the edge before we even get into the place."

"I was just confirming the absence of panties," he protests. "You are wearing a bra, right, Red?"

"Of course I am. I think you'd notice if I wasn't."

"I would," Shane chuckles.

"Everyone would," I giggle. "I'd have milk stains all over my dress."

"I bet there are loads of perverts who are into that as well," Conor grunts.

"I can get why though," Mikey says. "Jessie's milk tastes amazing."

I press my lips together as Conor rolls his eyes. "Why am I not surprised that you've tasted it, Mikey? You deviant."

"Um, I have too," Liam admits.

"Really?" Conor stares at him.

"How have you not, bro?" Shane laughs loudly and Conor stares at the three of them.

"Take no notice of them, big guy. You don't have to taste it if you don't want to," I whisper as I curl my fingertips through his hair.

"I didn't know it was a fucking option. I thought boobs were off limits until the babies don't need them?"

"Well, yeah. But sometimes things just happen," Mikey says with a shrug.

"It's not like we fucking suckle on them or anything," Liam adds.

"Well..." Mikey says and then he ducks as Shane throws the cork from our champagne bottle at his head.

"You really are a fucking deviant, Mikey Ryan." He laughs harder and even Conor is smiling now.

I slide onto his lap and wrap my arms around his neck. "Do you feel left out, big guy?" I purr.

He smiles at me. "Kinda."

"You can try some later," I giggle.

I have seen The Peacock Club during the daytime before, during non-business hours, but to see it at night is something else. It is elegant and classy, all chrome and black and gold and shimmering lights. I gasp out loud as we walk through the huge mirrored doors into the main room.

The place is a kinkster's dream. There are people dressed in regular clothes just like us, mixed among people wearing collars and leashes, bondage gear, masks and feathers and capes and glitter.

I freaking love it here!

"Good evening, Mr. Ryan. Mrs. Ryan." All of the bouncers greet us as we pass, before the manager comes over and does the same. Then she tells she has reserved us the best private booth and assigned us their best waiter too.

"We'll go find our booth," Liam says and Shane nods to him.

"I just want to show Conor and Jessie the main floor," he winks to Liam and Mikey who chuckle in response. Mikey, Shane and Liam have been here at night before to do some club business but it's Conor's first time here too.

Shane gives Conor and me a brief tour of the club. Conor keeps his hands on my waist at all times, as though he's worried someone might run off with me, but the people here are for the most part a very respectful community who adhere to the strict code of conduct that the club has in place.

On one side of the club there is a dance floor but it's obviously not for dancing. There is a huge bed in the center and currently there are three people on it. Two guys and a girl. Guy one is eating the girl's pussy, while guy two is railing guy one.

"Wow!" I stand and stare unashamedly. "This place is amazing."

"It's something," Conor says.

"Hmm." Shane rubs a hand over his jaw.

"You don't want to take Jessie there?" Conor glares at his brother.

"No," Shane replies with a laugh. "But only because you wouldn't be into it, would you, sweetheart?" He snakes an arm around my waist.

"No. I mean I quite like a little exhibitionism, but I'd feel too exposed doing it right there in front of a crowd."

"Thank fuck!" Conor mutters.

"But the rooms downstairs," Shane arches an eyebrow at me. I remember them from our visit. There are twelve rooms in the basement. They can be private if patrons choose for them to be. Alternatively, each of them has a two way mirror where a small group can watch the activities.

"I like the rooms downstairs," I say biting on my lip and looking at Conor.

"Yeah. Me too. I'm gonna lock you in one and fuck you all night while we leave these three deviants up here."

"Conor," I giggle as he presses a soft kiss on my neck. "Come on and let's catch up with the twins."

As I turn to move, Shane stops me, standing behind Conor and me, he wraps an arm around each of us and pulls us closer so we can hear him whisper above the noise. "One day, Con, we are going to take her together in one of those rooms. We're going to let people watch and you're going to fucking love it."

The very idea of that, along with the closeness of his and Conor's bodies, makes me almost pass out and I sway on my feet. Both of them wrap an arm around my waist.

"We got you, sweetheart," Shane breathes in my ear

"You liked the sound of that did you, Angel?" Conor asks as he bends his head low and his breath skitters over the shell of my ear.

"Uh-huh," I murmur.

"Fuck!" he hisses. "You two are gonna fucking kill me."

"But what a way to go, bro," Shane says with a wink.

If you've loved Jessie and the Ryan brothers as much as I have and you don't want to say goodbye – or if you just want to find out if Conor ever does go through with it, then look out for them in my super spicy short stories.

A Ryan Reckoning
    A Ryan Rewind
    A Ryan Restraint
    A Ryan Halloween
    A Ryan Christmas
    A Ryan New Year

ALSO BY SADIE KINCAID

Sadie's latest series, Chicago Ruthless is available for preorder now. Following the lives of the notoriously ruthless Moretti siblings - this series will take you on a rollercoaster of emotions. Packed with angst, action and plenty of steam — preorder yours today

Dante

Joey

Lorenzo

If you haven't read full New York the series yet, you can find them on Amazon and Kindle Unlimited

Ryan Rule

Ryan Redemption

Ryan Retribution

Ryan Reign

Ryan Renewed

New York Ruthless short stories can be found here

A Ryan Reckoning

A Ryan Rewind

A Ryan Restraint

A Ryan Halloween

A Ryan Christmas

A Ryan New Year

Want to know more about The Ryan Brothers' buddies, Alejandro and Alana, and Jackson and Lucia? Find out all about them in Sadie's internationally bestselling LA Ruthless series. Available on Amazon and FREE in Kindle Unlimited.

Fierce King

Fierce Queen

Fierce Betrayal

Fierce Obsession

If you'd like to read about London's hottest couple. Gabriel and Samantha, then check out Sadie's London Ruthless series on Amazon. FREE in Kindle Unlimited.

Dark Angel

Fallen Angel

Dark/ Fallen Angel Duet

If you enjoy super spicy short stories, Sadie also writes the Bound series feat Mack and Jenna, Books 1, 2, 3 and 4 are available now.

Bound and Tamed

Bound and Shared

Bound and Dominated

Bound and Deceived

ABOUT THE AUTHOR

Sadie Kincaid is a dark romance author who loves to read and write about hot alpha males and strong, feisty females.

Sadie loves to connect with readers so why not get in touch via social media? Follow links below.

Sign up to her newsletter for all the latest news and releases here

Join Sadie's reader group for the latest news, book recommendations and plenty of fun. Sadie's ladies and Sizzling Alphas

ACKNOWLEDGMENTS

Firstly I would love to thank the incredible readers and members of Sadie's Ladies and Sizzling Alphas. My beloved belt whores! You all rock.

And to all of the readers who have bought any of my books, everything I write is for you and you all make my dreams come true.

I'd like to thank my fellow authors, and friends, Mary and Mandy for their friendship and support - not to mention having to listen to me go on and on about the world of independent publishing.

To my fellow romance authors, but especially Vicki H Nicolson, Nicci Harris, Elle Nicoll and BJ Alpha - you all make this journey so much more enjoyable.

Super special mention to my lovely PA, Kate, who loves the Ryans as much as I do, and who played a special part in making these books what they are!

To my incredible boys who inspire me to be better every single day. And last, but no means least, a huge thank you to my husband, who is my rock, my biggest supporter and my very own Shane, Conor, Liam and Mikey Ryan rolled into one.

I couldn't do this without you!

Made in United States
Orlando, FL
16 November 2024

53958860R00203